Acclaim for An Inexpressible State of Grace

"Cameron Abbott's *An Inexpressible State of Grace* is a journey of self rediscovery and reinvention. Its first-person style is straightforward, no-nonsense, immediate, and intimate. The protagonist, Ashleigh Moore, shares her struggle with her failed marriage, the aftermath of her first great love, her attraction to a fascinating colleague, and the awesome legacy, for good and ill, of her father, the scion of a wealthy family who abandoned her before birth. Family secrets draw us into an intriguing tale of the discovery and rediscovery of love."

—Anita Campitelli
Author, *German for Music Lovers*

"With deft characterizations, an engrossing plot, and a marvelous sense about the volatility of secrets, Cameron Abbott has crafted a terrific follow-up to her first novel, *To the Edge.* Because of the author's narrative skill, this fine sophomore novel will go directly to the head of the class."

—Lori L. Lake
Author, *Different Dress, Gun Shy,*
Under the Gun, and *Ricochet in Time;*
Reviewer, *Midwest Book Review,*
The Independent Gay Writer, The Gay Read,
and *Just About Write*

An Inexpressible State
of Grace

HARRINGTON PARK PRESS
Alice Street Editions
Judith P. Stelboum
Editor in Chief

Past Perfect by Judith P. Stelboum

Inside Out by Juliet Carrera

Facades by Alex Marcoux

Weeding at Dawn: A Lesbian Country Life by Hawk Madrone

His Hands, His Tools, His Sex, His Dress: Lesbian Writers on Their Fathers edited by Catherine Reid and Holly K. Iglesias

Treat by Angie Vicars

Yin Fire by Alexandra Grilikhes

From Flitch to Ash: A Musing on Trees and Carving by Diane Derrick

To the Edge by Cameron Abbott

Back to Salem by Alex Marcoux

Egret by Helen F. Collins

Your Loving Arms by Gwendolyn Bikis

A Donor Insemination Guide: Written By and For Lesbian Women by Marie Mohler and Lacy Frazer

Extraordinary Couples, Ordinary Lives by Lynn Haley-Banez and Joanne Garrett

Cat Rising by Cynn Chadwick

Maryfield Academy by Carla Tomaso

Ginger's Fire by Maureen Brady

A Taste for Blood by Diana Lee

Zach at Risk by Pamela Shepherd

An Inexpressible State of Grace by Cameron Abbott

Minus One: A Twelve-Step Journey by Bridget Bufford

Girls with Hammers by Cynn Chadwick

Rosemary and Juliet by Judy MacLean

An Inexpressible State of Grace

Cameron Abbott

Alice Street Editions
Harrington Park Press®
An Imprint of The Haworth Press, Inc.
New York • London • Oxford

Published by

Alice Street Editions, Harrington Park Press®, an imprint of The Haworth Press, Inc., 10 Alice Street, Binghamton, NY 13904-1580.

PUBLISHER'S NOTE
This is a work of fiction. Names, characters, places, and incidents either are the products of the author's imagination or are used fictitiously, and any resemblance to actual persons, living or dead, business establishments, events, or locales is entirely coincidental.

Cover design by Lora Wiggins.

Library of Congress Cataloging-in-Publication Data

Abbott, Cameron.
    An inexpressible state of grace / Cameron Abbott.
        p. cm.
    ISBN 1-56023-469-5 (soft cover : alk. paper)
    1. New York (N.Y.)—Fiction. 2. Women lawyers—Fiction. 3. Birthfathers—Fiction. 4. Lesbians—Fiction. I. Title.
PS3601.B36154 2003
813'.6—dc21
                                                                            2003002442

for Michele

Acknowledgments

My heartfelt thanks to Naomi, Neal, Elizabeth, and Jeanne, each of whom provided some valuable contribution to this book. Thanks also to Judith Stelboum, and the incomparable copyediting staff at The Haworth Press. Finally, and most important, my special gratitude to Jane.

❧ Editor's Foreword

Alice Street Editions provides a voice for established as well as up-coming lesbian writers, reflecting the diversity of lesbian interests, ethnicities, ages, and class. This cutting-edge series of novels, memoirs, and nonfiction writing welcomes the opportunity to present controversial views, explore multicultural ideas, encourage debate, and inspire creativity from a variety of lesbian perspectives. Through enlightening, illuminating, and provocative writing, Alice Street Editions can make a significant contribution to the visibility and accessibility of lesbian writing and bring lesbian-focused writing to a wider audience. Recognizing our own desires and ideas in print is life sustaining, acknowledging the reality of who we are, as well as our place in the world, individually and collectively.

Judith P. Stelboum
Editor in Chief
Alice Street Editions

It was on that road and at that hour that I first became aware of my own self, experienced an inexpressible state of grace, and felt one with the first breath of air that stirred, the first bird, and the sun so newly born that it still looked not quite round.

Colette

❧ *Chapter One*

I drove into Providence just as the sun was starting to set, and was so mesmerized by the peculiar purple hue over the water that I nearly missed my exit. Well, okay, maybe David's phone call had something to do with it, too. To be fair, it wasn't really even the phone call—it was the guilt that distracted me, the lies upon lies culminating in a feigned reception problem. "Sorry, you're breaking up. I'll have to call you back when I get to the hotel," I'd said as I abruptly snapped shut the cell and pulled across two lanes of rush-hour traffic at the last minute. With horns blaring and conservative Northeasterners giving me the finger, I cut off a blue Volvo and zipped onto the off-ramp as if I were the only car on the road. Dad would have been proud.

Dad—damn, the thought of him invariably started a patter of little pinpricks to rim my eyes. *No, not now.* I don't cry; I just don't. Certainly not in public. It's fine for other people, even endearing sometimes, but for me, it's simply unacceptable. A sure sign of weakness that I long ago learned never to display. My brother Rob had taught me that lesson with devastating clarity too many times to count. I tried to shoo away the feeling by tapping into some anger at David. That was better.

But it was true—Dad would have been proud. He was the best driver I'd ever known—and in some ways, the worst. Taught me everything I knew about driving, the good and the bad. And he had no patience for the "defensive driving" campaign popularized in the 1970s. "Right down the pike, honey. Don't you worry about the other guys; they'll take care of themselves. You just watch out for you." I'd often thought how strange it was that he would espouse this philosophy behind the wheel, since it was so diametrically opposed to the way he lived the rest of his life. He had taken it on himself to watch out for everybody. *Shit, that was my turn.*

So I figured I'd check in and think of something to tell David about why my drive took three hours longer than it should have. I'd have to call the office first, though—Stella had probably been wondering about me. And that toad Dick Parsons—I was sure he'd been looking for me too. I'd left the slips from his two phone messages on my desk when I'd walked out today—just a rebellious little jab for him in case he happened to stop by my office. *That's right, you shit, your messages are so unimportant that I left them behind, completely ignored.* Okay, I was acting like a petulant teenager, but I didn't care.

I forced myself to concentrate on getting to the hotel in one piece, looking for my turn, and absently rubbed an itch under my nose. Veronica. I caught a wicked whiff of her still on my fingers and felt the guilt slam into my chest all over again. Damn.

She'd called me yesterday afternoon. Out of the blue—same as always. And just like every other time, I'd relented. My resolve, built up over the course of two weeks, had evaporated right on cue. "I've got to see you," was all she'd said, was all she'd ever said, with that defeated inflection that told me she hated making this call as much as I hated getting it. And all of the reasons I'd given myself for saying no, for just telling her to forget it, had melted into a noticeable pool of guilt-slicked cream between my legs before I could decline. *Well,* I'd told myself, *maybe this time I'll just see her long enough to say it in person.* I'd tell her that it's wrong, and that I can't keep on lying to David, can't risk my nearly dead marriage for the sake of some cheap thrills any longer.

Obviously, David isn't the only person I lie to.

The Providence Hotel was right where I knew it would be. I always seem to know where things are. Never anything that matters, of course, like my house keys when I'm running late, or my calendar when a judge is asking me to check my schedule for a trial date—but when it comes to places, I just seem to know intuitively where I'm going and how to get there. David calls me Magellan. But then I remind him that Magellan never made it back.

Once I got checked in—after an annoyingly perky "Thanks for staying with us" from the redhead at the front desk wearing a badge that proclaimed "Hi! My name is Stacey!"—I plopped my bag on the bed and opened my laptop. It was too late to call Stella for messages after all, I realized—but that was okay, she would have called me on the cell if there had been anything urgent—so I plugged in the Sony and accessed my office e-mail instead. Might as well take care of any last-minute emergencies in the office before calling David. Then I could spend the rest of the evening tackling my final prep for tomorrow's deposition.

Two e-mails from Stella warned me that Dick Parsons was again calling for me—he could bite my ass, after what he pulled at my partnership review. I scanned through a half-dozen junk messages until I saw something from Carla Oakes. Weird, she almost never e-mailed me at work. I saw then that it was a mass e-mailing to our entire class. "To the Class of '86, Flung Far and Wide" read the subject line. Carla always did have a touch of the tabloid in her. Far and wide was right—the last time we were all together in one spot was probably that beautiful June afternoon when, diplomas in hand, we were pronounced educated young women and set loose on an unsuspecting world. An afternoon I could never forget, as much as I'd like to. Since then, my classmates and I had left Northampton in the dust and roamed, literally, to the four corners of the Earth in search of whatever it is that young women seek—I couldn't name it for you, and I certainly never found it. Despite all those reunions in the intervening years, all those opportunities to reconvene, we never did seem able to come together again as a group. With all that wandering, very few of us ever found our way home again.

I decided to read the whole thing later—I really needed to call back David. I kicked off my pumps and flopped on the bed to dial.

"Ash? All settled in?" he asked without preamble, as if he'd been waiting by the phone.

"Yeah—how'd you know it was me?"

"Caller ID. Who else is going to be calling me from the Providence Hotel? So, what, was traffic tied up? I thought you'd be there hours ago."

"Yeah, there was a tie-up on Ninety-Five outside New Haven, but I also got a late start."

"Why am I not surprised?"

"Come on, you know how stuff comes up just as you're trying to leave the office. It's like bullshit is laying in wait for me, ready to ambush me as soon as I need to leave and get somewhere."

"Well, at least you're there now. No trouble finding the place?"

An indignant snort was my answer.

"Right, stupid question. So anyway, what are your plans for tonight?"

I knew he was just being his considerate self, but I immediately felt his question as an inquisition and had to pull back on the stiff retort I wanted to fling at him.

"Oh, I'll just go over my notes for tomorrow's deposition. It's no big deal—a damages expert. But it's complicated stuff."

"By the way, I made that appointment for us next week—on Thursday."

"What appointment?"

"The marriage counselor." Shit. "It was hard for her to work us into her schedule, but she stays late on Thursday, and since you asked for the latest time possible, I grabbed the eight-thirty slot."

I'd forgotten all about it. Gee, I wonder what that means.

"Look, David, it's a really hectic time for me. Don't you think we could—I don't know—postpone this or something?"

He was silent for a minute—brooding or gearing up for battle, I couldn't tell which. Either would be preferable to the hurt little boy routine that he'd been slipping into recently.

"What I think is that we need to sit down and talk about this. And since we don't seem to be able to do it ourselves, we need to do it with a professional."

"What you mean is me," I said. "I'm the one who won't sit and explore every little nuance in our relationship."

"Come on, Ash."

"No, I mean it. You seem to have no trouble telling me every two seconds that you want to have a baby, but when I say I'm not ready, I'm suddenly the one who isn't willing to work on our relationship."

"That's not fair." It wasn't. There was a lot more going on than just a disagreement about starting a family—but that seemed to bring it all into focus, at least for me. A handy proxy for everything else.

"Look, I'm sorry, but I have a few distractions at work these days too, you know. I just don't have the luxury of being able to sit through the marathon late-night talks you always want when I'm so tired I can't keep my eyes open."

"Ash, you agreed to give counseling a try, so that's all I'm asking you to do." He made his tone cajoling as he continued. "Maybe that way we can save our late-night marathons for something more enjoyable."

I hate it when he turns everything, even an argument, into an invitation for sex. I started to feel the beginnings of a headache.

"Let's not get into this now. I have a lot of work to do for tomorrow."

"Fine," he said shortly. "Just tell me you'll go, and you can bury your head back in your work."

"No, don't make this about my job. Any time you want to be the sole breadwinner in this house, you can just say the word."

It was a low blow, well below the belt, and I knew it. He was sensitive about the fact that I earned more money than he did as a dot-com executive. His options might someday be worth millions, but we both knew that the possibility was becoming more and more remote, and the downturn in the economy only seemed to fuel his frustration.

"Listen, I'm sorry," I said, meaning it. "This Parsons shit has really got me nuts."

"Oh, that reminds me: he left a message for you here. Doesn't he know you're out of town?"

Now my agitation had a legitimate target, so I let it out. "No, he's not on this case, thank God. That worthless shit—if he calls again, you can tell him to go to hell."

"Nothing would make me happier. Can I invite him over and beat him up?"

I laughed. God, David was good for me in some ways. "Sure," I said, "but save the gory stuff for me. You know that prick actually told Stella she shouldn't count on being a partner's secretary any time soon unless she was interested in working for someone else?"

"You don't think he's trying to lure her away from you, do you?"

"No, he'd never get rid of Louise, much as we all wish he would. It's more that he's trying to plant these little seeds around the office. Laying the groundwork, I think, so that it won't come as such a big surprise when he shoots down my partnership."

"If, not when. He's a long way from getting you voted down."

"Yeah," I sighed, my headache settling around my skull like a comfortable old overcoat. "Well, he's certainly doing his best." I stretched a crick out of my neck and leaned back against the headboard. "Any other messages I should know about? How about the mail?"

"No, nothing that can't wait. Oh, you got some lawyer-looking thing from Arizona. Why would they mail it to your home?"

"No idea—I don't even know anybody in Arizona. Open it."

"Wait a minute; let me get it."

Listening to him carry the phone into the den, I clicked on the TV and started flipping through the channels. I wondered if I'd ever tell him about Veronica. No reason to, I figured, since I was absolutely positive that I would never, ever sleep with her again. Maybe someday I'd tell him—in about, oh, fifty years or so—and we could have a good laugh about it. Then again, maybe not.

"Ash?"

"Right here."

"What's that in the background?"

There it was again—no, it wasn't an interrogation, just an innocent question.

"CNN. The Dow was down again today."

"Yeah, I know. So anyway, it says it's from someplace called Liddle, Barrington and Sweet in Tucson."

"Never heard of them. Read it."

"Okay, let's see. 'Ms. Ashleigh Moore,' blah blah. Boy, they sure don't know you. Nobody calls you Ashleigh."

"C'mon."

"Okay. 'Please be advised that this firm has been retained by Kenneth Gardner for the purpose of contacting you regarding the estate of the late Edna Williams Gardner.' Who the hell is Kenneth Gardner?"

Oh shit. The headache of a moment ago now took on a whole new dimension, blossoming into a full-fledged body bruising that slammed my gut and my skull with equal force.

"Ash?" I heard through the drumbeat in my ears. "What is it?"

I felt the tears well up, and with Herculean effort pushed them right back down into their hiding place. *C'mon, focus.*

"Honey?"

"He's my father."

"What are you talking about? Your father's—"

"No." *Shit, why is this so hard? Choke it out.* "He's my natural father. The father I've never met."

📖 📖 📖

"Parsons wants you in his office. He's been calling every ten min-utes since about eight this morning." Stella handed me a stack of pink message slips first thing Thursday morning, and I noticed the one from Parsons on top with a skull and crossbones that Stella had doo-dled on it.

"But—"

"I know. I told him yesterday that you were out of town at a deposi-tion, but it's Louise who's been calling. And don't get me started about how snotty she's been getting. You'd think *she* was the head of the corporate finance group. You know what she did yesterday, while you were gone?"

I had a thousand things to take care of this morning, after having been out of the office for two days, but I couldn't resist hearing the latest on Queen Bee, as we'd taken to calling Louise, so I took a sip of my coffee and nodded her on.

"Well, I was over by her desk getting some bills—you know how Parsons makes sure all the bills get reviewed by him even when it's not his client? So anyway, Alan comes by and needs to see Parsons about some meeting, but he's not in his office so Alan asks Queen Bee where he is. And she says, 'I'm sorry, he's in a meeting and can't be disturbed.' So Alan goes, 'I know. I'm supposed to be in that meeting. So where is it?' And Louise actually gives him a hard time about it. She just picks up the phone while he's standing there—you know how she does that, pretending she's answering a phone call?"

"I know. She keeps the ringer turned way down so no one else can hear it."

"Right. So she goes, 'You're going to have to wait'—like she's doing him some big favor and she'll get to it when she can. And then she actually keeps him standing there while she's supposedly taking care of some very important business for Dick."

"Yeah, like confirming a lunch reservation."

"Like nothing. I swear, I was standing right there and I don't think that phone rang at all. So anyway, Alan was getting fed up—you know how he gets—so he leans right over her desk and snatches up Dick's calendar to look for himself. Right out from under her nose!"

"Oh my God, he touched the Holy Grail. Bet she loved that."

"Oh, you know it. She just stops in the middle of a sentence to this pretend person on the phone, and says, 'It's not in there'—you know, the conference room number—then she goes right back to her phone call. Like she's got the time to tell him that, but she doesn't have the time to tell him what he needs to know."

"What'd he do?"

"Well, this is the best part. He gets down right in her face and says, 'You tell me where that meeting is *right now*, and *then* you can explain to the managing partner why you made me late for it!' So she huffs like, you know, it's this incredible imposition, and she says, 'I'm sorry, but we don't have you down for that meeting.'"

"We?"

"No shit. 'We'—like it's *her* meeting!"

"Unbelievable."

"Well, Alan just lost it—you should have seen it. It was beautiful. He straightens up and just starts screaming at the top of his lungs, 'I don't give a flying fuck what you've written down! Dick called me five minutes ago, so you goddamn tell me where that goddamn meeting is right this second!' You should have seen the look on her face."

"I hope it really was a fake phone call," I said. "I'd hate to think that some client heard that."

"It's like she doesn't get it that all of her bullshit just gets in the way of everyone else doing their jobs. You'd think that Dick would see that much."

"Dick's never going to do anything about it, because she doesn't interfere with *his* job, and he just doesn't see what the rest of us have to go through."

"Doesn't see or doesn't care."

"Yeah, that's probably more like it." I sighed and shook my head in wonder at the ability of a legal secretary to manipulate all of the lawyers around her. It was because we didn't have the authority to fire her, of course. Only Dick had that power over her—and over most of us, too.

"Anyway," I said, "I guess I should go see what he wants. Oh, by the way, see if you can get hold of my sister for me, find out a good time I can talk to her about something."

"Any time in particular?"

"This morning if possible." I picked up my coffee mug and started toward my office.

"Everything okay?"

I shrugged. "Just some family crap."

📖   📖   📖

Alan was waiting for me in my office an hour later, and he was the perfect antidote for my foul mood. One of my closest friends at Huxley Doyle, he'd made partner a few years ago and despised Parsons almost as much as I did. Lounging in one of the chairs opposite my desk and playing with a squeeze ball—one of the many toys from court reporter services littering my office—he displayed no reaction at all as I stormed in, slammed the door, and threw my writing pad on the desk.

"Let me guess. Parsons?"

"I don't want to talk about it," I said as I clicked open my Inbox to scan messages, fighting back the tears of anger and frustration that threatened to erupt. I hated that a smarmy little prick like Parsons could get me in this state, and willed myself to focus on the anger. Anger was easier—a strength instead of a weakness. Anger was my safety position, and I slipped into it easily. Years of practice.

"Deposition go okay yesterday?"

"Piece of cake."

"Who was it?"

"An economist for the other side. What a joke."

"What?"

"You wouldn't believe the shit this idiot came out with. Economics for morons."

"Yeah?" Alan grinned. He loved a good fight.

"He actually testified that, in his expert opinion, all government regulation is inherently evil and detrimental to societal welfare. So I questioned him on it—pollution controls, antitrust laws, you name it. Even drug laws and the minimum drinking age."

"What's that got to do with your case?"

"Nothing, but that's not the point. This guy's their expert. His credibility is on the line, and he looks like a fanatic coming out with this stuff. As far as he's concerned, if a government regulation even remotely touches on articles in commerce, it's bad for society. So what if a few hundred people die because of contaminated products, he says—the market will correct for it eventually. Can you believe it?"

"Sounds like a good day."

"Oh, you know it. We're going to destroy this guy in front of a jury," I said as I closed out my Inbox and turned to face him. "So, what's up?"

"Well, I met with Parsons yesterday about this new CRS matter."

"CRS?"

"Chasen Research Science."

"Oh yeah, I heard you had a hard time getting to the meeting," I said, smiling.

"Well, that's a whole other story. Anyway, the client was there too."

"No shit, Huff Chasen?"

"The one and only."

"Is he as bad as they say?"

"Well, you can decide for yourself. It's going to be your case, you know, but I got called in because Parsons wanted a litigator there for the first meeting."

"I know. I just came from a meeting with Parsons about it—sort of. Two minutes on the case, and an hour on why I'm not going to make partner."

"He came right out and said that?"

"No, it was all nicely couched in genuine concern for my well-being. But I got the drift."

"He's only one vote, you know. And he's not even in our department. I'm in your corner, you know—and so is Dennis."

"You really think that matters? The guy controls ten million in billings."

"But Dennis is the head of litigation, and every single partner in this department is behind you. Besides, the clients love you."

"Yeah, well, we'll see. Chasen's a client now too, and anything he knows about me at this point is from Parsons. So what's your take on the case?"

"Pretty straightforward. This guy Chasen thinks a competitor has been monkeying around with his FDA application for a new angioplasty device. Even thinks they may have gotten their hands on the FDA file."

"That would be pretty serious—theft of trade secrets, unfair competition, maybe even some confidential patent information in there."

"Right."

"What's Parsons got to do with it? He's no litigator. I don't think he knows what the inside of a courtroom even looks like."

"No idea. I think they're friends or something. Anyway, it looks like it'll be a lawsuit, so that's why they needed us—well, you. But I'm available to help if you need a hand."

"Thanks."

"One thing that worries me, though. Chasen seems to have it in his head that he won't really have to sue."

"What do you mean?"

"That the other side will cave in if we just rattle some sabers."

"Shit. Wonder where he got that idea—Parsons was shooting off his mouth, I assume?"

"Not while I was there. But they'd obviously been talking beforehand."

"I hate when the corporate guys do that. Why can't they get it through their heads that they need to leave the litigating to the litigators?"

"Tell me about it," Alan said. "And from what I saw yesterday, I really don't know if Chasen has the stomach for a lawsuit."

"Great."

"Parsons did the same thing to me in that insurance case two years ago. Pumped the client full of all this crap about how the insurance company would pay up right away as soon as we filed suit, and when they didn't—which I knew they wouldn't—our complaint gets hit with a motion to dismiss and the client bitches a blue streak about all the fees we rack up opposing the motion. Suddenly the client wants out because he's in over his head in a lawsuit that he never really wanted to bring in the first place. The client still owes us fifty thousand on that mess."

"I think the corporate guys just come from a different place. They're used to doing deals where the guys on the other side of the table want to cooperate, to make things happen. They just don't get it that by the time things get to the point of a lawsuit, the gloves are off and everyone's more interested in posturing and getting entrenched than in negotiating. No one takes kindly to a threat—you sue them, you just firm up their resolve to fight back."

"And then it's up to us to salvage the situation."

"Yeah, but by that time it's cost the client thousands more than they thought it would, so even a victory at that point feels like a defeat."

"And we get the blame."

"You got that right." My intercom buzzed just then, and Alan got up to leave.

"Yeah?"

"I've got your sister on line two," Stella said over the speaker. "She's available now if you want to take it."

"Take your call," said Alan as he tossed me the squeeze ball. I nabbed it with one hand and reached for the receiver with the other.

"Okay, I'll catch up with you later."

❧ Chapter Two

There had been so many times that I'd missed Gussie over the years, so many times that I'd wished I could just pick up the phone and dial that number I'd known by heart since nursery school, wanting so much just to hear her sing-song "hello-o," familiar as my own heartbeat. For the first few months after her death, it had been practically a daily ritual of masochism I'd put myself through. I'd feel the tears bite my eyes as my soul swelled with a feeling of utter abandonment, desolate orphanhood. I wasn't really an orphan, of course—Gussie had been my grandmother, after all, and my parents were alive and well. All three of them, so far as I knew, including the faceless stranger with the Y chromosomes. But Gussie had raised me as her own, at least until I was eight. She'd sprayed the Bactine on my knees and read *Charlotte's Web* to me long after I could read it to myself. She'd mothered me in countless ways that her own daughter never quite could. And over time, as the pain of her funeral receded, acknowledging her absence got a bit easier. Sure, I still put myself through the ringer of missing her from time to time, but less frequently. And the sense of guilt, at first lurking just beneath the surface with a hair trigger, slowly abated to a point where I had to dig a little to get to it. Still, no matter how much time went by, sooner or later I'd get to thinking of her, wanting to check in with her about something or other, and I'd tap into that pool of motherless ache just waiting for me, a well of regret lined by a hundred "if only's." Because, you see, I so rarely bothered to make those phone calls while she was still there to answer.

"Don't call me Grandma," the story went, part of the family mythology traceable to Robbie's early childhood—and no doubt embroidered over the years by Gussie's fanciful take on just about everything. "I'm too young to be anybody's grandma. My daddy named me Gussie, and if it was good enough for him, it's good enough for his great-grandson." Of course, I knew early on that the story was more fiction than fact. Her father had actually hated the name Gussie, according to Aunt Aurelia, and never called her anything but her given name, Augustina. I tended to believe Aunt Aurelia's version of most things, and on this one I knew she was right. I'd never met Old Granddaddy, as he was called—he was long dead by the time I came along—but his fondness for his daughters' names was as much a part of our family lore as his worship of the Roman emperors for whom he'd named them: Augustina, Margaret Aurelia, and Octavia. Bitch that I am, I always wished I'd had the opportunity to point out to him that he'd named two of his girls after the same man, that Augustus Caesar and Octavian were the same person. Just as well that I never got the chance, probably—Gussie would have taken the fly swatter to me for that one.

It wasn't just Aunt Aurelia's credibility that had me thinking Gussie's story was full of holes. The fact was, Gussie would not have insisted that Robbie call her by that name because, when it came to Robbie, she never insisted on anything. His shit just didn't stink; it never had. More likely than not, therefore, it was Robbie himself who came up with the name Gussie—out of garbled baby talk or sheer mischief, it didn't matter—and Gussie simply found it as enchanting as everything else that came out of his hallowed mouth. Whatever its genesis, the name stuck, and by the time Liz and I came along it didn't occur to us to call her anything else.

That being said, though, there was a certain ring of truth to her story too—especially the way she supposedly described Old Granddaddy as Robbie's great-grandfather. That was her way—everyone was something-or-other to everyone else, described not in terms of appearance or achievement but in relation to their spot on our complicated family tree. Gussie would never dream of simply referring to Ruth as Ruth. Ruth was always at least "Cousin Ruth," and more often than not she was "Cousin Ruth, your mama's first cousin once removed on my mama's side." Which meant, technically, that Ruth was Gussie's first cousin and my first cousin twice removed. But I digress.

When I went to college up North and found myself surrounded by New Englanders, it began to dawn on me that other people didn't walk around with an encyclopedic knowledge of their lineage hard-wired into their brains. I had never felt like much of a Southerner growing up—Washington, DC, may be south of the Mason-Dixon, but only on a map. I had cousins in Richmond, some even in Norfolk, and I was a veritable Yankee compared to them. But once I was up North, I became acutely aware of my Southern heritage, and it was never so apparent as when my friends and I would discuss our families. I realized then that I'd absorbed Gussie's photographic memory of our family tree—which, with all of the intermarriages, resembled more of a chain-link fence—and I'd unconsciously acquired her way of referring to my kin.

The difference became more pronounced when I was a law student. Sitting in Property class as a first-year, I was puzzled by my classmates' sweat in trying to work out the skewed lines of descent in the professor's hypotheticals. For me, raised on years of Gussie's stories referring to a far more tangled web of cousins, the answers appeared so laughably simple that my five-year-old cousin in Richmond could have gotten them. My second cousin Laurie, that is, the daughter of my mother's first cousin Harry on her father's side.

I may have been infused with Gussie's innate knowledge of our relations, but I knew early on that I didn't see my family, or my place in it, in quite the same way that everyone around me did. For as far back as I could remember, when anyone spoke of our family's generations, the accumulation of names in the family Bible, it was as if it all boiled down to me and Liz and Robbie (especially Robbie), as if we were the end of the evolutionary story. We were indoctrinated with the unspoken belief that we three were the culmination of everyone's efforts through the ages, the genetic destiny of all who had contributed to the chromosomal mix to bring about the crowning achievement of us. And although the message was tacit, it was relentless and unmistakable from all of the adults in my home—Gussie, Mom, Gramps (that's right; he didn't mind being reminded that he was a grandfather), and even Dad once he married Mom and got scooped up into the family's net. In countless ways, large and small, they let us know every day that we three were the most important people in the world. And while I can't say how Liz and Robbie translated that message— I have my suspicions, but I don't know for certain—I know that, for me, the whole idea just didn't jive with what I seemed intuitively to know about myself: that, far from a crowning achievement, I was more of a footnote in our grand family treatise. As a child, I had no words to express this notion—this disconnect between the me that I knew myself to be and the me that I saw reflected from those around me. I just knew on a primitive, preverbal level that they were fooling themselves. That I wasn't who they thought I was.

Growing up with Gussie's stories, we all learned everything anyone could care to know about our mother's side of the family. Gussie and Gramps, and their parents and siblings and so on and so forth—interrelated for at least the past three generations and making for some very confusing double and triple relations. Gussie, for example, was not only a blood aunt to Cousin Nance, she was also her aunt by marriage and her step half sister. Don't ask.

When it came to our natural father, however, that whole side of the family tree was bare—a maze of blanks that we couldn't possibly fill in without asking a lot of questions we simply couldn't ask in our house. Not without treading on an acre of landmines that we instinctively knew were hidden there. By the time the Vietnam War was ending, we'd all adopted the jargon we'd learned from Chet Huntley on the evening news, and knew that information—*any* information—about our natural father was situated in the DMZ and surrounded by hostiles.

We had one conduit to his particulars, however, in the form of Aunt Nell. She was our natural father's great-aunt, already ancient by the time we were born, and a veritable outcast among her own clan for having taken my mother's side in the divorce. She adored the three of us, worshiped my mother, and basically served as the lone representative of the entire Gardner family for all of us. She was the one who'd speak freely about Mr. Gardner—as I took to calling him when I was young, deciding that "natural father" wasn't fitting, since there was nothing natural about a man who'd leave his young wife and two kids with a third on the way. By the time I was a teenager, I'd switched to calling him the Sperm Donor—to Dad's delight and Gussie's horror—and as an adult, I didn't refer to him as anything at all, because I never thought about him.

Not that Aunt Nell had much to say about our father. Sure, she'd wax poetic about his grand lineage—most of which was her lineage too, after all. But as for the man himself, she kept pretty mum—which as a small child I took to mean that she didn't know much, but which I eventually credited to her innate sense of decency. If she had nothing good to say about someone, Aunt Nell was the type who'd rather say nothing at all.

Looking back on it, I can't quite figure why I was so keen to pump Aunt Nell for information about my father, when I was equally adamant in turning a deaf ear to Gussie's stories about the side of the family that was actually present in my life. Every time we saw Aunt Nell, I'd somehow try to get her alone and ask her a few questions about Mr. Gardner. But at the same time, when it came to Mom's side of the family, I'd just tune out. As soon as Gussie would start in on one of her endless tales about some long-dead relative, Gramps would sneak me a look and roll his eyes a bit, and I'd nod complicitly. Sometimes I'd even pipe up to challenge her story in some way—point out an inconsistency between this version and the one she'd recited the last time she'd told the story. I liked to think that it was just my way of seeking out the truth, rejecting stories that were so heavily embroidered that they bordered on the fantastical. But deep down, I knew that a big part of it was my ornery streak, which always seemed to come out in spades around Gussie. So often after her death, I'd wished with all my heart that I'd had the wisdom back then to simply accept Gussie for who she was, to understand and give in to her constant need for telling and fictionalizing our family saga. Most of all, as with so many other things, I'd wished that I could just go back in time to shake that heartless eight-year-old—to try to make her understand that some acts of cruelty, deliberate or not, can haunt us forever.

   📖 📖 📖

I guess I reached out to Liz that morning because there was no Gussie for me to call anymore. That's who I really wanted to talk to—from the minute David had started reading me that letter—but, as usual, I was about ten years too late. Gussie would have hemmed and hawed, but eventually I could have wheedled some information out of her, and I know I would have gotten sound advice on how to handle the whole thing—whether I should tell Mom ("Not yet," I could hear her gentle voice in my ear. "Good Lord, let's think this thing through first"), whether I should tell Rob and Liz about it ("Well, he's their kin as much as he's yours, isn't he?"). And the big one I'd been mulling over for the past day and a half, whether I—or we—should respond at all. The Gussie in my head saw the pros and cons, as I did. "Well, that no-good so-and-so never was worth a plug nickel," she was saying (with the unspoken "like I told your mama a hundred times" pointedly implied), "so don't you go calling him. He can just jump in a lake." But her pro voice was just as persuasive: "You've got a good head on your shoulders, Ash. You can hear him out and *then* tell him to go jump in a lake." God, I missed her.

"Liz?" I said as soon as I punched up line two.

"Yeah, what's up?" Hurried, but not impatient. That was a good sign.

"You sitting down?"

"Shit. What?" Her tone was cautious—looking out for me. She was always going to be my big sister.

"No, I'm fine," I assured her, not really knowing how to say it. "It's just, well, I got a letter from some lawyers in Arizona."

"Yeah?" A whisker of impatience now flecked her tone. Get it over with.

"They want to talk to me. Or us, maybe—that's what I want to talk to you about."

"Ash," she sighed, "could you just get to the point?"

"They represent our father, the Sperm Donor." Okay, I was back to my teenaged self. So be it.

She was silent for a long moment. I could envision her sitting there in her office amid stacks of unread manuscripts, mulling over a sudden tumult of competing thoughts, pulled every which way as she tried to get a handle on the whats and whys. The same gyrations I'd been tossing myself through over the last two days. I let her take her time.

"What does he want?" Her tone was neutral, giving away absolutely nothing of what she felt. Neither hopeful nor disdainful, although I was pretty sure she was feeling plenty of both, and a whole lot more. As had I—until my conflicting emotions, like a storm of charged electrons, had eventually resolved themselves into the posture of seeming repose that I assumed now. But it was only an illusion; the storm continued to rage beneath, and imperiled my carefully balanced equipoise as I waited her out. Liz got to the same place I had much more quickly, but her perch there—her manifestation of calm—was no more secure than mine. Of that I was certain.

"He wants to talk to us. About Grandma Edna."

Another beat. Then, "I don't get it. She's been dead for, I don't know, ten years or so."

"Well, it's something about her estate. That's what the letter says."

Janelle, my junior associate from down the hall, picked that moment to sashay into my office and flop herself in one of my chairs, draping one leg irreverently over the arm. She either didn't see my expression imploring her to leave, or she didn't care. Oh well.

"Look," Liz said, her tone tinged with more of an edge, "what do you want to do about it? What does Rob say?"

"I haven't talked to him yet. He's my next call."

"Oh. Well, let me know what he wants to do."

Typical. She wasn't going to take a position until she knew how everyone else felt about it. I tried not to bristle at her obvious maneuvering—leaving it up to me to get the consensus. It sometimes seemed that Liz should have become the lawyer instead of me.

"Well, since he's going to ask me what you think, why don't you just tell me? Should we call them?"

"I don't want to talk to them. You do what you want."

I shouldn't have been surprised, really, but her attitude ticked me off nevertheless. When it came to the big stuff, Liz was perfectly content to sit back and watch. To say that Liz was not a risk taker was an understatement. That game plan worked very well for her when we were kids—she was spared most of the punishments that Robbie and I had routinely endured, because she almost never directly participated in our escapades. She'd go along for a while but invariably would come to the point where she'd just sit back and watch. In adulthood, I often thought that her safety zone had evolved into a fortress, as isolating as it was protective.

When that truck had plowed into Dad's Oldsmobile last year, it was Liz who had gotten the first call from Mom and Liz who had planted herself at Mom's side through those hopeless hours at the hospital—but it was Robbie and I who had been forced to give the unthinkable instructions to the nurse for the machines to be turned off. And at the funeral home, although we'd agreed that we'd spare Mom that final image of Dad, Liz had hung back at the last minute and, once again, left it to me and Robbie to walk into that softly lit back room to identify the body for cremation. I don't know what irked me more: the fact that Liz's manner always seemed to put the difficult tasks on my shoulders or the possibility that the weakness I saw and despised in her might reflect my own.

I sighed into the phone instead of biting her head off, and held up a hand to Janelle to indicate I'd be with her in a minute.

"Okay, well, I'll let you know what we decide," I said.

"You're not telling Mom, are you?"

"I don't know. What do you think?"

"Not right away. See what Rob thinks."

As I hung up, I turned to find Janelle leafing through an issue of *Amicus Lawyer*—the one containing my article on lender liability. I could tell when she came to the article, because her eyebrow cocked rakishly and she puckered up in a mock whistle.

"Whoa, girl. The hotshot lawyer strikes again." She grinned.

"Yeah, right," I mumbled. "Save it for your bedtime reading. It's guaranteed to put you right to sleep."

"I won't be the only one doing a little bedtime reading with this picture. Girl, you look *good*," she said as she held up the page displaying my picture.

"Oh, please." It was a good picture, but I wasn't in the mood for Janelle's antics at the moment.

"I'll bet that little paralegal from Dorsey Kimball is going to drool all over this one," she said.

Veronica. Definitely a topic of conversation I wanted to avoid, especially with Janelle, who always seemed to know far more than she was told. At least she was discreet.

"I don't know what you're talking about."

"Uh-huh," she said as she put the magazine back on my desk. "Well, you can deny it if you want, but I'm telling you, that girl has the hots for you, and I have a feeling she's the kind who gets what she wants. If she hasn't already."

It was the same game we'd played for years. Janelle says something provocative, just to see what kind of rise she can get out of me, and I retreat into studied neutrality. It never seemed to fool her.

"You're full of shit."

She laughed. "You keep denying it, girlfriend, but I know what I saw while we were on that Bank Street case with them last fall. Now what I want to know is, when are you gonna talk to me about it? It's not like I keep anything from you."

"God knows that's true." Janelle had the annoying habit of filling me in on every juicy detail of her endless sexual exploits, whether or not I wanted to hear them. Whether or not I had a thousand other things to do.

"Veronica Mars is a friend of mine. That's it." Technically speaking, it was the honest truth at that moment. And whatever it was that she and I had been doing for the past two months, it was a closed door now—no need to delve into it with Janelle. Or David.

"Come on, I sat through two months of document production with you two. I saw how she creamed her pants every time you walked into the room, so don't you tell me she's just a friend. I don't know how far she got, but I sure as shit know where she was heading." She swung her leg back over the armrest and sat up straight. "Are all you white girls this dense? You want me to draw you a map?"

She would, too, if I gave her half a chance. I snatched up my legal pad before she could grab it.

"Very funny. How many times do we have to have this conversation before you get it that I'm not looking? Putting aside the fact that I'm straight, doesn't the fact that I'm married mean anything to you?"

"The question is whether it means anything to Veronica—which I already know it doesn't. And whether it means anything to you. The jury's still out on that one."

No shit, that was the question all right. But it had nothing to do with Veronica, and everything to do with what was between me and David. Or wasn't.

"I don't have time for this, and neither do you. Don't you have a brief to write? Something about promissory estoppel?"

She just laughed and slumped back in the chair smugly. "Hmm, I hit a nerve? Maybe you can tell me why you blush like that every time I mention Veronica Mars."

"You know, since you seem to have so much free time on your hands, I'm sure I can find another research assignment for you."

"You pulling rank on me?"

"Damn straight."

Janelle got up and pretended to fluff her jericurls. "You can call me anything but straight. But we'll pick this up later."

"In your dreams," I mumbled as a turned to the stack of papers on my desk.

"Not my dreams, baby. Don't flatter yourself."

It was next to impossible to get my head into work after Janelle left, but I really didn't have a choice. Parsons had scheduled a two o'clock meeting with the client on the CRS case—without consulting my schedule, of course—and I'd need to develop at least a passing familiarity with the issues before that time. Calling Rob would simply have to wait—no big sacrifice, since I really didn't want to speak to him anyway. But Janelle's comments had provided a whole new venue for distraction, one that she had been relentless in exploring over the years, and that I'd been equally diligent in avoiding. Of course, these days her friendly banter was hitting much closer to home. One of the ancient Greeks—Aristotle, probably—had described fear as a function of power and proximity. Sitting at my desk, pretending to review the notes before me, I felt the interplay of the two viscerally: Janelle's prodding was uncomfortably close to the truth, and the power of that truth to upend my life seemed at the moment to be exponential.

It was unsettling to realize how deliberately I'd avoided thinking about the consequences. I'm paid a hefty salary to think precisely along those lines, to analyze the likely impact of each strategic move. With Veronica, I'd told myself over the last few months that it had "just happened"—a phrase I'd also rehearsed when envisioning a confrontation with David. Part of me knew, as David would surely know, that there was always a reason—that these things didn't just happen. They don't emerge from nothing—a sly smile, an intoxicating kiss, fade out—as if I weren't even a part of it. As if the rest of the tale, the seismic activity beneath the surface, was immaterial. In those scarce moments of brutal honesty with myself—and, believe me, they're thankfully infrequent—I knew that any affair, no matter how casual, doesn't simply happen out of the blue to unwilling or uninvolved participants. It's odd, really, how the standards of honesty that I maintain without any difficulty in my professional life manage to fly right out the window when it comes to my dealings with David—and myself.

The truth was, it hadn't just happened. I'd known exactly what I was doing, and exactly where I expected it to lead, right from the start. And I'd been partly right: I knew I wouldn't feel any real emotional connection, and I didn't. In some sense, I'd ensured the outcome by allowing it to be Veronica with whom I'd tested the infidelity waters—someone with whom I'd never fall in love. If I never fell in love with her, I'd never have to face any of the nasty doubts about myself that I'd so carefully sidestepped since college. There would be nothing but some hot sex, I told myself—and there wasn't.

The problem was that I'd failed to consider how even hot sex might make me reconsider my marriage and everything that wasn't there. Veronica wasn't the issue; she was gone. The issue was me and David, and we were still here, still playing our game of best friends who happened to be married.

Much as I wanted to talk to Janelle about it, I dreaded doing so. She was a close and trusted friend, but I knew she'd latch on to the lesbian angle, and I definitely didn't want to dwell on that. Veronica could just as easily have been a man, right? The point was that I went outside my marriage, and that said a lot about my marriage. In the end, of course, I guess it said a lot about me too, but I just couldn't deal with that right then.

Strangely, I think maybe it was Veronica who understood the situation best—saw what we were doing for what it was and what it wasn't. When I'd told her on Monday that I was willing to see her before my trip the next day, I'd been firmly committed to ending it. And it had been a good plan, as far as it went. Of course, I didn't think much past those first few moments when we'd be alone.

This time she was waiting for me in the lobby of the Excelsior—she'd already gotten us a room—and we rode up in the elevator together. Her eyelids were heavy, nearly half-closed, and she shook her long blonde hair behind her shoulders before leaning against the back elevator wall, her tightly sweatered breasts a pair of prominent beacons—God, they were inviting. I was so focused on them that I barely heard her whispered "Come here" as soon as the elevator doors closed. I'd reached out toward her, telling myself it was just for a quick embrace, nothing more. Really. But she took my hand and, before I knew it, she'd brought it to her chest to dust against those amazing orbs, smiling into my eyes as she watched my reaction to feeling her straining hard nipples against my fingers. I didn't have a chance to decide whether I'd back away—she instantly grabbed my other hand and deftly slipped it into her loose-fitting slacks, under the waistband of her panties, and directly into her sopping wet center, which she immediately began to rotate in fluid circles around my helpless fingers. "Do you see how much I've missed you?" she'd pleaded in my ear. I retrieved my hands just before the elevator doors opened and deposited us onto the seventh floor, my head and clit awash in a fog of thrumming urgency.

Afterward, it was so easy to say everything that needed to be said—everything that the previous two hours had exposed as patently absurd. Sure, she'd agreed that the whole situation was impossible. Laying on her side with one leg pulled up slightly—to ensure the most advantageous view of her delicious round ass, of course—she'd nodded when I'd said we couldn't keep doing this. Seemed almost to purr as she rolled over and arched her back in a stretch, her gravity-defying breasts reaching for the moon for a moment before she sat up and absently smoothed her hair.

She hated lying to her boyfriend as much as I hated lying to David, she'd said. And she had a harder time than I did trying to find excuses for her sudden absences from the office in the middle of the day. Besides, it was expensive getting a hotel room in Manhattan every few weeks. Although I always paid her for half—she'd use her credit card, so that David wouldn't see the charges on my bill—the cost was still exorbitant, especially on her paralegal salary.

Most of all, it was going nowhere, and we both knew it. Neither of us wanted anything out of it, neither wanted or expected anything from the other. I certainly wasn't going to leave David, at least not for her. *I'm not gay,* I told her. *I have nothing against it, but that's just not who I am.* I may not be happily married, but I'm happily heterosexual. And whatever this was—lust, erotic play—it wasn't lesbian. She'd assured me that she wasn't gay either—held up her boyfriend as living proof—but she'd agreed that it wasn't working anymore.

The appalling truth was, I didn't even like her very much. Sure, she's gorgeous, and the fireworks she evoked in me were phenomenal, but once I'm sated and the fog dissipates, I know that I could never enjoy so much as an hour in her company. She cares nothing for history or current events, doesn't read books or newspapers, watches only slasher movies and mindless sitcoms, and we have absolutely nothing to talk about. You'd think that we might at least share a common interest in the law, but she's as unplugged from her work as she's plugged in to her sensuality. I tried once to have a normal conversation with her, just because it seemed the right thing to do as we were recovering from some particularly bone-shattering orgasms one afternoon. I guess I was just trying to fill the silence, to distract myself from wondering what the hell I was doing. I started it off with an innocuous query about whether she was working on any interesting cases, now that the Bank Street case was over. "No, they're all boring," was all she'd said as she rolled toward me and started fondling my breasts again.

And Tuesday, on what was to be our final afternoon together, although she'd agreed that we couldn't continue seeing each other she still had nothing much to say. In a way, she saved me the trouble of explaining it. I like to think that maybe she intuitively understood, but I have to admit that it's just as likely she had nothing to say because we are, simply and fundamentally, incapable of conversation. We had no language but sex.

Now that it was officially relegated to the past, I was left in a place where I'd never wanted to be: with no distraction, I had only myself to look at—wondering what I was doing in my marriage, questioning its worth, doubting my ability to remain in it. Not because of Veronica, but because of me. Because whatever I thought I was seeking in those lovely arms, it wasn't about what I'd found there; it was about what I was leaving behind.

If only I'd thought about it from all directions, taken it to its only logical conclusion, before I'd ever gotten involved with her. But of course, some part of me didn't want to think it through that deeply, didn't want to admit that a little sexual dalliance on the side might really be functioning as anything more. I didn't want to consider that it could represent anything other than a neatly compartmentalized exploration of some secret diversion that had nothing to do with the rest of my resolutely straight life. I couldn't go there after all, couldn't really delve into it, without making the connection I'd spent half a lifetime avoiding—and, in the end, without bringing it around to Claire.

No, it has nothing to do with Claire. That bizarre chapter of my life was closed and long since buried. A schoolgirl crush. A moment of confusion during college, nothing more. I'd repeated those phrases to myself so often that they spontaneously popped up in tandem with any fleeting thought of her over the years. As a litany, they'd become my mantra, my truth, and I'd cloaked myself in their comfort for fifteen years.

📖   📖   📖

By 1:30, I'd been only moderately successful in putting aside the distractions that were buzzing into my concentration, and—despite skipping lunch and postponing a bathroom break to the point of agony—I'd only gotten through about half of the CRS file. Naturally, therefore, Louise chose that moment to call and inform me that I was late for the meeting.

"What do you mean? It's not for another half hour."

"The clients came at one."

I did my best not to rip her a new asshole as I gathered my papers, the phone cradled in the crook of my neck. "Well, that doesn't make me late—it makes them early. I'll be there in a minute." I really had to go to the bathroom.

"We need you there now. It started half an hour ago."

We?

"Yeah, well, thanks for letting me know," I said as sarcastically as I could.

"I posted the change on the computer calendar. It's up to you to check it."

That did it. She picked the wrong day for this bullshit. "No, Louise, it's up to you to inform me or my secretary when there's been a change. My time's supposed to be spent doing billable work for the clients, not logging onto the calendar every five minutes because you can't be bothered to pick up the phone. Now where is the meeting?"

"I'm in the middle of something—I have to go. You can find it on the calendar."

She hung up before I could throw the phone through the window.

After clicking through various screens, locating the room, and then dashing down the hall—only to wait an interminable two minutes for the frigging elevator—I finally emerged on the forty-second floor and made a beeline to the ladies' room. It was either that or give Parsons something to really yell about. Tearing around the corner, I slammed through the bathroom door—and ran smack into a woman on the other side. If she'd been an inch closer, she would have been clocked by the door. As it was, I nearly decked her as I barreled in, and I had to grab her with my free arm—the one that wasn't laden with a stack of papers—to help keep her on her feet.

"Sorry," I mumbled as I stood there for half a beat to make sure she had her balance, my urgent bladder for the moment taking a back seat to civility. The look on her face as she stared back at me told me that I'd just made a complete ass of myself—which, of course, I already knew.

"No problem," she muttered. I scooted past her, hastening to a stall, and heard her leave without another word. As I emptied my bladder as quickly as possible, I dismissed the thought of how attractive the woman was and tried to collect my thoughts for the meeting—the meeting for which I was now officially late.

Given how fucked up the day had been so far, it should have come as no surprise when I walked into Conference Room D a minute later to find Parsons (who dramatically looked at his watch) seated to the left of a middle-aged man trying to look ten years younger—and both of them across from the woman I'd almost totaled in the ladies' room. As I entered, she looked up and smiled—a courtesy she hadn't bothered to bestow back in the bathroom.

Huff Chasen was large, probably six-three, and reptilian in a way that certain big men have when they've logged a successful career of using their size to get their own way. It was more than the quiet intimidation lurking just under the surface of his massive bulk, and more than the gleam of his eyes at half-mast sizing up his audience—particularly me. No, if I had to put my finger on it, I guess it was the air of resolute willfulness in which he cloaked himself that made me want to go home and wash my hair the minute I met him.

I wasn't alone in my initial assessment of him. Huff Chasen was known for having a long string of business associates and adversaries strewn across the country who didn't trust him any further than they could throw him, and for good reason. His reputation as a bully was well earned, and these days it opened more doors than it closed. Unfortunately, one of the doors that welcomed him had Huxley Doyle written on it.

He rose as I approached the table—I suspected he never missed an opportunity to tower over someone, especially a woman—and after he shook my hand a little too long I had to force myself not to wipe his sweaty residue on my suit jacket. "Huff Chasen," he said with false good humor. "Good of you to join us."

He said it with just enough irony, with a smile that was just oily enough, that I knew Parsons had filled him in plenty about me, none of it good. As a general rule, I try not to make snap judgments about people, but in Chasen's case I couldn't help it. I hated him on the spot.

"Ashleigh Moore?" the woman interjected as she stood up with a hand outstretched toward me. "Nice to meet you. I'm Renee Silver, General Counsel of CRS."

General Counsel? No shit—she didn't look a day over thirty-five, a veritable baby in Chasen's cutthroat world. Maybe she's a superstar, I thought, one of the anointed few from the top of her class at a prestigious law school. All it took was one look at the predatory gleam in Chasen's eye as he watched her shake my hand for me to get a sinking feeling about the key to her success, and it had nothing to do with legal talent. Chasen was also famous for the eye candy draped on his arm at the many social functions he attended. Why should the litmus test for General Counsel be any different? Either she was sleeping with him, or he wished she were. Snap judgment number two: I didn't trust her.

It was going to be a long meeting.

📖   📖   📖

"To the Class of '86, Flung Far and Wide." The e-mail's subject line caught my attention again later that evening after I'd finally done a little office housekeeping and deleted the garbage from my Inbox. It had been a particularly horrendous day, what with Parsons taking little bites out of my ass at every turn and two emergency motions suddenly blowing up in my face—both minor matters that I gladly dumped on junior associates, but I'd have to review and edit them extensively—all topped off by an excruciating two-hour meeting on the CRS case. Of course, I'd never gotten around to calling Rob. Hit by a quick stab of guilt for having ignored Carla's e-mail, I decided that Rob could wait. In truth, I didn't mind putting off that call.

> Don't hate me for flooding your inboxes with a mass mailing, but I missed the deadline for the Class Notes flyer, so it's this or nothing.

Typical Carla, so involved with thousands of projects that she never quite got anything done. I had to smile as I thought about how many times she'd stormed my room in Comstock in the middle of the night to beg me to type a paper that was due the next day, because she hadn't gotten around to starting it until midnight.

I scanned the lengthy message with something between interest and disgust. Everyone's life seemed so much happier than mine, so much more normal. Debbie Douglas had another kid. Anne Breckenridge was named CFO of her company in Atlanta. A few downbeat items were sprinkled in—Janice Murphy was getting divorced (*gee, couldn't have seen that one coming,* I thought, recalling how wasted she'd gotten at our last reunion). The whole e-mail was making me nauseous and I wasn't even halfway through it. I was tempted to delete the whole thing—but just as I reached for the mouse, my eye latched onto the one name for which I'd secretly scoured the Class Notes flyers through all these years.

> And would you believe it, I finally tracked down none other than Claire Michaels! Well, to be fair, she tracked me down. No, she didn't fall off the map. She's in Chicago. Isn't that the same thing? Anyway, we had a nice long chat, and she told me she's running her own lab now at Meers-Boothe, and sends regards to one and all.

Ignoring the clench of my stomach, I clicked on the "To" line and, sure enough, there it was, buried within a stack of several dozen others: Claire's e-mail address. I had some vague notion of Meers-Boothe as a big pharmaceutical company and, with a little surfing, I was able to locate its Web site. A few more clicks landed me on the About Us page, which got me to Claire. An impressive list of her credentials— grad school at Stanford, various research positions at a St. Louis outfit, and finally her own lab at Meers-Boothe. I was both relieved and disappointed that there was no picture. I didn't know if I was prepared to see any Claire other than the ones in my ragged yearbook—the twenty-one-year-old with a viola tucked snugly under her chin and a look of utter peace on her face; the candid shot of a stoney-faced blonde walking purposefully across the Quad with a book in her hand; and, most of all, the unapproachable beauty whose cryptic half-smile in her formal head shot had haunted my dreams with maddening regularity for the past fifteen years.

❧ Chapter Three

I turned off the hot water and made myself stand in the cold spray a few moments, partly for the sheer torture of it and partly to dissuade David from joining me. I could hear him puttering around at the sink, just waiting for an invitation. He'd never be so bold as to simply suggest we go back to bed for some lovemaking—he'd long ago adopted a strategy of subtle physical cues in the apparent hope that the suggestion would come from me. But it never did, not in months now, and the more he wanted it, the more I didn't. I honestly didn't know which was worse—the guilt of tacitly rejecting him, the guilt of keeping his hopes alive by avoiding the inevitable discussion, or the guilt I was sure to feel if I said yes and simply went through the motions. It had already been a long week, and it was only Thursday—doling out research assignments on the new CRS matter, reviewing the crap that the junior associates came back with, and endless meetings with Renee Silver.

She was a real puzzle—friendly and almost warm one minute, but then masked the next in a cool professionalism that bordered on icy. She was very bright, that was clear, and I found something about her intriguing, but I couldn't seem to get beyond the hard exterior she appeared determined to maintain around me. *Maybe she just doesn't like me*, I thought—*maybe Parsons has already poisoned any chance of her seeing me in an acceptable light.* The thought was disturbing to me, partly because I was so acutely aware of how attractive she was. She had these amazing hazel eyes that seemed to fire with intensity at times—but I didn't want to think about that. She was a client, after all—and Parsons' client at that. No, I didn't want to think about that at all.

"No run this morning?" David asked when I finally emerged from the shower chilled to the bone.

"No," I said, grabbing the towel maybe a little too awkwardly. I didn't like the eager expression on his face as he looked me over, or the sight of his Pavlovian cock as it started to ask for attention. "I'll try to hit the gym tonight."

He turned back to the mirror and continued to shave while I toweled off. I could tell by the slump of his shoulders that he was disappointed. He really deserved better.

"Remember, we have that appointment tonight at eight-thirty."

Shit, that's right. The last thing I wanted right now was to hash through our relationship with some therapist who'd insist that we get in touch with our feelings. Hell, it seemed I spent most of my time around David telling the cacophony of my inner voices to shut the fuck up. How could I get into what I really felt and wanted when I didn't have a clue myself?

"You know," I tried to keep my tone light, "tonight is really bad for me. This new case Parsons has me on has really blown up this week, and I'll probably have to work late. Isn't there any way we can reschedule for a weekend?"

"We've been through this," he said, keeping a lid on the exasperation I sensed in him. "Her weekends are booked solid. The only regular appointment she could give us was a weeknight. And you were the one who asked for eight-thirty."

"What do you mean 'regular'? I can't commit to a block of time each week."

"Well, you don't just show up and have your marriage fixed just like that. It's a process. We need to give it some time."

"I know. It's just . . . I don't know. How long are we talking? Weeks? Months?"

"Why don't we just get there first, and see how it goes?"

He was right, and I knew I was being unreasonable, but I couldn't let go of the feeling that I was being put upon. "Whatever," I muttered.

"You know, I might finish up early tonight. Maybe we could go out for a nice dinner before the appointment." He caught my eye in the mirror and smiled.

"I don't know. I really want to get to the gym if I can get away early."

"Okay."

I dressed on automatic pilot and got out of there in record time. I can normally shower, dress, and get to work within an hour of my 6:00 a.m. alarm, but recently I seemed to be cutting a good fifteen minutes from my usual time. And I was sure it wasn't because the taxis were speeding.

Safely ensconced in the back of the cab, I exhaled slowly and tried to organize my day. Rob—I'd already put off that call for a week, and it couldn't wait any longer. CRS meeting with Renee Silver—goddamnit. Edit the motions—I hoped they'd be in decent shape. Deal with the Arizona lawyers—maybe, depending on what Rob wanted to do.

Claire. No way, I wasn't going to open that can of worms, not now. Hey Claire, guess what? I dreamed about you last night. We were back at Smith, and you broke my heart all over again.

I hated that dream, hated waking up with the feelings so raw and fresh that I seemed to have relived my entire senior year in the span of a single night. I hated having to dig myself back out of it each time, pushing aside layer upon layer of sensation throughout the day in order to surface once again in a here and now that was infinitely less painful but no less complicated.

Two voice mail messages were waiting for me as soon as I got to the office: one from Renee Silver—her velvet voice practically caressing the words as she explained she'd be arriving half an hour early for our meeting—and the other from Rob, who got right to the point as usual. "What's this damn business about our father? Call me."

I pulled out the Arizona letter to scan it again as I kicked off my pumps. I really hate business attire and would wear jeans and a T-shirt every day if it weren't for Parsons and his ilk. Most of the Huxley Doyle partners agreed with Dennis, the head of our litigation group, that the attorneys' personal comfort was more important than appearances—especially since most of our clients had adopted a "business casual" dress code themselves. Who were we supposed to be dressing up for? But Parsons called the shots around this firm, at least when it came to associates, and while Dennis could get away with the occasional khakis and golf shirt, I couldn't afford to incur Parsons' wrath.

It was predawn on the West Coast, but Rob kept market hours and was usually in the office very early. He answered on the first ring.

"I guess Liz called you," I said. We were long past perfunctory greetings.

"Yeah, and thanks for letting me know." I could hear the challenge in his voice already. "So what's this about?"

"All I know is what the letter said, that it has something to do with Grandma Edna's estate. And I was about to call you."

"Well, why'd he write to you?"

I should have guessed that he'd feel slighted. As the oldest, he'd always acted, and no doubt felt, superior to me and Lizzie. I was sure that, in his mind, it was an outrageous insult that the lawyers had bypassed him altogether and written to the youngest of us. But I'd learned long ago not to rise to Robbie's bait—as a child, it could earn me something painful, and as an adult it got me a dismissive putdown. So I didn't bother to point out that the letter hadn't been written by Gardner but by his lawyers. Nor did I state the obvious—that I couldn't begin to guess their motivation. Discretion was always the better part of valor in dealing with Rob, even from a remove of 3,000 miles.

"Look, do you want me to fax you the letter so you can see it yourself? Give me your number."

"No, it doesn't matter. Just call them up and see what they want."

I bristled at the order. Who the fuck did he think he was, dictating instructions as if I were his secretary? My time is billed at $350 an hour, and I sure as hell wasn't going to hop to it on his command.

"Well, I was thinking that we could call them together," I said calmly. "Liz doesn't want to, but I can have my secretary set up a call for the two of us, if you want."

"I don't want to talk to him."

"No, the lawyers."

He was silent a minute—one of his little control games, keeping me on the hook waiting for him.

"You know, there could be money in this."

I didn't see that one coming. "What?"

"Grandma Edna. She was loaded."

"You're kidding. How come I never heard about it?"

"You never met her."

"So what? Don't tell me you remember anything about her—you were barely five years old when he left."

"I remember," he said quietly. Stella picked that moment to poke her head in my office, but I waved her away. Robbie had my full attention now, and I hesitated to breathe too audibly for fear I'd chase away his sudden confessional mood. In all these years, I could count on one hand the number of times Robbie had ever admitted to remembering anything about those years with our father. And I'd have a few fingers to spare.

"She used to come visit sometimes," he continued. "She always wore lots of furs and jewelry. And perfume—I remember the perfume. And she'd send money at Christmastime, even after he left. You must remember that—the Christmas money."

"Vaguely." Not really.

"And Gussie said something once, one Christmas."

"What?"

"She was talking to Gramps in the kitchen, and I don't think she knew I was on the basement stairs."

"What'd she say?"

"Something about how you'd think she'd send more than a measly fifty bucks, seeing as how she had all those millions and knew we were all cramped in that tiny house."

It was a lot to take in, and I didn't know quite what to think. So I pressed on, hoping to squeeze every ounce of information out of this unexpected trip down memory lane.

"When was this? How old were you?"

I heard him sigh on the other end, and knew I was close to pushing it too far. As always, I was the one going left when everyone else in my family went right, marching blindly into the forbidden territory they all avoided.

"I don't know, ten or twelve. Old enough to remember. Anyway, all I'm saying is that it's worth calling these guys, because Grandma Edna had bucks."

"Don't you think it'd be worth calling them just because she was our grandmother?"

He snorted on the other end. "Yeah, right. Just see what they want," he said before hanging up without a good-bye.

I'd barely had time to put down the receiver, and no time at all to mull over the call, when Janelle walked in and stood beside my desk.

"I've really had it with that Queen Bee. I'm telling you, the minute the secretarial evaluations are handed out, she's toast."

"Not now, Janelle, I—"

"Here," she interrupted, placing on my desk something that looked like a rock. "It's a crystal. I picked it out especially for you. It'll give you good energy."

"Huh?"

"You hold it in your hand. The vibrations, you know."

"Oh, thanks." *Give me a break.*

"What's with you? You look like Parsons just did you up the ass."

"No, that was my brother."

"Ha, what does the Boy Wonder want?" she asked, easing herself into the chair across from me and immediately propping her feet on my desk. Janelle had only met Rob once, when he happened to be in New York on business and graced my office with a surprise visit—to borrow money. She took an instant dislike to him, even without the benefit of knowing anything about our history. "I just don't like his high and mighty attitude toward you," she'd said. She didn't know the half of it.

"I had to talk to him about a family thing."

"Yeah?"

It went against the grain to mention family matters to anyone outside our clan, but I only hesitated for a moment. It had already been a morning of unprecedented disclosures, and Janelle was practically family to me. I moved the rock—crystal—to the side of my desk as I considered how to begin.

"You know how I've never met my natural father? That he left just before I was born?"

"Yeah. A real piece of work, that one. You've got some real winners in that male line of yours."

"Yeah, well, it seems he wants to talk to us—me and Liz and Rob."

"No shit."

"Really. He had some law firm in Arizona write me a letter asking me to contact them."

"Why didn't he just write the letter himself? Or pick up the phone?"

"I don't know. Maybe he's ashamed of himself, walking out on us like that."

"He should be. I hope you give it to him good." I smiled—Gussie couldn't have said it better herself. She'd also roll in her grave to know that I was comparing her to a black lesbian. "So what are you going to do?"

"I guess I'm going to call them."

"Any idea what it's about?"

"Not really. All they said was that it was about my grandmother's estate—my grandmother on my father's side."

"Did she just die?"

"No, that's the weird part. She's been dead ten or fifteen years."

"So her estate must have been settled long before now."

"Right. And here's the real kicker: Rob says she had a lot of money."

"How much?"

"A lot. Millions, according to Rob."

"But you don't think so."

"I don't know what to think. I sure didn't hear anything about a rich relative while I was growing up."

"You never met her?"

"No, that whole side of the family was out of the picture before I was even born, except for my Aunt Nell, but she didn't have much to do with the rest of them. And I know she didn't like my Grandma Edna."

"But still, you'd think it would have come up at some point."

"Well, maybe not," I said as I absently fingered the crystal.

"What do you mean?"

"Oh, you know how nobody in my family ever talks about my natural father. It was like the big taboo subject in my house."

"But how could they keep something that big a secret?"

"I don't think it was a secret. I just think that the subject of my father was a sore spot for my mother, so we didn't mention him around the house—or anywhere else."

"But if he had money, or she did, I can't believe the subject didn't come up. I mean, you told me how tight things were for you growing up, how you might not have gone to college at all if you hadn't gotten that scholarship to Smith."

"You don't get it. We never talked about him. I mean, *never*. Practically the only thing I only know about the guy is that his name is Kenneth Gardner."

"But your name's Moore."

"My last name changed when Dad married Mom and officially adopted me."

"So let's get back to the money. How did Rob know she had bucks?"

"Well, that's kind of strange too. He said he overheard my grandmother say something a long time ago. But that means that he's known all these years, and he never said anything. I mean, I guess I understand why the adults in the house never mentioned it. That's the way they always were. But I didn't think Rob would be like that too."

Even as I said it, I knew better. Rob was very good at keeping secrets. In some ways, better than all of us. But they were always secrets that were in his best interest to keep.

"He never talked about your father growing up? He must have remembered some things."

"No. I don't remember the subject even coming up very often, but I do know that the one or two times I asked him, he said he didn't remember anything."

Janelle righted herself in the chair and stretched her legs. "Well, girlfriend, I think you've got a phone call to make."

"Yeah, I guess so. It's probably nothing."

"By the way, who's that woman I keep seeing you meeting with? You were in the conference room with her yesterday."

"Renee Silver—a client. Why?"

Her face broke into a Cheshire cat smile with perfect white teeth, and the glint in her eyes was unmistakable. "Oh, no reason."

"Come on, give."

"I've just seen her around, that's all."

"Yeah, right." I didn't like her insinuation, or the way my pulse quickened when she said it.

"No joke, Ash. She's hot; you think I'd forget a face like that?"

"I'm sure you're wrong. Actually, I think she might be sleeping with that big guy who was with us last week."

"Huff Chasen? You're kidding."

"Just a feeling."

"Well, all I know is that I've seen her in a couple upscale women's bars on the East Side. If you'd come out with me some night, you'd see for yourself."

"Don't start."

"I'm only looking out for you, you know."

📖   📖   📖

"Eighty-sixth and West End," I said when I finally managed to flag a cab and climb in the back. "Take the highway."

"No, Teenth," the driver snapped in his heavily accented English.

"There's construction on Tenth. Take the highway."

"Eeeth!" he said, his clipped accent exaggerated by irritation. Maybe he was having a bad day, but mine had been no picnic either, and I was late for an appointment that I really didn't want to keep anyway.

"Eighth is jammed with theater traffic at this hour. Take the highway."

I don't get it, I really don't. If you're a cab driver, you have exactly one thing that you need to be able to do—get around town efficiently. The cabbies don't make money on long rides—they pay a huge cut of the meter fare to the fleet from which they license the hack. The real money is in tips, and I know something about living on tips: the best money comes from a lot of short trips, not one long trip. It's in everybody's interest—the driver's and the passenger's—to make the trip as quickly as possible. So why do I have to remind him to avoid midtown traffic?

"Lady, you driving? No, I drive. I say Eeeth."

Maybe it's the blonde hair, or the fact that I'm a woman, but the cabbies who don't seem to know the city's traffic patterns very well are invariably the ones who take offense when I suggest the fastest route. As if I'd just displayed the most brazen temerity and insulted their masculinity. For God's sake, I wasn't ridiculing his penis size, I was telling him the route that I, the customer, wanted to take. Fuck this.

"Tell you what, pal, take whatever street you want, but I'm only paying ten dollars for this ride. It's up to you how much of that ten comes out as a tip. The faster you get me there, the more of it goes toward the tip."

He muttered something incomprehensible as we turned north on Eighth Avenue and promptly landed in a monstrous traffic jam.

"Good choice," I mumbled, glancing at my watch. Ten past eight—no way I'd make it on time. I slouched back into the seat and mulled over the topics I was planning to avoid.

Renee Silver immediately came to mind. I'd have to put that one on a shelf far out of reach. Once I'd been tipped off by Janelle's gossip, I hadn't been able to help it—I'd spent our entire meeting today looking for clues. A meeting that had stretched into lunch. A lunch that I'd then proceeded to turn over in my mind at odd moments throughout the rest of the day.

Okay, be logical about it—systematic—and apply a little of that analytic ability for which clients pay the big bucks. For starters, Renee was beautiful. No big deal there; I'm surrounded by attractive people all the time, both women and men. Still, there was something particularly compelling about her beauty, some indefinable luster to it that enhanced the thick brown hair and brought out the shine of her hazel eyes. They were powerful eyes, framed with long dark lashes that I swear had never seen mascara. Some people are born that way, with a cover girl complexion on a face that makeup would only distort.

But it was more than just her lovely features. It was the whole package, from the functional yet stylish black suit—size six, I'd guess—to her composed, purposeful expression. Pure business, it said outwardly; yet there were those few moments, especially today, when I could swear she'd let down her guard for an instant, when I thought I saw a little crinkle at the corner of her eye, as if she'd been quietly laughing at an inside joke.

Like when she'd suggested that we continue the meeting over lunch. "A little bistro I know around the corner. Very quiet," she'd said in that soft low voice, and her eyes did that crinkle thing as if to imply that she was letting me in on a secret. And even though we were supposed to be going over the legal theories for the trade secret claim, the fact was that we spent nearly the entire lunch trading war stories and playing "do you know?" I'd been so surprised to hear that she was a Holyoke grad, just a year ahead of me, that I couldn't help but start us down the path of swapping names. And by the time she'd mentioned her tenure at Farnsworth Crowley after law school, we were knee-deep in the personal information end of the pool, with no hope of swimming our way back to the CRS business.

"Sure, I remember Charlie Porter," she'd said in answer to another "do you know" volley. "He sat in the office next to me for three years. And he married a classmate of mine from Columbia law."

"Doris Baker was in your class? I did an internship with her at Legal Aid before I started here."

"Oh God," she smiled—and what an amazing smile it was—"I can just see her doing that kind of work. Did she actually go back in the pens?"

Legal Aid is the public law office in New York that provides lawyers for indigent criminal defendants, staffed by an army of goodhearted but woefully underpaid young lawyers and law students who gain enormous practical trial experience in handling hopeless cases for hopeless clients. The worst part of the job—if you don't count the fact that you're always broke and on the losing side 99 percent of the time—is the fact that you meet your clients, usually for the first time, just before arraignment in the jail cells behind the criminal courtrooms. The cells are aptly called the pens because the men are treated like animals and the place stinks worse than the elephant house at the zoo.

"Yeah," I said, enjoying immensely the delight in her face, "I was with her on her first trip to court. The minute we walked back there, she was ready to lose her lunch from the stench. And then her client went batshit when he found out she was just a law student intern—started banging on the partition and screaming about his constitutional rights. I thought he was going to bust through and grab her!"

Renee laughed out loud; it was the first time I'd heard her do so, and the sound was so unexpected that I lost my train of thought. No matter. Renee picked up the ball.

"Oh, I wish I could have seen that! So what made you go into civil practice after your stint at Legal Aid?"

"My stint at Legal Aid," I deadpanned, and she smiled. "No, seriously, it was exhilarating and all that, but I just couldn't see being responsible for something as important as some guy's liberty, having it depend on me doing my job well. And that was before New York reinstated the death penalty. Imagine how much worse it would be now—some poor slob's life could be at stake." I shook my head. "No, I don't want that much responsibility. Same reason I didn't go to med school."

"So you'd rather be responsible for millions of dollars?"

"It's just money." I shrugged. "And no matter how much is at stake, it's usually just a drop in the bucket to the client. I think of it as Monopoly money, and try not to get bogged down in all those zeros."

"Same here," she said. "When I was in private practice, I remember being bowled over by the size of the claims we were litigating, but it seemed that the bigger the numbers, the less the client seemed particularly concerned about it. I mean, of course they cared, but they'd be less involved with micromanaging and second-guessing me."

"Yeah, it's the same for me. I don't know if that's a function of the clients or the claims."

"What do you mean?"

"If it's because the clients with big claims just have so much business and too many other lawsuits to get really involved with a single case, or if their disinterestedness is a part of the reason for their success—they delegate effectively and leave the lawyering to the lawyers."

"Good point. Well, I hope you'll find with CRS that it's more of the latter," she said, retreating an inch behind her wall of professional composure. I saw an opportunity to get some of the lowdown on CRS—and, I acknowledged to myself, her relationship with Chasen— so I slid my foot in the door before she could close it all the way.

"I get the feeling that Chasen's plenty diversified," I said casually as I stirred the foam of my cappuccino.

"Oh, I suppose so, but I don't really know. I just got here a few months ago, and I've been treading water ever since, just trying to get a handle on the things that require my immediate attention. I get the feeling it's just the tip of the iceberg. There seem to be whole areas of the corporate holdings that I don't know anything about."

I found that odd; it made no business sense for Chasen to keep her out of the loop. He'd have to let his corporate counsel know about all of the company's affairs, as a matter of self-preservation. Part of her job was to watch his back, and she couldn't do it if she didn't have a clear view of the territory. I said so, and she nodded.

"Look," she said quietly, "I'm the new kid on the block. I'm in no position to tell him how to run his company, even if he has given me a fancy title and a nice office. Maybe he's just easing me into the job."

Maybe, but I doubted it. And maybe he was hoping to ease her into more than just her job.

Interrupted for the moment by the waiter with the check, we turned our attention to paying the bill. "No," I said as I took the check from her hand, "this one's on me."

She smiled and let me take it. "On one condition."

"What's that?"

"You let me buy the next one. And you have more than cappuccino for dessert."

"But I love cappuccino."

"Well, next time, you can't have any unless you also have some of that decadent chocolate cake."

"Are you trying to corrupt me?"

She snagged me with a look that, for just a second, was piercing in its intensity. Then the moment was gone, and we both looked away. I didn't have any idea what had just happened, but I was profoundly disturbed by it. And so, it seemed, was she.

Frankly, I was disturbed by the entire lunch, in recognizing how much I'd enjoyed my time with her, and how deliberately I'd worked at getting her to loosen up with me. I still didn't really trust her, and felt certain that there was a lot of the CRS picture I was missing. But most of all, I didn't like the unexpected elation I felt when it became clear that she wasn't personally involved with Chasen. I didn't like the feeling, and I didn't like what it might mean.

Which, of course, brought me right back to my mental list of topics to avoid tonight. As I sat in the back seat of the cab—now stuck in traffic on Tenth Avenue, the cabbie having finally given up on Eighth but still unwilling to take the highway—I started once more to sort through the reasons that Renee disturbed me.

I'd only known her a week, and we hadn't even struck up much of a friendship yet; but even as I touched on the thought, my mind immediately flashed on her parting handshake that afternoon, warm and prolonged, as she smiled into my eyes and said she was glad I was on the case. Okay, that might have been a little close to the personal line, but let's face it: it was perfectly innocent. Except that she'd held onto my hand just a beat longer than professional decorum would dictate, and she'd looked into my eyes with such openness and—admit it— *engagement* that the moment had lingered for me long after she'd left. It wasn't really a come-on. I know a come-on, and that wasn't it. Lunch with Renee was something else entirely, and maybe that was part of the intrigue. There was nothing obvious about her. She wasn't barging across the line; she was deftly poised right on top of it—leaving herself open to interpretation, which might say a lot more about me than about her. Carefully balanced on the line, she usually leaned on the side of calm and reserve, but occasionally she shifted her weight to suggest that some deeply personal feelings might reside beneath that immutable exterior. Her perfectly composed features, lovely as they were to look at, were simply a mask through which I was permitted to glimpse, in a few brief and intoxicating moments, the woman within. And it was the unpredictability of those moments—the thrill of the unexpected glimpse—that had me reliving our lunch for the rest of the day.

I simply didn't know where I stood with her from one moment to the next. Which Renee she'd be, which Renee she'd let me see. Distant and then thoroughly engaging in the skip of a heartbeat.

Just like—oh God, I thought as the cab pulled up in front of the West End brownstone—*just like Claire.*

📖　　📖　　📖

"What do you expect to get out of this?" the woman seated in front of us asked after a few long seconds of silence. Dr. Mbaye, her name was, and David had assured me that she came highly recommended. I looked her directly in the eyes and tried hard to keep my face neutral, afraid that she'd misconstrue any discomfort on my part as an acknowledgment of her bizarre appearance.

Whatever I was expecting a marriage counselor to look like, this wasn't it. The woman before me couldn't have been more than five feet tall, and her natty Afro and bug-eyed expression reminded me of Buckwheat on *Little Rascals.* My political correctness shuddered at the comparison, but there it was. Still, I kept my eyes glued to her face so as to avoid looking at her arm—the one I'd inelegantly reached out to shake hello just a few moments before, only to notice too late that it was a metal hook that she was extending toward me. I didn't know that people still used such things in this age of robotic prosthetics, and I certainly didn't want to be caught staring at it.

She seemed perfectly at ease with the ensuing silence, apparently happy to wait us out. David had made this appointment, so as far as I was concerned, David could get the ball rolling. Only forty-seven minutes to go.

"Well," he said, and then cleared his throat, "I guess we've hit sort of an impasse in our communication, and we need a little help to get us back on track."

What the fuck, David, just speak English—it's not some board of directors for you to double-talk. I let the anger wash over me, even tried to gin it up a notch or two. Anything to avoid giving in to the other emotions that were clutching at my throat. Anger was good. Anger was my safety.

Dr. Mbaye simply nodded, her face open but unreadable. I guess they teach those skills in therapy school, or wherever marriage counselors go for training—how to make people keep talking without letting them in on what you're thinking. Sort of like negotiating a deal. I found it unsettling to stare at her, and even more unsettling to feel her staring back at me—it was David who was speaking, after all, so she should look at him. I glanced down at the crazy pattern on the hooked rug—oops, probably shouldn't call it that. Certain that she'd read my mind just then, I quickly turned my attention to the African mask hanging on the wall over her chair.

David cleared his throat again. "I guess the main sticking point has been over when we're going to start a family." Not whether—when. Damn him. He gave a little chuckle before continuing, with his head cocked to the side in that little-boy posture I'd once found endearing. "We hardly have time to discuss it, much less get to work on it."

It was getting pretty warm in there; maybe it was the heavy drapes in front of the windows and the heat of the table lamps, which seemed to have been positioned around the room to lend the place a living room appearance. That's what it was, in all probability—the living room of an old West Side apartment, which Dr. Mbaye and her colleagues had converted into a cozy therapy office. It had an air of having been well used, as if a tide of humanity had walked its rugs and flattened its sofa cushions over the years. The air was getting heavier—and the constriction of my chest wasn't helping.

David seemed to have found his stride, and I tuned him out as he started in on a long pity-party about his love for me. I'd heard it so often before, I couldn't help but wonder if he was saying it for her benefit or his own, unsure of whom he was trying to convince. We'd played out this scene so many times in private that I didn't need to be here to know where it was going, where it always went—to that perverse place where everyone has to conclude that his life would be complete if only I had remained the adoring wife I used to be; if only I weren't me. He got rolling on his solo dance for Dr. Mbaye, and I knew I was still in the room only because I could feel her gaze on me, penetrating but not challenging. No, the real challenge for me was to get enough air in my lungs, because the heat of the lamps and David's rambling monologue were using up all of the oxygen. The stifling air was choking the anger out of me and threatened to make way for everything the anger had kept in check. I had to get out of there.

Her eyes never left me—I could feel them bearing down hard as I glanced at my watch. David paused for a moment, and the silence echoed in my ears as I willed him to resume the next part of his speech. But he didn't. Instead, he sat there beside me on the sofa and let the silence embrace us both. And when I finally lifted my head to meet her gaze, I saw in her face not the big round eyes I'd expected, but something new, something that reached inside me and touched a place I didn't want her anywhere near. As if she'd read my soul in braille.

"What is it you don't want to say?" she asked me quietly, eyes unwavering.

No, please, not here, not now. But the words seemed to come out of nowhere, slipping past my lips with a will of their own before I could think about it.

"I don't want to be married anymore," I whispered as I felt the first tears spilling down my cheeks.

Chapter Four

I first met Claire at the start of my junior year at Smith. My room-mate Shelly and I had lived in Comstock House for our first two years and, like most of the residents, we figured we'd be there for the dura-tion. I'd come back to campus in early September that year, about a week before the start of classes, to receive training for helping out the new students in orientation—and also because I needed to look for a job. Money was very tight, since my scholarship covered tuition only, and even with Mom and Dad and Gussie and Gramps pooling their nickels to help out, there wasn't a lot to go around. I had been the third in line for college, after all. Even though both Rob and Lizzie were out by the time I started—Lizzie had, in fact, accelerated her de-gree to finish in three years—they had both received only partial scholarships, so there was virtually nothing left in the family kitty by the time it was my turn.

I'd gotten lucky—a four-year full-tuition ride, and a good job my first two years waiting tables at the vegetarian restaurant next to cam-pus. But junior year would be tough because I had too many after-noon classes—I couldn't squeeze the restaurant's mandatory weekday shifts into my heavy class schedule. So I had to look elsewhere, and spent the first three days of that orientation week tramping from one Northampton business to the next searching for work. It wasn't until Wednesday that I resigned myself to the fact that the only jobs I could fit into my schedule would be night jobs—and in Northampton, that meant a bar.

"Just do it," Shelly had said on the phone when she'd called that af-ternoon from her home in Boston. "You'll make most of your money in tips, so you won't have taxes taken out. Where else are you going to get that kind of money, in cash, for a few hours of night work?"

"What if they change the drinking age?" There had been talk that it might happen sometime that year; if it did, I couldn't even go to a bar, much less work in one.

"Don't worry. Even if they raise it to twenty-one, they're going to grandfather in all of us who have already turned twenty."

She was right—I'd heard something about the legislature toying with the idea of letting the twenty-year-olds keep their drinking privileges.

"I don't know," I said. "I've never worked in a bar."

"Well, your options for night work are pretty limited—unless you want to be a hooker."

"Very funny."

"I'm not joking, Ash." I wasn't in the mood to hear her feminist line on prostitution at the moment. She'd regaled me with it often enough the year before, when she'd taken that Modes of Feminism course. I just couldn't see empowering myself in that particular way. Let someone else take sex back from the patriarchy.

"Look, can we get serious for a minute? I don't know if I'm really the cocktail-waitress type."

"Oh, come on, you'd be perfect. All that long blonde hair, a skimpy little dress showing off those legs—you'd have the guys eating out of your hands."

"Sounds like we're back to the hooker idea. No thanks."

"Well," she said carefully, "that's not the only kind of bar around, you know."

"What do you mean?"

"You could always try a gay bar. There's one right off campus."

"Oh, get real."

"No, I'm serious. Why not?"

"Isn't it obvious?"

"No, really. The Cave—it's, like, a ten-minute walk from Comstock. I've been there; it's nice."

"I don't believe this. When did you ever go to a dyke bar?"

"Last semester—and don't call it that. A bunch of us from that Women Writers class went there a few times. Played some pool, drank some beer; it was fun. You'd fit right in."

"What's that supposed to mean?"

Shelly laughed. "Only that some of the women who go there are really crunchy granola types. You'll feel like you're back at the vegetarian restaurant."

"Keep it up, pal. I'll have you choking down some Tofu Delight before exams. Which reminds me, when are you coming back?"

"Saturday, probably. The campus starting to fill up yet?"

"Not really."

"How about next door? Janice is getting a new roommate, you know. Claire Michaels."

"You know her?"

"Yeah, she's cool. I had a class with her last fall. You're really going to like her."

I doubted that. Shelly had an abysmal track record when it came to predicting such things.

"Well," I offered, "she'd better be willing to put up with Janice's boyfriend, or she'll be moving out before I have a chance to get to know her."

"Rick got an apartment near Amherst; Janice will probably spend most of her time at his place."

"Really? Think she'd be willing to take you with her?"

"Oh, come on, we're not that bad!"

"Puh-leeze, you're worse than bad. You have no idea how peaceful it's been around here without you two talking like a cheap romance novel every minute."

"Yes, but I'm cute."

"That you are," I laughed, "and I'm a saint to live with you."

"Well, Saint Ash, I hate to cut this short, but Dad is making me pay for my own calls now, and you're not worth another dime. Go get a job at the Cave—I mean it."

It took only about an hour after that phone call—and a glance at my depressing checkbook—for the initial shock at the idea to give way to acceptance. By the time the Cave opened for happy hour at four, I was waiting by the door and trying to dispel the feeling of being an impostor.

"What can I do for you, doll?" asked a large woman in a suede vest as she approached the door and proceeded to pull an enormous

keychain from her belt. It looked very heavy, but she deftly flipped
through the keys.

"Hi," I said. "I'm, um, looking for a job."

"Uh-huh." She turned to unlock the heavy wooden door, and the
darkness inside stank of cigarettes and beer. "Hang on a sec while I
get the lights," she said from somewhere behind me. "There we go."

When the lights came on, I was surprised to see that the place was
nothing more than a very ordinary-looking bar. Nothing like the
S&M parlor I'd been imagining on my walk over, the room had a cozy,
neighborhood kind of feel, with a pool table on the left, a small dance
floor in the back, hardwood floors, and a well-polished mahogany bar
on the right.

"Have a seat," she said, nodding toward the high stools at the bar.
"I'll be right with you." She took off for the back to disappear through
a side door, and soon I heard the hum of the air-conditioning kick on.

"Whew," she said as she made her way behind the bar, "they said
this heat would break last night. Could have fooled me."

I nodded from my perch on the barstool, and felt a little less self-
conscious about the sweat stains on my tank top.

"I'm Kat, by the way," she said, extending a hand across the bar. I
shook it, for once unafraid to apply the firm grip that Gussie had
taught me. "You shake a person's hand," she'd say, "you let them
know they're shaking hands with *somebody*."

"Hi. I'm Ash."

"What can I get you while we talk? I'm having a Tab."

"Sounds good to me." I immediately liked her. She fit every stereo-
type I'd ever imagined when I thought of lesbians—tall, short brown
hair, a good fifty pounds overweight. But there was also something
very sweet about her, and a down-to-earth friendliness that was very
engaging. I decided right there she'd probably make a good boss.

"As far as a job goes, how old are you?"

"Twenty."

"Birthday?"

"January fifth."

She nodded. "That should be okay. If they change the law, it probably won't happen until the start of the new year. So even if they don't

grandfather you, you'd only have to miss a week. Now," she looked me up and down, "what I really need is a bouncer, but I don't suppose I could use you there. I just lost the best one I ever had; she decided she was straight, again, and now her boyfriend doesn't want her working here." She passed me the Tab and thought a minute. "But I'd been planning to put one of my bartenders on the door, and that would leave open a slot behind the bar. You interested?"

"Well," I said, deciding that honesty was the best policy, "I've never tended bar before. I've been a waitress though." I was willing to take the honesty bit only so far, and decided I should just keep quiet for now about being straight.

Kat chuckled. "You think this place has cocktail waitresses? Hell, I'd have to put up a chain to keep out the guys, and the feminists would probably burn me down."

Well, that was that.

"You know how to tap beer?"

How hard could it be? I nodded.

"Well, that's mostly what you'll do. We don't get too many requests for mixed drinks. Just the usuals—you know, gin and tonic, rum and Coke, scotch and water—and the shots are premeasured." She chuckled at my quizzical look. "Here, I'll show you."

She lifted a bottle from a shelf under the bar ledge and tipped it over a shot glass. The top of the bottle was equipped with a large plastic contraption with a spout, and, sure enough, the amount of liquid that poured from it precisely filled the shot glass but didn't overflow it.

"See? Nothing to it. Think you can handle it?"

"Sure," I said. It looked like fun.

"I can give you three weeknight shifts to start, and we'll see how it goes. If things work out, you can pick up some weekends too. That's when we're really busy once the semester starts, so the tips are good."

"Okay." I couldn't quite believe it had been this easy.

"I pay shit, though, I have to warn you. Four-fifty an hour, and I have to take out taxes and stuff."

"I know." That was what I made at the restaurant, where the tips were generally pretty lousy.

"But you're going to do fine on tips; the girls are going to love you. Women, I should say."

Well, I wasn't so sure about that, especially once they found out I was straight. But it was worth a shot, especially since I had no alternatives.

"Sounds great," I said, hopping down from the stool. I couldn't wait to tell Shelly. "When do I start?"

"How about tonight? Come by around seven, and I'll go through the basics with you. Plan on Thursday and Sunday too, okay?"

"You got it. Anything in particular I should wear?" I hated to sound like such a novice, but I was.

She smiled at me with an air of maternal indulgence. "What you're wearing right now is fine. It gets pretty hot in here when the dancing gets going."

"Okay," I said, reaching into my pocket to pay for the Tab.

"Put your money away. Employees drink for free."

"Well, thanks, Kat, I really appreciate it." I reached out and shook her hand.

"It was just a Tab," she said with a smile.

"The job," I laughed. "See you at seven."

The world was looking considerably brighter as I dashed back to the Quad. I had a job, and would start having some money in my pockets starting that night! I noticed that the streets were starting to fill up with some of the returning students—maybe business would be good tonight.

I approached the lovely Georgian facade of Comstock with my mind busily combing through my closet to pick out the tank top and shorts I'd wear. It would definitely work out—my first classes on Thursday, Friday, and Monday weren't until noon, so I'd have plenty of sleep and study time after my late nights. And the money was going to be at least as good as what I'd made last year at the restaurant—maybe even better, once I picked up some Friday and Saturday night shifts. I had to call Mom and Gussie right away. I'd leave out the part about it being a gay bar.

I burst through the door and took the stairs two at a time. As I reached the top landing, my mind pondering how to convince Gussie that good girls did indeed work in bars these days, I rounded the corner going full throttle—only to run head-on into a statue of a woman emerging from Janice's room. She was tall—well, taller than me—wearing a yellow bathrobe with a matching towel wrapped turban-style on her head, and she stood rooted to the spot despite my full-body assault. I was knocked backward by the contact, but she stood there immobile and stared at me as if I'd just swooped in from Mars.

"Oh, hi. Sorry," I fumbled as I tried to regain some composure. When in doubt, fall back on your manners, I heard Gussie remind me. "I'm Ash Moore. You must be Janice's new roommate."

"I must be," she said neutrally. Her face was immutable and absolutely devoid of expression—no friendliness, but no disdain either. And her look was so direct, so unyielding, that it made me even more uncomfortable than I already was. I tried to break through again.

"Claire, right? My roommate, Shelly, said you were moving in. You had a class with her last year?"

"Yeah," she said, looking down the hallway to the bathroom. "Look, I'm on my way to brush my teeth," she held up her toothbrush as if to prove the point, "so . . ."

"Oh, right. Sorry." God, what a bitch. "Well, welcome to Comstock."

"Thanks," she mumbled as she walked away. I turned toward my room, looking forward to telling Shelly that her abysmal record was intact.

📖 📖 📖

Claire Michaels. There was her Meers-Boothe Web page, with her e-mail link at the bottom. It would be so easy to just click on it and send her a quick hello. Easy, but a huge mistake.

"Honey?" David called through the den door. Shit—busted.

"What?" I said, trying not to sound irritated. The weekend had been rough enough on him, on both of us. *Just go back to sleep,* I willed him. But he wasn't reading my mind very clearly tonight—he opened the door a crack and popped his head in.

"What are you doing in here? It's two o'clock in the morning."

I quickly clicked the screen to my home browser page—no need for him to see whose name I'd been staring at.

"Nothing, just surfing. Thinking."

"Do you feel like talking about it?"

"No, I'm all talked out." That was the truth. I didn't want to jump back into that snake pit of a discussion for the rest of my life. We'd been hashing through it for more than a week already—every night since that first therapy session, in fact—and the crescendo we'd hit this weekend had been more than enough fun, thank you.

"Ash, come on, don't just clam up on me. We have to talk this through."

"No, we don't. Just give it a rest, okay? I'm sick of talking about it."

"I know," he sighed. "I'm tired too. But the longer we let things fester, the worse it'll get."

"David, all we do is talk." *And isn't that part of the problem? That he doesn't hear me when I say that talking isn't getting us anywhere because we just go around in circles?* "I'm just not up to it. Please, just go back to bed."

"All right. But I want you to know that I'm willing to do whatever it takes to see this thing through."

That did it. He'd played that pity-party on my last nerve, and I let him have it.

"Do you hear yourself? 'See this through'—you seem to think that means we end up happily married. That if you talk at me long enough, you'll convince me of it."

"Well, what other choice do we have?"

"Have you listened to a word I've said? We want different things—to me, 'seeing this through' might mean that, at the end of that road, we say good-bye. And when you refuse to hear that, it just makes it that much clearer to me that I can't keep going like this. I'm sorry, David, I really am, but that's just the way it is. And no arguing or talking or seeing it through is going to change it." I sighed, regretting the forcefulness of my words, irritated that I'd let him get to me again, that his obstinacy had once more brought me to this point.

"Just go back to bed," I said quietly. *Let me crawl back inside my head and try to sort this thing out.*

He stood there in the doorway and nodded, but I had no faith that he'd heard me this time either.

"You're right," he said. "Let's just drop it for now. You should get some sleep too, okay? You'll feel better with a good night's sleep."

I decided to start reading the apartment classifieds first thing in the morning.

📖 📖 📖

One thing I love about the law, probably the main thing, is that it's constantly evolving. Like most people, I'd always assumed that "the law" was just a list of rules written down in a book somewhere, and that law school was a place where I'd be taught to memorize them. The reality, I was happy to discover, was far more intellectually challenging. Law school didn't teach me the law at all: it taught me how to teach it to myself. Because that, I learned, was what lawyers do: they teach themselves the law every day. They have no choice. The law changes from one day to the next, with each new case that applies a seemingly settled rule to a new set of circumstances to give it a new twist.

When I first started law school, I couldn't imagine why we were being asked to read a stack of centuries-old opinions by long-dead judges. Who cared what some judge in the eighteenth century decided about some guy's claim for lost profits because his millstone didn't work? Why didn't they just give it to us straight, hand out the list of rules that I figured must be compiled in a book somewhere? I guess it was well into my first semester that it began to dawn on me that there is no such book, that "the law" is found in the opinions themselves, in the unique twist that each case gave to the principle under discussion. That's when I started to fall in love with the law, with all of its warts. I saw it as organic—living and breathing and mutating with each new case, striving to make sense out of the chaos. I saw it as beautiful.

We live in a common-law country, after all. Except for the handful of areas governed by statutes, which are indeed lists of rules written down in a book—the criminal code, for example—most of the laws pertaining to our everyday lives are handed down in decisions from judges. As law students, we learned how to read those cases, how to glean from them the kernel of wisdom that would apply to the next case—what principles the judge was relying on, and what facts of this particular case led to this outcome. As lawyers, we're presumably armed with this ability to teach ourselves "the law" in any given area, and for each case we set about employing those skills to discover the legal principles that will be helpful to the position we need to advance. Sometimes we're in pursuit of making new law—to get the judge to twist it our way.

As a result, my job makes me somewhat of a detective-historian. Any given case that I read is nothing more than a snapshot in time, expressing the legal and moral imperatives of its age, and filtered through the unique facts presented. It applies to my case only by analogy: the more comparable to the facts and circumstances of my case, the greater its applicability.

The real jazz happens when the research leads me to two conflicting, seemingly incompatible propositions of law—equally applicable, at least on the surface, but wholly at odds with each other. That's when the creative juices kick in; that's when I'm put to the test—finding the key distinction for the case I don't want applied, or unearthing the pivotal rationale underlying the case that I like, the fundamental precept that would swing the judge my way. Because "the law," whatever that is, lies somewhere between the two polar opposites and is discernible only by means of triangulation, with reference to both.

Not so different from "the truth," at least in a courtroom. When two witnesses to the same event have a totally different recollection of it, we hear the testimony of both and know that "the truth" lies somewhere in the middle. Cross-examination works in much the same way—the direct examination reveals only part of the story, and it's not until the opposing counsel picks at the holes in the story through cross-examination that the full measure of a witness's testimony is fleshed out for the jury to evaluate.

In essence, the whole legal process, from formulation of a legal theory to evidence at trial, works through a system of triangulation, of checks and balances, to arrive at a full-bodied legal claim applied to a three-dimensional story. It's a long and arduous process, frustrating in the sense that one never fully arrives at what *really* happened, the elusive "truth," but I think it's the system that comes closest to getting there. And it's exciting—intellectually and emotionally. The law is alive and deeply human, responding every day to our evolution as a species, as flawed and beautiful as we are.

That's why I retreat into my work when all hell is breaking loose around me. Not because of the obvious distraction afforded by its consummate demands, but because of the solace I derive from its grace. I see in it the ultimate flowering of our collective genius. I turn to my work for its poetry, and to restore my faith in humanity.

My faith was in need of some major restoration that Monday morning. I got to the office early to go through the research memos I'd assigned to two junior associates on a new real estate case, and I plowed through them mercilessly, marking up both of them so heavily that the blue ink covered almost every spare millimeter of space on the page. I have no patience for lawyers who do a half-assed job. They're bastardizing something I revere, and when I'm presented with their schlock work, I take it as a personal affront. That's why, when Charlie Donovan appeared at my door just after ten, I lit into him before he could sit down.

"What the hell is this supposed to be?" I snapped as I held up his research memo.

"Huh?" He looked like a deer caught in the headlights.

For a moment—just a brief one—I considered letting him off easy. He was just a second-year associate, so fresh out of law school that he probably still remembered some of the questions on the bar exam. But his research memo had been a waste of everyone's time and the client's money. I could have simply rewritten the damn thing, but I had an obligation to teach the juniors, and he'd never learn anything if I just did his work for him. So I walked him through the concepts he'd missed, questioned him in the formal didactic model, until I saw the light begin to dawn in his eyes. It took longer than it should have, but I viewed the time as an investment: the better he understood how to conceptualize and embark on the research I needed, the more likely he'd hand me something useful in the next round, and the better he'd grasp what was expected of him in the future.

By the time we finished, more than an hour later, he looked completely dejected, and I felt bad for him. But he'd have to get the hang of this pretty soon, or he'd be out of a job. I wouldn't be doing him any favors to let it slide.

"Look," I said, "everyone makes mistakes, and I probably make more than most. What you need to do is sit and think about an assignment for a little while before jumping in—think about what you've been asked to do, and try to see how it fits into the big picture."

"I got it. I'll redo this for you right away," he said, standing up.

"Just be glad you wrote it for me instead of Dennis." Dennis Williams was a sweetheart of a guy, and he'd probably be a lot more tolerant than I was—but then again, he might remember it when it came time for junior associate evaluations, and that might hurt this kid's career. I tried to insulate the juniors who worked for me as much as possible until I felt they were ready to show their stuff to the higher-ups.

I was no gentler with the next lamb who came in for slaughter, and her grilling took even longer. But by the end of the critique, I had the feeling that she too had learned something from her mistakes and, if I was lucky, she might even be able to hand me some research I could actually use. Around one, once I'd dispensed with my bitch duties, I closed my door and took out the long-neglected letter from Arizona. I didn't want to make that call, but I'd already been through the apartment ads, and there were no more excuses for procrastinating.

"Liddle, Barrington and Sweet."

"Mr. Barrington, please."

"Just one moment. Who's calling please?"

"Tell him it's Ashleigh Moore."

Annoying Muzak played for me while I sat on hold. You'd think they'd at least put something interesting on the hold line, like sports scores. Oh well.

"Ms. Moore, Oscar Barrington here. Thanks so much for getting back to me." His deep baritone resonated with a down-home country kind of accent—not Southern exactly, but with a definite twang.

"What can I do for you, Mr. Barrington?"

"Well," he chuckled, "I think it's more a matter of what I can do for you."

"I don't follow you." I didn't particularly like his avuncular tone—or maybe I was just seeing him as an extension of his client. I picked up Janelle's crystal and rubbed its smooth surface. I could use some good energy right now.

"Okay, I'll get right to the point. As you know, we represent your father, Kenneth Gardner." He paused, and I resisted the urge to correct his reference to my father—I was here to listen. "He'd like to speak to you and your brother and sister. About your grandmother's estate."

"Yes, I got that much from your letter. What about it? I understand she died some time ago."

"Well, I'm not at liberty to say." Funny, the twang was suddenly gone—he was now pure Princeton. I tried to keep my impatience in check, figuring I'd get nowhere with this guy if I pissed him off.

"You're his lawyer, aren't you?" I asked. "I'm not represented by counsel; you can speak directly to me." I threw in that last bit in case he was concerned about the ethical rules. Lawyers are generally supposed to deal only with other lawyers, and not the parties themselves, unless a party doesn't have a lawyer. Barrington seemed to have missed the point entirely, however.

"No, you don't need a lawyer for anything, Ms. Moore." He obviously didn't know I was a lawyer and I figured I might as well keep him in the dark about it for a while longer, in the hope that he'd speak more freely. "May I call you Ashleigh? I feel as if I know you already. Kenneth speaks so highly of you."

Whatever game this guy was playing, he was going in blind, and seemed unaware of the fact that Kenneth Gardner couldn't possibly have anything to say about me—he'd never met me. I decided to play him right back, to see where it went.

"Sure. And, by the way, may I call you Oscar?"

"Please do." He took a beat too long on that one. A bit rattled at my presumption? Good.

"So what's this about, Oscar?" I'd had so much fun saying his name the first time, I came back for seconds.

"Well, I can only say that I've reached out to you on Kenneth's behalf, as a courtesy to him. He'd very much like you to call him. He'd like to talk to the three of you. Beyond that, he'll have to tell you about it himself."

"I see." Except I didn't. I had a million questions—why didn't Gardner just contact us himself? Why was the letter written just to me?—but I knew there was no point in trying to tease any further information out of this guy. And too many questions might spook him, and Gardner. No, if I was going to keep the door open on finding out what this was about, I'd have to make them think we might actually call. "I'll have to talk to my brother and sister about that, of course. Where can we reach him?"

He gave me a number. "That's his home—just outside Tucson."

"Well, it might be easier for us to call during business hours, if you have an office number for him."

"No, he's retired these days. You can get him at home most any time." He was back to the folksy twang, which now struck me as somewhat forced.

📖 📖 📖

Janelle stopped in after lunch and dropped a card on my desk. I put my stack of CRS documents to the side and picked it up.

"Lambda Legal Defense," I read from the card. "So?"

"So the firm's bought a table at their annual dinner, and you're going."

"Okay. Why am I going?"

"Because it's a worthy cause. Plus, I want to play a little I-told-you-so."

"I give up. What are you talking about?"

"Lambda is a gay legal group. But don't get in a huff, a lot of straight people support it too. And I think you're going to see some familiar faces there. One in particular."

"Oh, are we back on this again?"

"Honey, I'm telling you—"

"Look, Renee Silver is definitely not gay. I had lunch with her last week, in fact, and—"

"Oh, yeah, I heard about that—over two hours, wasn't it? Must have been some lunch."

It was, but I wasn't about to admit it. I looked at the card again.

"Next Thursday? Sorry, I'm busy." I really was, too—Thursday was Mbaye night. And although the two sessions I'd attended so far had been anything but enjoyable, it still provided a handy excuse to blow off a dinner that sounded like something I should avoid.

"Don't give me that. We have to fill the table, and Dennis wants a good turnout from our department. I already told him you'd be there."

Shit. I really didn't want to have to explain something like this to David. But then again, if I was serious about this separation, I'd have to stop worrying about what he would say and start keeping my comings and goings to myself. *Maybe I'll even have found an apartment by then.* I looked at the newspaper on the side of my desk, with only two items circled.

"Come on, a few drinks, some rubber chicken, a lot of laughs— we'll have fun. Alan and Susan are going too. You can even bring David if you want."

I'd have to deal with this sooner or later, and decided in that moment to just go for it. Actually telling someone might even make it a little more real for me.

"David wouldn't be going. In fact," I took a deep breath, "I think I'm leaving him."

Janelle just stared at me, mouth gaping, and then turned to close the door. Amazingly, she wasn't bursting with gossip-digging energy, and she didn't smirk; in fact, she was remarkably calm. She lowered herself into the chair opposite me and waited for me to speak. She didn't have to wait long.

"It's been coming for a while, I guess. Things just haven't been right. I can't really explain it, so don't ask me to."

"Well, I can't say that I'm surprised. But why now? What did he do?"

"No, it's me. It's definitely me." She waited patiently for me to continue—I knew she wouldn't let me off that easily. "It's just . . . there's nothing there anymore. I'm not even sure there ever was. Does that make sense? Sometimes it's like—don't take this the wrong way—but sometimes he even disgusts me."

"Wow."

"And we've been going to this marriage counselor, where—"

"Wait, back up. You? Went to a marriage counselor?"

"Well, yeah. It was his idea."

"I'm sure. But I still can't believe you're going."

"I didn't want to, but it really isn't that bad. I mean, it's horrible, actually, but I'm glad I'm doing it. I really think I feel better afterward. Well, not better. I feel pretty awful, but I'm clearer, I guess, like I have a better sense of things."

"Holy shit."

"Look, it's not exactly something out of the blue. I've been feeling this way for a long time. I knew I was thinking about it, but I'd never been able to put it into words. Not to him, not even to myself."

"So you told him? You came right out and said you were leaving?"

I nodded, feeling the familiar stinging around my eyes. I picked up the crystal again.

"Boy, she must be some therapist."

"She is, but that's not it. She doesn't really pry and poke at me—it's more like she just sits there and lets it come to me. Lets me feel things."

"Something I'm sure you love to do," she said with a smile.

"Yeah, no kidding. You should see her—she's this African woman about two feet tall, with this wild Afro and a hook on her arm."

"Excuse me?"

"You know—I guess she lost her lower arm or something. The thing she uses for a hand is a metal hook."

"You're shitting me now."

"No, really. My first thought was that she's probably great at making people feel better because anyone who comes in must think, 'I may be in bad shape, but at least I'm not *you*!'"

Janelle laughed. "Shit, girl, you sure know how to pick 'em. So are you going to keep going?"

"I don't know. David wants to, of course, but I don't really see the point."

"Closure, honey. It's called closure."

"I know. It's just—I don't really want to."

"I think that means you should."

"Probably."

"Maybe you could go to her yourself. You know, for individual therapy."

I didn't like that idea, not one bit. "I don't think so. I'm really busy, you know, and David might take it the wrong way—like I'm admitting that the problem is me and if I get fixed we can still be together. I mean, it *is* me, but I don't want to be fixed—I want out. And what I don't want is David thinking that I'm working on getting back together with him or something." It was bullshit, and I knew it. What I didn't want was to look at my own shit too closely. And with David sitting there, I might not have to.

"It's not about David, you know. It's about you. Taking care of yourself."

"I know." I turned the crystal in my hand. "I'm looking for a new apartment."

"Wow, this is really serious. What are you going to do about dividing up your old place, and all your other stuff?"

"I don't know. We're not there yet."

"Honey, you're a lawyer; you're supposed to think about these things. When push comes to shove, I'm telling you right now, David's going to take no prisoners. He'll line up a lawyer before you can blink, and he'll take you for everything."

"I don't care. He can have it all; I just want out."

"That's just your weariness talking; don't do anything until your brain takes over. You find yourself a place for now, and we'll get you a lawyer to deal with everything else. I know some people who do matrimonial; I'll make a few calls."

"I really don't want to deal with that right now."

"I know, but I'm not going to let you get taken to the cleaners."

The phone rang just then, but I ignored it.

"You know," she continued, "he's the one who should be moving out. You bought that apartment with your own money, if I recall."

"We're both on the title, so it's his as much as mine."

"But once you leave, it'll be harder to reclaim it later."

"Look, I'm disrupting his life enough right now—I just don't feel right about making him move out too."

"It's a bad idea."

Stella buzzed my intercom line.

"Yes?"

"Renee Silver is on line one. She says she needs to speak to you right away."

Janelle arched an eyebrow. "Well, speak of the devil." Ignoring her, I lifted the handset.

"What does she want?"

"I don't know," said Stella. "I said you were in a meeting, but she asked me to put her through anyway."

"Okay. Tell her I'll be with her in a second."

Janelle took her cue and stood up. "I guess you can find something to keep your mind off David, huh?"

"Janelle, seriously, knock it off about Renee. She's a client of Parsons and I don't want any shit floating around the office about her. Especially now."

"I'm just teasing you, Ash. I know you know what you're doing."

I wouldn't be so sure about that. I waved her out as I reached over to punch line one.

"Something weird is going on," Renee said when she called again on Wednesday afternoon. "The Amtec stock is still going up, and there's nothing on the wires to explain it."

"Did you talk to Huff about it yet?" When she'd first called me about the sudden rise in Amtec's stock on Monday, I'd suggested she bring her concerns directly to Chasen. Amtec was the competitor that Chasen believed might have gotten hold of the CRS application to the Food and Drug Administration. If he was right, that might explain the sudden spike—but only if there was some kind of public buzz about it. My sense of Chasen was that he always had his ear to the ground about everything impacting his business and would know the inside scoop about any stock shift in the industry before it ever started.

"Well, that's part of what's so strange," she said. "He told me not to worry about it—seemed pretty calm, in fact."

"Who's doing the trading? Institutional investors?"

"It's hard to say, but I don't think so. At least they didn't start it. As far as I can tell from my contacts on some of the trading desks, it started with a few core blocks before everyone else hopped on the bandwagon."

"Must have been some big blocks."

"Not huge, but big enough to be felt."

"We should move up our schedule for going into court," I said. "If they've gotten their hands on the CRS file somehow, someone knows and is manipulating the stock. The whole sector can take a hit when this thing blows up."

"That's what I was thinking. Probably Monday—no way you could get papers together by Friday, and I don't want my lawyer dead before the lawsuit even starts. So take the weekend, and we'll file on Monday."

Great, another weekend in the office. Just my luck. I put the classified ads for apartments to the side of my desk—I'd only circled three listings anyway. Well, at least I'd have a little more time than usual—pulling together papers for a temporary restraining order was a labor-intensive process and usually had to be accomplished very quickly.

"Okay, but when will you have time to review it?"

"Over the weekend—I'll be there with you. Breakfast Saturday morning is on me."

"You don't have to do that—that's what you hire us for."

"And I know how tough it is to throw together a TRO on a moment's notice. Besides, you'll need my help on the affidavit."

That was true. And I had to admit that the junior associates at my disposal wouldn't be nearly as efficient as Renee—their learning curve was too steep. Time was of the essence here, and right now the firm's interest in training junior associates was outweighed by the need for speed and proficiency.

"Deal," I said. "Nine o'clock Saturday morning. And I like my bagel with salmon spread."

"You got it," she said. I could practically hear the smile on her face.

📖   📖   📖

I walked down to Alan's sunny partner office a little after five, needing a short breather from the TRO papers. He was buried under his own pile of documents, and I felt the beginning of a headache just looking at his desk.

"I hear you're in for a long weekend too," he said as I sat down on the leather sofa along the wall.

"Word travels fast. What are you working on?"

"Rewriting a brief for Dennis. Considering the shitty shape it's in, it'll probably take the rest of the week and most of the weekend."

"Sometimes I think 'weekend' is just shorthand for 'the phone doesn't ring as often and you can wear jeans to the office.'"

"You know it. By the way—totally unrelated—did you hear, Parsons has called for a meeting of the litigation partners next Friday?"

My headache blossomed to a seven on the Richter scale. I really didn't want to know about it, but like a driver passing a gruesome accident on the highway, I couldn't help but probe.

"Any idea what's on the agenda?" I asked.

"I think we can both guess. The partnership vote is only two weeks away."

I nodded resignedly. "He's laying the groundwork to line up votes."

"It'll be a hard sell. Dennis loves you—so do the rest of us. He won't get anywhere trying to sow dissension in your own department. I think he's more interested in feeling everyone out, to get a sense of how much opposition he'll be facing."

"He wields a lot of power in the firm. He can shave people's points: how many people would have the balls to stand up to that? Just for the sake of a lowly associate?"

The firm's profits were allocated at the end of the year by means of a cryptic, nearly incomprehensible system of assigned points among the equity partners—multiple points for some, fractions of points for others, all adding up to 100 percent of the pie to be divided among the equity holders. The only thing anyone really knew for certain about the system was that a committee of three—the biggest rainmakers in the firm, including Parsons—held the key for reallocating the points, and therefore the profits, among their partners. It was a lot of power in the hands of a very few, who made their decisions behind closed doors and answered to virtually no one.

"Yes, but it's still a partnership," Alan said, "and majority vote rules. No one wants the firm broken into warring factions. It's in everyone's interest that we all hang together."

"Oh, come on, everyone's interest is in their own wallet—they can just as easily hang together behind Parsons."

"I don't think it'll play out that way. Dennis is not going to sell you out. It's a power thing for him too at this point. He'll never cave in to Parsons."

"It's been a power thing from the start. It's all about whose dick is bigger. No wonder there are no women on the Management Committee."

"I guess that's true, but Dennis calls the shots in litigation, and we're all behind him—and you. No way the firm would shoot you down when your whole department is unanimously supporting you. That's the kind of politics they just won't want to get involved in."

"I hope you're right," I said, not believing it for a minute.

"You can always buy a lottery ticket—win big, move to Vermont, and just tell Parsons to fuck himself."

"You know what's really pathetic? If I won the lottery, I'd probably still show up for work the next day."

"You're right; that's totally sick. Me, I'd show up the next day just to clean out my office and flip fingers at everyone."

"No, I mean it. I don't think my life would change very much at all. Maybe I'd buy a nicer apartment"—yes, I'd definitely do that, considering my current living arrangements—"but I love what I do. Why would I change that?"

"You know, I believe you. I think you're the only person I know who would actually keep doing this even if you didn't have to."

"But you're right, I'd love to tell Parsons to fuck himself."

He laughed, and picked up his pen to resume work on the brief. "Wouldn't we all."

I ran into Janelle in the hall on my way back to my office, and she walked me there. "I've been meaning to ask you," she said, "whatever happened with your phone call to those guys in Phoenix?"

"Tucson," I said, and shot her a look that put off any further questions until we were in private. She shut my office door when we got there, and picked up the squeeze ball from my desk. Everyone loves my toys.

"Sorry. I was going to ask you in an e-mail, but then I thought better of it."

"I appreciate that." We didn't really know if the firm monitored our e-mail, but there was always that possibility, and I didn't want news of my family matters spreading around.

"So, did you make the call?"

"Yes, but they didn't have much to say. Just that our natural father wanted to speak to us about his mother's estate. They gave me his number."

"Did you call?"

"No. I left messages for my brother and sister about it, to see if they want to talk to him with me. Liz doesn't. I still haven't heard back from Rob." Liz's message had been brief and to the point. "I don't want to talk to him. Don't ask again."

"Look, she died a long time ago, right?"

"So I'm told."

"So there's got to be a probate file for her estate somewhere."

"I suppose so."

"What is it with you? You're not thinking like a lawyer. Get your hands on that file, and you can arm yourself with some information before you talk to this lowlife. See what's what before you just start wandering in blind."

"I thought of that, but it would take some time. The last I heard, she was living somewhere in Texas." At least I thought she was, but I wasn't sure of anything at this point, and didn't really have anyone to ask.

"If that's where she died, that's where her estate was probated."

"Right, but I can't just run off to Texas to try to find a probate file. I don't know anything about probate in Texas."

"Girl, you're going to drive me to drink. We can line up a Texas lawyer to look into it for you and hunt down that file."

"That's going to take a while."

"So what? He's waited thirty-five years. He can wait a few more weeks."

I knew she was right. I wasn't thinking clearly—and that was one thing I was determined to change. I'd never consider going into a negotiation without preparing, and I'd do well to handle this Gardner thing the same way. In some sense, I'd been appointed by Liz and Rob to act on their behalf, and it was time I started acting like the lawyer I am.

"You know anybody in Texas who does trusts and estates work?"

"Now you're talking. I've got just the woman—a friend of mine from law school. A regular cowgirl."

"Tell her to leave her six-shooter at home. All I want is a little peek at the file."

"Honey, she doesn't go anywhere without her gun. Don't look at me like that; I'm serious. She says it's a status symbol down there. Anyway, if I know Shawanna, she's on a first-name basis with everyone in the county clerk's office and brings 'em cookies on their birthdays."

"Shawanna?"

"Shawanna Tulaine. You got a problem with a black cowgirl?"

"Not me. How much is this going to cost me?"

"Nothing. Let's just say she owes me a few."

"I'll bet."

"You got a problem with a black lesbian cowgirl?"

"Do you know anyone who isn't a lesbian, Janelle?"

"Sure, Dick Parsons. But that's okay, we don't want him. So, you want me to call Shawanna?"

"Yeah—and thanks."

⊞ ⊞ ⊞

It always struck me as some kind of divine conspiracy that my birthday fell in the dead of winter, when there were no Baltimore steamed crabs to be had, while Robbie the Anointed One got to stuff himself full of the delicacy on every single one of his birthdays, for no better reason than the fact that he'd been born in July. For as long as I could remember, my very favorite food in the entire universe was steamed crabs, with fried chicken from the lunch counter at Reade's Drug Store a distant second. As a result, my birthday was celebrated every year by a family jaunt to Reade's, while Robbie's was an occasion for all of the aunts and uncles within driving distance to descend upon us for an outdoor feast around the newspaper-covered picnic table in Gussie and Gramps' backyard.

Gramps would drive out to Neptune's to pick up a bushel or two of hot crabs that had been swimming in the Chesapeake just a few hours earlier, and the car would smell of that delectable Old Bay scent for weeks afterward. To this day, all it takes is a single whiff of steamed crabs to bring me back to the summers of my childhood—an Orioles game on the radio, Gussie passing out paper towels and yelling at the kids to eat some vegetables, Robbie hoarding his claws and stealing a few of mine, and Mom complaining about the flies while Gramps shrugged them off with the observation that "they don't eat much."

Robbie's eleventh birthday came during the same summer that Louie Plough moved in down the block from our house. Like me, Louie was seven, but he was big for his age, and he took an immediate dislike to me because I could throw a baseball farther than he could. It took only one pickup game among the kids on the block before the humiliated Louie announced that he wasn't going to play with us anymore, and that he didn't want any of us playing either. That didn't sit so well with me and my friends—baseball was a religion to us, with Jim Palmer as the high priest, and there was just no way we were going to let Louie cancel our summer on the dirt field behind the elementary school. But Louie was very persuasive, mostly because he beat the daylights out of us when we next tried to put together a game, so our baseball outings that summer were relegated to the few Saturdays when we could get a grown-up to come out with us. Even Louie wasn't stupid enough to mess with a grown-up.

With no baseball to be had, that early Saturday afternoon of Robbie's birthday found me sticking close to home as we waited for the family to start arriving for the crab feast. Dad was already dating Mom by then, and he showed up early to help with the preparations. Mom and Gussie were flying around the tiny kitchen cooking beans and ears of corn that no one but the grown-ups would eat, and Gramps had already left for Neptune's. I wasn't about to venture outside the backyard gate, since I saw Louie playing in his yard three houses down, and he'd think nothing of thrashing me right in front of Gussie's house just for the fun of it.

Even if Louie hadn't been lurking in the vicinity, I didn't feel much like seeking out one of the neighborhood kids for a game of catch. I'd been whisked to the doctor that morning for some ailment or other—Gussie liked to run to Dr. Krauss at the first sign of a sniffle—and I'd gotten a shot in my throwing arm. It was too sore to do much more than hang limply at my side, so I kept my running around to a minimum and occupied myself in Gussie's garden.

The previous January, Dad had made the insulting mistake of giving me a Barbie doll for my birthday. He didn't know me very well at that point, so he probably had no idea that I hated dolls and had been praying for a catcher's mitt. He got with the program by the time my next birthday rolled around, and presented me with a model steam shovel that I absolutely adored. But the Barbie, well, that had been a bust—although under Gussie's critical eye, I had accepted it with as much polite grace as a seven-year-old could muster.

I'd found one productive use for the thing, however—the hard plastic legs, pointed at the toes to fit in those little high-heeled shoes, were a perfect tool for digging tunnels. And that's exactly how I spent that Saturday afternoon before the crab feast—out back in Gussie's garden with my Barbie in hand, my left one, to dig out a fort behind the rosebush. There had been a little drizzle the night before, so the dirt was a mixture of damp topsoil and peat moss—a perfect habitat for some interesting beetles, which I soon discovered scurrying for cover.

One in particular stood out. It was long like a slug, but had a zillion furry-looking legs sticking out and, most amazing of all, it actually seemed to have a face—a real honest-to-God face, with a mouth and two big round eyes. I picked it up for closer examination, and was delighted to see that it didn't appear to be afraid of me. It just sat there in my hand, calmly staring back at me, with its furry legs caressing my palm. I named him Jack.

I could hear through the back door that some of the relatives were starting to arrive, and that meant that Gussie was going to shout for me any minute to come get washed up. Unwilling to leave Jack just yet, I wedged myself farther behind the rosebush to study him more closely, and pushed the bangs out of my eyes, heedless of the little sweat-drenched wisps that ended up sticking out every which way from my forehead.

"Whatcha doin' in there, peein' in the garden?" Louie yelled from just outside the gate. I'd been too engrossed in Jack to notice that he'd left his yard to come searching for mischief.

"Shut up," I said, feeling very grown-up to have picked up this phrase from Robbie. I burrowed more deeply into the overhang from the bush, and willed him to go away.

"Ashleigh's peein' in the garden!" he sang out to no one in particular. "Ashleigh forgot her diaper!"

Ignoring him and praying that he'd shut up before Gussie heard him and called me in, I returned my attention to Jack, who still seemed to be staring at me. He had two little antennae protruding from just above his eyes, and when I lifted a finger to wave at him, one tiny antenna dipped down and up, as if to wave back at me. All thoughts of Louie Plough disappeared at that point—I had myself a talking bug. I smiled down at his wide-eyed little bug face, and I swear to God, he smiled back at me.

"What's that?" I heard right over my head. I looked up and there was Robbie towering over me, Orioles cap on his head and a bored expression on his face. I looked quickly toward the gate—Louie was gone, thank goodness. He was stupid, but not stupid enough to pick a fight with me in front of my big brother.

"Nothing," I said, closing my hand to shield Jack from his eyes. But Robbie wasn't so easily dissuaded.

"Let's see," he said, and crouched down to crawl partway into my hiding place.

"It's just a bug," I pleaded. "Leave me alone."

He punched me squarely on the spot where I'd gotten the shot. I didn't know if he'd remembered my shot and done it deliberately, or if he just had an uncanny skill at honing in on a weakness. Either way, the pain was excruciating. Although I knew better than to cry in front of Robbie, the tears welled up before I could stop them.

"Hand it over," he commanded, "or you'll get another one."

I knew he meant it, so I opened my hand slowly—just enough to let him see that it really was just a bug—and tried to keep it out of his reach. But Robbie was a lot bigger and faster than I was, and he leaned over and snatched Jack out of my hand before I knew it.

"It's just a stupid bug," he said, peering at Jack with mild interest. "He's got little antennae just like you." I tried to pat down my errant bangs, without much luck. "Gussie says it's time to come in."

"Give him back," I said, and realized my mistake too late. I'd shown him that I cared about Jack—always a dangerous proposition with Robbie.

"No." He stood up, Jack clutched in his hand. "Wipe your face, you're covered with dirt."

I felt the tears threatening again and looked up at him—but I knew better than to beg.

"Bet he'll make a real loud squish if I squeeze him," he said in a low ominous tone that I'd begun to think of as his "dark voice." I knew not to mess with him when I heard that voice, so I sat there, afraid to breathe. He held up Jack between his thumb and forefinger, stared me in the eye, and dared me to say boo. And I just couldn't help it.

"No!" I screamed, reaching out to grab his leg, but he danced away and laughed, with Jack held high over his head. Out sprang the tears again, and I knew that Jack's fate was sealed. The smile left Robbie's face as he ceremoniously lowered his hand to hold Jack out before my eyes and, glaring at me with a mixture of defiance and glee, he proceeded to crush the tiny creature between his fingers.

"Come on, bug-head, time to go in," he said as he wiped the guts on his jeans. "You let Gussie see you were crying and I'll hit your shot again."

I steered clear of Robbie the rest of that afternoon, my throbbing arm an insistent reminder of what he'd done to Jack. But by early evening, all of the kids were gathering on the basement steps for a stair-jumping contest, and I felt safe enough among all my cousins to join in the game. The rules were simple—the kid who jumped from the highest step won. Little Amy and Denise, Cousin Ginny's girls, were only four and they couldn't make it from higher than the second step. Cousin Boo and Frankie Junior were teenagers and considered themselves too big to play, so they refereed. That left the rest of us as the main competitors: Robbie, Lizzie, and me, plus our Richmond cousins Jenny, Pammie, Alice-Anne, and Danny.

After three rounds, Robbie was looking like the winner, since he'd made it from the seventh step, a good four feet high. But Lizzie was close on his heels, and in the last round a rare daredevil streak seemed to inspire her—she was preparing to jump from the eighth step. We three were the last to go, so we were alone at the top of the steps, with all of the cousins down in the basement waiting for us. I stayed on the top landing, waiting my turn and watching Robbie and Lizzie two steps below me. I could tell they were mostly shielded from the view of the other kids by the basement ceiling—only their legs were showing through the banister. Robbie was arguing with Lizzie, telling her that she couldn't jump from that step because it was too high, she'd break her neck, and Lizzie was telling him to piss off and leave her some space.

"Oh, I'll give you some space," he said—and with that, I saw him give her a good hard shove right in the middle of her back. She tumbled headfirst down that flight of hardwood stairs, threw out her arms to brace the fall, and squealed with agony in the same instant that we all heard a loud crack like a tree limb breaking. Robbie and I just stood there dumbfounded, staring at Lizzie lying in a crumpled heap at the foot of the steps, and watched as Alice-Anne rushed to her side. Then the commotion erupted all at once—Danny yelling "Lizzie? Lizzie?" and Alice-Anne squatting on her knees beside Lizzie and shaking her shoulder and Pammie yelling "Don't touch her!" and the sound of half a dozen grown-ups stampeding toward the basement door with Gussie leading the way and shouting, "What in tarnation was *that*?!"

Robbie turned to look at me as the herd of grown-ups pushed past us on the steps, his eyes crackling with barely restrained energy, boring holes deep through my skull. "She fell," he said quietly in his dark voice—as if only to me.

"What the hell were you kids up to?" Uncle Dink thundered as he grabbed Cousin Boo by the arm.

"We were having a jumping contest. And I guess she just fell. She was way up there," Boo was saying, pointing to the spot where Robbie stood soldierlike on the stairs. Lizzie was awake and crying her head off by now, and Gussie picked her up just like that and held her to her breast.

"That right, Robbie?" Gramps asked from somewhere behind me. Robbie looked up to him and nodded, wide-eyed and shell-shocked. "Yes, sir. I told her that step was too high for her, but she didn't listen." I was in his line of vision, halfway between him and Gramps in the doorway, and he lowered his gaze to fix it on me. "Tell him, Ash." Gramps didn't appear to hear the threat in Robbie's voice, but I did. I nodded, and looked past him at Lizzie cradled in Gussie's arms, her cries softened to hiccups and whimpers, and her right arm hanging at a peculiar angle across her chest. Mom was on the phone with Dr. Krauss and announced that we could rush her right over to his office.

"I'll take her," said Gussie in her brook-no-argument voice. "Caroline, you come with us," she ordered Mom, and started up the stairs with Lizzie still clutched to her chest. Uncle Dink and the rest of the cousins fell in step behind her. Gussie gave Robbie a good long look as she passed him on the steps. "We'll talk about this some more when we get back home."

Robbie and I let everyone pass us on the stairs, and as I turned to follow Frankie Junior at the end of the line, Robbie reached out and grabbed me on my throbbing arm. "Remember," he said as he gave it a good squeeze, "she fell."

It wasn't long before the events of Robbie's eleventh birthday found themselves incorporated into the family lore. "Oh, that was the year Lizzie fell and broke her arm," Gussie would say before launching into a heavily fictionalized version of how she'd heard the arm snap from the living room and was flying down the basement stairs before anyone knew what was what. Robbie was always portrayed in this tale as heroically trying to stop Lizzie's foolishness. As far as Lizzie was concerned, the whole thing was just one big blur—except for the part where Gussie let her have as much ice cream as she wanted for days on end. For me, that day would always be remembered as the one when I found a bug who smiled at me—until Robbie killed him, along with a little piece of my innocence.

📖   📖   📖

"Is that supposed to be some kind of message about me?" David had asked at our session on Thursday. He'd turned to me, demanding an explanation—needing me to clarify it for Dr. Mbaye. But I didn't have any answers to offer him. I'd looked to the good doctor for help, not even bothering to keep my eyes away from the hook in her lap, but she'd just sat there.

"You think I'm a bully like your brother? Is that it?" David had pressed. Then he'd turned to Mbaye to make his case. "I've never threatened her; I've never laid a hand on her with anything but love," he'd explained calmly. "Tell her, Ash."

I'd wiped the tears from my face, irritated that I'd gotten side-tracked onto this tangent in the first place, and shook my head. No, it wasn't about David—it was about me; it was about my fucked-up family. And I had no idea why it had come up now.

"You love her fiercely," Mbaye had said neutrally.

"Damn right I do. That's why we're here."

Mbaye had simply looked at me, giving me the space I needed to fill in the blanks, but there were just too many of them to fill, and all the time in the world wouldn't help. Still, I was struck by the way she'd described his love. Fiercely. It was an ominous word, and apt—it connoted some of the desperation in him that had sometimes felt like an assault. But how could she know that?

📖   📖   📖

Frankly, I was relieved that Renee didn't make it in on Saturday morning after all. A tiny bit disappointed too, I had to admit, but I focused on the relief and convinced myself that it was by far the dominant reaction. It had been a hellish few days of work, topped off at night by David's punishing, petulant silence yawning in the living room like a hungry beast—he'd been in a snit ever since our session on Thursday, thinking that I'd accused him of abusing me. I think I preferred his cloying chatter. Well, maybe not. At least we'd reached a sort of truce on the apartment situation Saturday night—I'd take my time finding a new place, and he wouldn't try to talk me out of it. It was better than nothing. Meanwhile, he'd graciously offered to sleep in the den, and I'd accepted. It wasn't that I couldn't stand his presence in the bed, not really, but it was pretty crowded in there, what with me, him, and all that guilt cuddled up with us.

Other than negotiating our temporary living arrangements, the only time we'd spoken all weekend was when he'd overheard me on the phone with Rob on Saturday night.

"So you're going to just call this guy on your own?" David had asked.

"Looks like it. Rob and Liz don't want to talk to him."

"You'd think Robbie would be jumping at it—the prospect of all that money." His use of the diminutive for Rob's name didn't go unnoticed by me, and I was pleased at the implicit put-down. David was well aware of the story about my brother's announcement, sometime during high school, that everyone in the family had to call him Rob instead of Robbie. Maybe he just favored the short, clipped sound of "Rob," but I always believed it had something to do with the childish sound of "Robbie," as if it commanded less respect. And Rob was all about respect. In any event, from that day forward, no one was allowed to call him Robbie—except for Gussie, of course, who would forever see him as a darling cherub. And except for me, but only behind his back.

"He doesn't really think there's any money. Believe me, if he did, he wouldn't leave it up to me."

"Well, when are you going to call?"

"Not until I get a copy of the probate file. I want to know what I'm dealing with before I talk to him."

"I know you'll get to the bottom of it, honey," he said with that puppy-dog look that made my skin crawl.

As a result of the deafening silence that had ensued for the rest of the evening, I'd had a hard time falling asleep, and by the time I dragged my ass into the office on Sunday, I was happy to bury myself again in the TRO papers.

When Renee called from the lobby early Sunday afternoon, I had pretty good working drafts of the affidavit and brief to show her. I went downstairs to bring her up—building security required a personal escort during off-hours—but I barely recognized the woman standing beside the guards' desk. She had her long dark hair tied back in a clumsy ponytail, and was dressed in ratty jeans with the tail of her button-down shirt hanging out. Scuffed sneakers rounded out the picture. The whole effect was an androgynous mix of casual tomboy and graceful femininity. In a word, breathtaking, and I cursed my ever-inappropriate libido for the powerful reaction I felt as soon as she smiled at me, her hazel eyes dancing with a cheery hello.

"I see you're my kind of girl," she said lightly, stopping me dead in my tracks before I realized she was referring to my own jeans and workshirt. I tried to return her smile, but my heart was hammering so loudly that I wasn't sure I'd managed it.

"Well, since I blew off breakfast yesterday, I thought I'd bring you a tuna sandwich for lunch today," she said, holding up the bag in her hand. "Shall we?"

What? Oh, the elevator. "Yeah, let's head upstairs, and you can take a look at the draft affidavit while I eat."

"Sounds like a plan."

We set up shop in my paper-strewn office, and she reviewed the affidavit while I choked down a few bites of the sandwich between sips of Diet Pepsi. Her attention was so focused on the papers that I was afforded the chance to sneak a couple of long glances at her perfectly chiseled features. A few strands of dark hair had escaped her ponytail and were hanging beside her face, partially obstructing my view, but I could just make out the severe knit of her brow furrowed in concentration. Now and then she lifted one of her long tapered fingers to bite at the cuticle—a gesture that I found both incongruous and thoroughly endearing. As picture-perfect as she was when she knew she was on display, it was this other woman—the one who didn't know she was being watched—that I found utterly riveting. Shit, this was no place to start acting like a crushed-out adolescent.

"I like it," she said when she reached the last page, and almost caught me staring when she looked up. "Especially the language where you describe the threat to our confidential business information. It's very powerful."

I could feel myself start to blush and reached for the Diet Pepsi to wet my suddenly dry throat.

"Thanks. I figured we'd better hit them hard right up front, start painting them as the devil right away. But I need you to fill in those blanks in the first few paragraphs, where we go into the corporate structure."

The phone started ringing just then, so Renee merely nodded and picked up a pen to start working while I reached for the phone.

"Ashleigh Moore? This is Shawanna Tulaine in Austin."

"Oh, hi. I was going to call you tomorrow."

"No need, sugar; the cavalry is here." Unlike Barrington, Shawanna had a Southwest drawl that sounded genuinely homegrown. "I did a little poking around after I got Janelle's call last week, and I think I found what you're looking for."

"You found the probate file already?"

"Well, hold your horses, honey; we'll see. I got a little friend down at the county clerk's office, and she went through their database—you know, the one that only the clerks get to use? I'm telling you, it's just plain silly how they don't have a centralized system for the lawyers to access."

Oh brother, this woman likes to talk as much as Janelle. This could take a while, I thought.

"So, lucky for us, she had a little down time, and she went looking for Edna. And lo and behold, she called me back on Friday to say she found her!"

"What, you mean she's alive?"

"Good lord no, she's dead as a doornail. I mean she found her file. But it's not here in Austin—she died up in Dallas, back in 1990. Those old records are stored someplace else altogether—some warehouse or something. So I got hold of the records clerk up there and arranged to get me a copy of the file pulled from the warehouse. I've got to remember to send that nice woman some brownies. So anyway, when they pull the file, she said they'll make me a copy and I'll send it on up to you soon as I get it."

"Wow, Shawanna, that's great. How long do you think it'll take?"

"No idea, sugarplum. She promised she'd get on it right away—let's say I was very persuasive—but I don't know how quick that might be."

"Look, I really appreciate all you've done. Can I pay you for your time?"

She let out a whoop—I wondered for a moment if they were rounding up the cattle in her backyard.

"No, no, baby. You just tell that Janelle that I expect to see her at the next Gay Law convention, and she'd better make some serious time for me. You got that?"

I smiled. I could see they'd make quite a pair. "I got it. And thanks again, Shawanna."

"Any time, sugar."

"Probate?" Renee asked as I hung up. "I didn't know you did Surrogate's Court practice too."

"No," I said, reaching out for the papers she'd marked up already. "It's personal. A family thing."

"Oh, I've been through that."

"You've been an executor?"

"No, a beneficiary. My great-aunt's estate, back when I was in high school and college."

"Really?"

"Yeah, what a headache."

"How do you mean?"

"A dozen distant relatives we'd never heard of came crawling out of the woodwork to challenge the will. It was tied up in court for years."

"Must have been a big estate."

"Big enough, but most of it went to a trust to fund some women's shelters in Syracuse. By the time it was over, I got enough to pay off my law school debt, but that's about it. Anyway, all the court fights turned out to be a good thing for me, in a way; that was my first real exposure to the law, and it's why I decided to go to law school."

"No kidding. You'd think it would have the opposite effect."

"Well, I saw what the whole process did to my father. He was her favorite—my great-aunt's—and he was determined to honor her wishes by setting up those shelters. So he fought everyone off, didn't cave in to their demands for a piece of the pie. It got pretty ugly, but the worse it got, the more he stood his ground to do what he knew was right. At first I thought he was being stupid—we could have all gotten a lot more money if the trust wasn't set up. Even I knew that, and I was still in high school when the whole thing started. But eventually, I saw him as kind of noble, and that what he was doing was pretty admirable. I guess that experience showed me both sides of lawyering—the good and the bad—and I decided I'd go to law school to do some good."

"So now you work for Huff Chasen." I couldn't resist that one, but she took it in stride.

"Well, things don't always work out as we plan," she said softly. I nodded, but her comment took me aback momentarily; it was the first time I'd heard her say anything remotely critical of Chasen, the first I'd heard her acknowledge his sleaziness, albeit tacitly. She was his General Counsel—no matter how dirty he might be, she owed him a duty of loyalty. But, of course, I owed him the same duty—I was his lawyer too.

"Anyway, I've been there, so if you want someone to talk to . . ." She left the invitation hanging. I looked into her wide open eyes, the slight curve of her mouth in a little half-smile, and was tempted to take her up on the offer. But something held me back. Old habits die hard.

"Thanks," I said with a shrug, and returned my eyes to the brief in front of me.

It was pretty obvious that I wasn't going to pursue the topic, and she seemed to take it as a dismissal—more than I'd intended. I could practically feel the wall behind which she suddenly retreated. A wall that appeared to be made of ice—the temperature in the room cooled distinctly.

"I think I'll run around the corner for an iced tea," she announced, standing up and heading toward the door. "I'll be back in a little while. This visitor's pass will get me back into the building, won't it?"

"Yes," I said. I looked up and caught her eye as she stood in the doorway. Yep, her mask was securely in place—no flicker of connection whatsoever. *I didn't mean to insult you; I didn't mean to cut you off. It's just that I'm fucked up and so much is going on.* Damn her, she wasn't reading my mind very well; she walked out without another word.

Chapter Six

Renee Silver called at ten o'clock Monday morning—just an hour before I was to leave for court—to say that Chasen had pulled the plug on the TRO.

"What do you mean 'wait'? Doesn't he realize that we—"

"I know," Renee said. "I've been explaining it to him for the last hour. He understands the implications, but he's convinced that it'll blow over, and he wants us to do some more fact investigation before we go into court."

"But once we file, we can get all the information we want through discovery. And if Amtec's stock continues to go up, the whole sector could get dragged under when it blows up."

"Look," she sighed, "I agree with you. And I've said all that, but it's his call, and that's the way he wants to play it. He knows the business better than either of us, so we're just going to have to trust that he knows what he's doing."

"Well, I wish he'd had this brilliant idea before we blew our entire weekend putting together the papers."

"You and me both. But at least they're ready to go, whenever he gives the green light."

Fat consolation—I could have been looking for an apartment all weekend. Instead, I had the pleasure of busting my ass in the office, somehow managing to kill off my budding friendship with Renee in the process—only to come home each night to the King of Sulk.

He'd pulled a fast one on me when Dr. Mbaye had called Sunday night to say she had to reschedule our Thursday appointment this week, asking if we could make it on Tuesday instead. David had said he had a Tuesday board meeting that couldn't be changed—but when I mentioned that I was free, he'd jumped on it.

"Fine, you go by yourself," he'd said. "Maybe you'll finally start getting to the bottom of whatever's going on with you." I'd wanted to throw it right back in his face, point out that maybe the reason we weren't getting anywhere with this stupid counseling was that he used up all the time complaining about me instead of looking at his own shit. But I wasn't up to another argument with him, so I'd just shrugged and told him I'd go without him, silently promising myself that this session would be my last.

"By the way," Renee continued, "I think I found something we can follow up on."

"What?"

"Well, I pulled up some of Amtec's recent SEC filings to see what insider activity has occurred over the last few quarters."

"So?" Company executives who exercise options and buy or sell company stock are required to disclose the transactions to the public and the SEC. Nothing illegal about it, unless they fail to disclose, or they do something at a conspicuously fortuitous moment—like selling just before the stock goes in the toilet, thereby giving rise to the inference that they knew it was about to go south based on inside company information.

"So one of the insiders who cashed in on some options and sold out last year is also mysteriously absent from their last quarterly filing."

"He left the company?"

"So it seems."

"Let me get this straight. This guy cashes in his chips when the stock is low, and now that he's out, it's going through the roof. I'm betting he's not a happy camper."

"I'm betting you're right."

"Who is he?"

"His name is Irwin Knowles. But get this—he was the vice president in charge of research and development."

"Holy shit."

"Feel like a trip to Baltimore?"

"Baltimore?"

"I want to go talk to him, face to face."

I liked her style, and was tempted to say so, but she was sounding considerably warmer than she had over the weekend, and I didn't want to jinx it.

"When do we leave?" I asked.

"Let's go on Friday, and plan to stay over on Saturday too, if we need to."

"I'll have Stella make the reservations."

My dislike of Claire Michaels ripened into something just short of loathing soon after classes started that fall semester. It was mostly a function of her aloofness, which struck me and everyone else in Comstock as a form of conceit. She kept to herself, choosing not to watch television with us in the common room or join in any of our after-dinner games of Yahtzee. She wasn't snippy about it, never outright condescending or rude, but her entire demeanor—her erect posture, her unrelenting expression of glacial neutrality—created the impression that she walked through life in a different dimension, in a universe wholly apart from ours.

It's not as if we didn't try to include her in things. She was often alone in her room during those first few weeks of classes, her roommate Janice spending every spare moment enjoying a passionate reunion with her boyfriend at Amherst. Shelly and I often stopped by their room on our way somewhere, to invite her along for a drink in town or an evening of study at the library. But she invariably declined our offers—politely, but without any explanation, which I took to mean that she had no other plans but nevertheless preferred her solitude to our company.

I saw her around campus from time to time, but she was usually alone—sitting quietly with a book, or striding across the Quad with her purposeful don't-bother-me gait. Once, outside the bookstore in the basement of Seelye Hall, I came across her actually having a conversation with someone—a sophomore who was carrying a violin case in one hand and twirling her long brown hair with the other. The scene was remarkable to me because, frankly, it was hard to imagine Claire having any interaction with another person. But there she was, talking to this sophomore as if they might even be friends. I walked past them without acknowledging her, firmly convinced at that point that Claire was indeed capable of friendship—just not with me.

What changed it was that Friday night toward the end of September. I'd finally gotten to the point where Kat was willing to give me some weekend shifts at the Cave, and I came home from that first Friday night shift around two-thirty in the morning with my T-shirt soaked with perspiration and my pockets stuffed with cash. It had been a good night, but I was bone tired, and wanted nothing more than to strip off my clothes and fall into a comalike sleep. As I climbed the stairs to my room, I sent a silent thank-you to the gods for giving me a night with the room to myself; Shelly had taken the bus to Amherst with Janice.

The blissful quiet of my room lasted all of thirty seconds—I had my rancid T-shirt halfway over my head when a sudden pounding at the door threatened to wake the entire house.

"Jesus, shut up!" I called through the door in a stage whisper. I pulled my T-shirt back on and crossed the room in two strides to open the door. There stood Carla Oakes, the perennial procrastinator, and I knew instantly what she wanted.

"Please, Ash, you've got to help me. I have to hand in this paper tomorrow, and—"

"No. No way," I said, shaking my head and backing away from her. "I just got off work and I'm going to bed."

"No, I'll type it—you can sleep."

"Not with you typing, I can't. Look, just borrow the typewriter—take it back to your room and do it there."

"Margaret will kill me. She's got tennis practice tomorrow morning—she has to sleep."

"Well so do I!"

"But you can sleep in tomorrow."

Well, not really. I was starting to fall behind in my reading, and was counting on using the weekend to get caught up.

"I don't get it, Carla. Why do you always wait till the last minute like this? Hey, wait a minute; tomorrow's Saturday. What professor gave you a deadline on Saturday?"

"My Soc class. But, actually, the deadline was today. I got her to give me a twenty-four hour extension, but it's got to be in her office by nine tomorrow morning."

"And you haven't started it yet."

"Well, I've *started*." She held up a sheaf of handwritten scribbles. "But it needs to be fine-tuned a little while I type it."

I sighed—the prospect of Carla's hunt-and-peck tapping all night, and the inevitable chatter that would accompany it, draped an extra layer of fatigue over my exhaustion. "Shit, Carla, I just can't. Tell you what—give me your key, and I'll go sleep in your room. You can work in here."

Carla lived in Wilder—right there on the Quad beside Comstock. I could be asleep in ten minutes.

"Deal," she said, marching over to my desk to dump her papers and dig out her keys. "Just try not to wake up Margaret."

I stuffed fresh clothes and underwear into my knapsack, and was just looking for my toothbrush when we heard a thunderous crash next door. Carla and I took a beat to stare at each other, the indecision plain on both our faces—check in on Claire, or screw her?—but then I heard a weak whimper on the other side of the wall, and the faint sound of someone saying my name.

Carla and I flew out to the hall and tried Claire's door—it was locked. I pulled my college ID from my pocket and carded the door, grateful for the old locks that were so easily picked. We piled into the room and found Claire sitting awkwardly on the floor beside her desk, books strewn all around her and the three wall shelves over her desk hanging at a precarious angle. Sitting there looking so vulnerable, she still somehow maintained a dignified composure.

"Claire," I said, forgetting all about hating her and rushing to her side. "What happened?" I knelt down but didn't dare touch her.

"Are you all right?" Carla asked, standing beside us.

Claire looked up and gave her a blank stare. "Obviously not." Then she lowered her eyes to me, and fixed me with a stare that suggested she wanted to ask for help, but couldn't.

"Where does it hurt?" I asked softly, holding her gaze. She didn't flinch, and I thought I saw something else in that look—something like gratitude.

"My ankle," she said. "I twisted it when I fell. I think it might be broken."

"Carla, why don't you climb up there and take care of those shelves," I said. "We don't want them falling on her now. Claire, when you're ready, I'm going to help you get up, okay?"

She nodded, and we watched Carla climb onto the desk. After a moment, Claire looked back at me, and when I caught her eye, she looked down. "Thank you," she mumbled.

"No problem," I replied, just as quietly. "I heard you call my name—how'd you know I was up?"

"Well, you were pretty loud, you know." Then, amazingly, she smiled at me. Well, okay, it was more of a half-smile, and full of irony, but at least it was a start. Suddenly I didn't feel so tired.

"Oh, sorry about that." My face felt hot, as if I were embarrassed, but I had no reason to be.

"No problem," I thought I heard her say.

"Okay, all clear," Carla announced as she removed the last shelf.

"You ready?" I asked Claire. She nodded, and slipped an arm over my shoulders as I grabbed her around the waist. I gave her a count-down, and on three I lifted, and she pushed, and together we clumsily got to our feet, with Carla calling out directions the whole way. Claire winced as she tentatively tried to put weight on her left foot, and shook her head—it was no good. So we hobbled over to her bed, where she gingerly sat down.

"We've got to get you to the infirmary," Carla said. I knew she was right, but there was no way Claire was making it there on her own. Luckily, it wasn't far—right here on the Quad—so she might be able to lean on us.

"Look," I said to Claire, "do you want me to go find some ice, and see if that'll help? Maybe after you ice it for a little while, we could give it a try."

"I'll go," said Carla before Claire could answer. "Be right back." She was out the door in a flash, and I let her go—she needed something constructive to do, I told myself.

"I feel like such an ass," Claire muttered after Carla was gone.

"What were you doing rearranging your bookshelves at three in the morning?"

She gave me a withering look, but then broke into a smile, as if conceding she couldn't quite pull it off.

"Nothing as industrious as that. I was just getting my microbiology book from last year—I had it on the top shelf, so I had to climb on the desk, and—well, I guess I slipped." She raised her arms in a little half-shrug.

"Do you think you'll be able to make it across the Quad? You really should have that checked out before morning."

"I know. But I don't see how, unless you carry me." My heart started hammering for some reason—I couldn't tell if she was joking. She had a way of keeping me off balance, and the feeling was both pleasant and terribly uncomfortable.

"Look, you can lean on us—we'll take it slow, okay?"

"You'd do that for me?" she asked.

"Of course."

At that, she broke into a genuine, full-faced smile, the real McCoy, and the effect was overwhelming—like a bolt of warm sunlight breaking through an overcast November sky. Her pale blue eyes lit up, and her entire face was transformed, animated in a way that I found utterly engaging. It suddenly struck me that she was beautiful. How odd that I hadn't noticed it before—all this time she'd been just a remote, unapproachable woman with some serious social defects. I'd never bothered to notice how attractive she was—until now. The realization was very disturbing, and got my heart pounding even harder for some reason. I turned away and busied myself with picking up the books littering the floor.

"You really don't have to do this," she said.

"Oh, it's just a few books."

"No, I mean taking me over there. It's late—I'm sure you want to go to sleep."

I stopped and turned to face her, afraid that she was implying that she didn't want my company.

"I want to go with you," I said simply, my eyes locked on her. I didn't look away, and neither did she. She nodded quietly.

📖   📖   📖

It was stifling in there, and I couldn't help but wonder if Dr. Mbaye kept it that way for a reason. Maybe it helped people open up or something. But it didn't work that way for me—it just made me uncomfortable, and talking about Claire only made it worse. *How did I get started on all that anyway?* I wondered. For damn sure I wouldn't have gone into it if David were there—and I was suddenly very relieved that his board meeting for tonight couldn't be rescheduled. Wouldn't he love to know that I was using our marriage counseling time to talk about Claire?

But it wasn't just me—Dr. Mbaye had something to do with it too. She's the one who brought it up, really, picking up on David's comment last week that our marriage had been my only real relationship. Boy, had I fumed at that—how dare he insinuate that my college relationship had been insignificant simply because I didn't talk about it. If he doesn't see it, it doesn't exist or doesn't matter. In some way, I suspected he knew better—knew *me* better—and that's what really pissed me off about his comment. As if he were deliberately trying to minimize it because he was well aware that the things I refuse to talk about tend to be the most important ones.

Whatever David had been thinking, it was clear that Mbaye had picked up on it in a flash—and I guess that's why she'd delved into it tonight, when he wasn't here. The real question was why I'd let her take me there. I didn't want to think about Claire, or Smith, or any of that. Especially now, when I was so fucked up just trying to disengage from David and sort out what I really wanted. Wasn't the issue supposed to be me—the me of today, not fifteen years ago? Weren't we supposed to get to the heart of what was happening in my marriage, and why I just couldn't do this anymore? This ancient history served no purpose but to fuck me up some more, I realized—and that's why I stopped talking about Claire all of a sudden. No, the tale wasn't over—it had hardly begun—but I wasn't going to keep going down that path. It was a painful distraction that would lead to nothing productive, nothing that I wanted to think about, so I simply stopped talking.

But then Dr. Mbaye changed gears on me, and took all the indignant wind out of my sails. Took me, in fact, to a place infinitely more troubling, right here in my own backyard.

"Who is it that has you thinking about Claire?"

📖 📖 📖

My favorite class in grade school, the one I blame for turning me into an unmitigated school junkie, was fourth-grade geography. Up until that point, classroom time had been little more than a mild diversion from my relentless pursuit of mischief. I'd spent more hours than not in the principal's office for everything from spitball contests to playground fights—miraculously bringing home report cards with top grades in every subject except Conduct, but never really feeling much interest in anything but having fun.

All that turned around as soon as my fourth-grade teacher, Mr. Hackman, passed out those geography books. From the first map, I was hooked—immersed in a world of longitude and latitude. I'd lay awake at night in the room I shared with Lizzie, my mind soaring over the vast distances to India or Antarctica, mentally identifying any spot I chose and getting there through a simple function of left and right. The whole world was laid before me in a comforting combination of north, south, east and west—I could imagine where everything was, and where I was in relation to it.

Something about the grid of a map has always felt very familiar to me. It taps into the grid that seems to have been permanently implanted into my personal circuitry. I've always been able to tell what direction I'm facing, even when the sun isn't shining, even when the clouds are obscuring the moon and the stars. I never questioned this innate ability—I guess I always assumed that everyone walked around with their own inner compass, that it was no more remarkable than being able to identify the color red. I didn't exactly know what people meant when they said they were lost—I guess I figured that they simply didn't know the address of their destination. It never occurred to me that they might not know where they were.

Once I learned about the navigational tools of the ancient mariners, their method of pinpointing their location and direction from an observation of the stars and use of a sextant, the world took on a whole new dimension for me—quite literally. I was fascinated by their method of triangulation, their way of identifying a place on Earth by reference to a point outside the grid. No longer limited to a series of lefts and rights on a two-dimensional plane, my mental wanderings at night could embark into a third dimension: up and down were added to the equation. Suddenly, the entire universe was available to me, and any point in space could be traced back to my location through a simple combination of left or right, and up or down.

High school physics opened things up for me even more, and put all of creation at my imagination's disposal, because I could envision not only this universe but other dimensions as well. As some theoretical physicist had hypothesized, my three-dimensional universe might just be the "surface" of a four-dimensional "ball." If so, then my universe was round, and if I traveled in a straight line out into the far reaches of space, I would eventually just end up right back in my bed in Washington, DC. The possibilities were staggering, and limitless.

Thursday afternoon, with my back to the sun streaming through my office window, I stared at the online map of Chicago, tracing with my eyes the path from the interstate to Meers-Boothe. It was a simple combination of lefts and rights, of norths and wests, between me and Claire. But the distance between us couldn't really be measured in miles. It was an impenetrable paradox: for all my youthful cartography, for all the comfort I derived from knowing my place in the universe and envisioning the worlds beyond, I didn't know the way back to Claire.

That afternoon found me near the bottom of the pile of work that I'd put aside over the weekend in order to draft the CRS papers. That still left this week's accumulation of piles, but I could only do what I could do. Staying late last night had helped some, and had also provided the perfect excuse to avoid the talk that David was itching to resume—grilling me on my session with Dr. Mbaye on Tuesday. He now seemed to feel that, with me having seen Dr. Mbaye individually, the ball was firmly in my court for resolving our marriage problems—

and that really pissed me off. Work was a helpful distraction, and the phones had obediently stayed silent today—except for the call from Renee around noon, worried that Amtec stock was still going up. One more thing I could do nothing about; that list was getting pretty long.

Since I'd already had a session with Dr. Mbaye this week, I was free after all to attend the Lambda dinner that night. What I really wanted to do was sleep, but that was out of the question as long as I was still living in the apartment with David. We'd either fight, or he'd guilt me to death. No, if I could put aside work for the evening, I decided I should probably go to the dinner.

By the time Shawanna called around four, I was toast. My head was pounding heavy artillery, the afternoon sun streaming through my windows was uncomfortably hot, and to top it off I could feel my period coming on. Just perfect.

"Sugarplum, have I got something for you!" Shawanna sang out.

"You got the file?"

"In my hot little hand. Copies all made and ready to overnight to you. It's too big to fax, but you want me to tell you the down and dirty?"

Did I? Or did I want to just read it for myself? Of course, I might not be here tomorrow by the time it arrived—Renee and I were leaving for Baltimore in the early afternoon. And I could tell that Shawanna really wanted to spill the beans. What the hell—I let her.

"Okay, what's the story?"

"Buckle your seat belt, girl, your grandma died filthy rich."

Really? So Rob was right about that. "How rich?"

"Buy-the-Dallas-Cowboys-with-her-spare-change rich. Three hundred and fifty million, but that was twelve years ago. Wisely invested, that loot could have easily doubled by now."

I didn't actually drop the phone, but I might as well have—I didn't hear another word after a certain point. That number was bouncing around in my skull, looking for a place to sit down, but it just didn't fit anywhere in there.

"But there's a catch. You still with me, sugarplum?"

"I think so." I hoped so.

"Well, pay attention, because this part here's important."

As if three hundred and fifty million wasn't? "Okay, I'm listening."

"You're not in it."

"I'm not in what?"

"The will, honey. You're not there."

I let that news settle in for a minute. I hadn't really believed I would be included in Grandma Edna's will. The lawyer in me knew that if any of the three of us had been named as beneficiaries, we would have been contacted about it twelve years ago. But still, some small part of me had hoped that maybe there had been some kind of mistake back then, that Gardner actually had an ounce of honor and was setting out now to right some wrong that had been done to his children.

His children. What a joke—I hadn't thought of myself as his child since I was five years old. I would never admit to Liz or Rob that I'd had such a foolish thought. It was embarrassing enough to acknowledge it to myself, to concede that, for just a second, I'd fallen into an adult version of the same trap that had ensnared me with aching regularity through all the years we had lived with Gussie—when I'd curl myself into a tiny ball under my covers and pretend that Mommy was about to come into my room and tell me not to cry because I had a daddy after all, a daddy who was happy to have me as his baby girl, and he'd come home to us soon and say it had all been a big mistake.

Shawanna was still talking and I missed most of what she said, so I had to ask her to repeat it.

"I said, it's weird the way this thing reads. I'm no trusts-and-estates lawyer, but it looks to me like somebody went out of his way to cut you out of this thing. Anyway, you ready for the real kicker?"

"You mean there's more?" This just kept getting better and better.

"The lawyer on the papers—the guy who drafted it?"

"Don't tell me—"

"None other than Kenneth Gardner."

📖   📖   📖

There is very little on which the members of my family—immediate and remote—can ever agree. We're a disparate bunch, with a wide array of big personalities thrown into the mix. With all of our intermarriages, you'd think we'd resemble one another more than most families, in personality as well as looks. But just the opposite was true. Oh sure, there were a few common traits running through the bloodline—hard-headedness comes to mind—but for the most part, we were all about as different from one another as we could be and held widely divergent opinions on most things.

When it came to one's chosen profession, however, the various branches of my clan found a rare point of commonality. From Uncle Dink to Cousin Laura, from Aunt Tavia to Cousin Ruth, there was never such unanimity of opinion as on this single and oft-recited precept: All lawyers are scum. The message was drummed into us relentlessly, from early childhood—maybe prenatally—in both subtle and explicit terms.

I'd be watching television before bedtime—me, Lizzie, and Robbie sandwiched between Gussie and Gramps on the long sofa, Mom in the chair by the coffee table—and as soon as the character of a lawyer came on, Gussie would solve the whodunit by announcing, "He's the baddie." Gussie always sat in the same spot on the sofa, the far left-hand side by the end table, where the reading lamp cast the best light for her to do her nails or read her magazines. She'd be busying herself with something or another during the show, but even with only half an ear tuned to the set, she'd zero in on the story enough to disparage the lawyer. And everyone would nod in agreement.

When Dad married Mom and we moved out of Gussie's house to our own down the block, he carried on the grand family tradition without missing a beat. "You can steal more money with a briefcase than a gun," he liked to say. Dad and Mom clicked on many levels, so deeply suited for each other that at times they seemed almost to read each other's minds, but this shared aversion to lawyers was a tract of common ground that they highlighted more than most. Some families share racial or religious antipathies. Especially in the 1960s and 1970s, when Washington, DC, was a melting pot ready to boil over, I knew more than a handful of kids who thought nothing of repeating distasteful jokes that they'd heard around their dinner tables—jokes that, as we grew older, as kids and as a nation, most of us learned to revile. But my family was staunchly Democratic and, despite our Southern heritage, adamantly liberal. We didn't tell jokes that belittled racial or religious groups, we didn't use those ugly epithets, and we felt superior to those who did. No, our put-downs were saved for only one group of people—the lawyers.

It always struck me as a bit odd, this loathing of a vocation that, so far as I could tell, had done nothing to us—at least not professionally. Sure, I knew that the Sperm Donor had been a lawyer, but it wasn't his job that had broken my mother's heart; it was the man himself. And I knew that his father had been a lawyer too at one time, and was a judge by the time he'd married my mother—but, again, so what? There had also been plenty of lawyers on Mom's side. Gussie was full of stories about the great statesmen among our ancient kin, all the way back to Chief Justice Marshall on Old Granddaddy's side, and Justice Taney on her mother's. I translated these jumbled messages into the admonition that the law had once been a grand profession, peopled by great and selfless men, but that it had become perverted in modern times, and was today the bailiwick of shysters and hoodlums.

I think that's a big part of why I put off law school for as long as I did. Although I'd secretly rooted for Perry Mason on those evenings in Gussie's living room, I kept my fascination with the courtroom to myself. In college, I'd taken history courses and logic as a cover, and didn't let on that part of what I was seeking in those classrooms was a back door into the mysteries of the law. My graduate work in history had also been a subterfuge. And when I finally announced that I was going to law school, I knew it was a stroke of profound rebellion. My family had nothing to say about it by that time—I'd put myself through Smith and two years of graduate school in American history before finally answering the siren call of the law. I know they felt betrayed by my choice—I felt it too, because those old lessons die hard, and the voices of our childhood can never really be stilled.

And let's face it, I was running from more than my true vocation in those years before law school. There was a lot of dust to settle, and I waited it out as best I could by burying myself in the political battles of Adams and Jefferson. By the time I felt able to rejoin the living and survey my surroundings, the thought of disappointing my family held a lot less power over me. I knew what real disappointment was—had practically written a multivolume treatise on it by then—and I knew they'd get over it. Gussie had accepted my news about law school with her customary pragmatism: "Well, just make sure you'll be one of the good ones." Mom and Dad had just shrugged—I think they told their friends I'd joined the Peace Corps.

When it came right down to it, I think it was David who had given me the last ounce of impetus I'd needed. We'd been dating about a year by then, and he understood the entropy I'd been feeling in my graduate program. Always respectful of my family, and downright reverent when it came to Gussie, he'd nevertheless pointed out at regular intervals that the decision was mine, and if I truly wanted a career in the law, I should just do it. Once I'd made the decision, there was no looking back, and David was right there with me, cheering me on as I moved forward with the LSAT and law school applications. I don't suppose my connection to the nest was any different from anyone else's—even without purse strings, I was tethered to my family by hundreds of immutable bonds that took various forms but all boiled down to the simple notion of allegiance. At the end of the day, there's Us and Them, and the big life decisions mark us as one or the other. In deciding to go to law school, I'd taken a bold step across the Rubicon—a metaphor that Old Granddaddy would have appreciated—and I'm not sure they ever forgave me.

❧ *Chapter Seven*

The Grand Ballroom at the Hyatt was packed when I got there. I was late, having taken the time for a quick run in Central Park and a shower at home. Frankly, once I was out of the shower, I considered just bagging the whole thing and going to bed, but I'd promised Janelle and Dennis that I would be there. Besides, David came home while I was drying my hair, and the last thing I wanted to do was spend another evening under the weight of his accusatory glare. I dressed quickly in dress pants and a silk top—panty hose at that hour was too much to ask of me—and I slipped out the door with the reminder that I'd be at a firm function for the evening. No need for David to know the nature of the event.

Janelle spotted me at the coat check desk and immediately appropriated me with an arm around my waist.

"Thank God you're here. I was ready to give up on you. There are just *way* too many men here for my taste."

I surveyed the room and had to agree—the suits outnumbered the women by about three to one. Then again, some of those suits might be women; I kept that observation to myself.

"Where's the bar?" I asked.

"Now you're talking, girlfriend. Come with me." Janelle in the lead, we threaded our way through the groups and stood five people deep in a cluster around the bar.

"I don't see anyone else from Huxley yet," I said as we waited. "I'd better not be the only one who showed up after all. I could be home in bed right now." Or arguing with David.

"Don't even think about it. Dennis and Alan are over there," she cocked her head to the left, "with Charlie Donovan and some of the other junior associates." I scanned the corner and found them next to a group of middle-aged men. It looked like a scene out of a Victorian gentlemen's club.

"Bet they're having a great time."

"Oh, you know it. Alan's on his third scotch, and Dennis has already complained that there are no women here."

"Do you know which table is ours?" There were about 200 tables, apparently numbered in random order. It could take an hour just to find our assigned seats.

"Sixty-seven. Don't worry, I've got us covered," she said as she squeezed up to the bar. "Two vodka martinis," she told the attractive young bartender.

"Make mine a Johnnie Walker Black," I corrected. "Double, on the rocks." If I was going to make it through this stupid dinner, I was going to need some serious liquid reinforcement. With an appreciative eye, I watched the bartender make the drinks—she was quick and fluid in her movements, and gave me two generous shots. I know how hard it is to make bartending look easy, and she had it down pat. Janelle noticed the wink she gave me when she handed over the scotch.

"You go, girl," she whispered, turning away from the bar.

"No thanks," I said, wondering if I could devise a convenient excuse to get out of there. It was warm, and the crush of men towering over me was beginning to get to me. I'm not normally claustrophobic, but it was pretty tight quarters in there—maybe I'd feel better when we sat down.

With Janelle in the lead, it was taking us a long time to weave through the crowd toward our group and, without thinking, I was sipping my drink to quench my thirst—with the result that my scotch was half finished before we were anywhere near our destination in the far corner. I was just considering whether I should go back now for a refill, when I suddenly felt a hand on my arm. I turned to look up and found Veronica's green eyes boring into me. Janelle continued through the obstacle course, oblivious to my predicament—which was, of course, a good thing.

"Hi," said Veronica, sliding her fingers down my arm to clasp my hand. The crush of bodies filled in the gap between me and Janelle, so she was by now totally out of sight. I'd have to make my way over to the Huxley Doyle group on my own.

"Hi," I said, and gave her hand a little squeeze before letting it go.

"So is this some sort of political statement?" she asked. I guess I gave her a quizzical look, because she jumped right in to explain. "Coming to a gay fund-raiser." She had a sort of smirk on her face, as if she'd caught me at something.

"No more than it is for you, I guess. It's a worthy cause, and Huxley Doyle bought a table."

"Well," she said, the smirk now erased by a smile, "you look good enough to eat."

"Veronica—"

"Relax, honey. I'm just kidding." She reached out for my arm again, and gave it a friendly tug. "Go find your friends. I'll catch up with you later." And with that, she disappeared into the throng.

I finally emerged from the worst of the huddled masses to find Janelle in the corner wagging a finger at me. Busted—just great. Tempted to turn around right there and fight my way back to the bar, I eventually concluded that I was better off facing Janelle than running into Veronica again, so I pushed on.

"I can't leave you alone for a second, can I?" Janelle asked with a wink. The evening was only half an hour old, and I'd already collected more winks from women tonight than I'd received the entire year from men.

"Can it, Janelle. I mean it."

"Can what?" asked Alan, sipping his drink. He had a sloppy grin, but otherwise appeared sober.

"Has anybody figured out which table is ours?" Dennis interrupted.

"Janelle says she knows where it is," I offered, happy for the change in subject.

"Isn't that your new client over there?" Dennis asked, looking toward the middle of the room. "The one with CRS?"

I peered in the direction of his gaze and heard Janelle choke on her drink beside me. Through a break in the crowd, I caught a quick glimpse of Renee standing by herself with a wine glass in her hand. The temperature in the room suddenly shot up about twenty degrees, and I nearly missed one of the junior associates asking, "What's CRS?"

"A client of Parsons," Alan answered. "That trade secret case."

My respite from the conversation was short-lived—Dennis addressed his next question directly to me. "Parsons giving you a hard time?"

My view of Renee was blocked again by a very animated group of men enjoying a good laugh over something. At least someone was having fun.

"Not on the case," I said, "but in every other way, well . . ." I didn't want to get into it.

"The answer is yes," said Alan. "He's being a royal asshole about this partnership vote."

"Well," said Dennis, "don't let him get to you. We're in your corner." I appreciated it, I really did, but it wouldn't do any good to point out to him that I might need more than just a corner. "I'm just keeping my head down and doing my work," I said. The rest was out of my hands.

"Girl, I need a refill, and so do you," said Janelle. "You fellas hold down the fort—we'll be right back."

I knew what she was up to, but seeing Renee—even running into Veronica again—seemed preferable to hanging around for the premortem on my partnership odds. I let her steer me directly toward Renee and felt my cheeks start to burn the minute Renee caught my eye through the crowd. Her look was one of surprise—maybe even disbelief—which was quickly displaced by a big smile. She waved and started making her way toward us, so we finally met up near the corner of the bar.

"I'm so glad to see you," she said. "I had no idea you'd be here."

"The firm bought a table," I said hastily, feeling the need to explain. I introduced Janelle and Renee, and before I could utter another word, Janelle announced that she was on her way to order a drink and did Renee want a refill?

"White wine, thank you," she said.

"More of the same for you, Ash?"

"Yeah, but get it with soda—I'm thirsty." It was awfully hot in there.

"You got it. Of course, I'd get better service from that cute bartender if you were standing beside me, but I'll do my best."

"What was that about?" Renee asked as Janelle took off.

"Nothing. Janelle just likes to throw shit my way."

"Well, the bartender is cute."

I didn't really have anything to say to that, so I changed the subject. "So what brings you here?" That seemed safe. Then again, maybe not.

"Oh, worthy cause and all that," Renee replied. "Actually, I did a pro bono case for Lambda two years ago, so I get invited to all the dinners."

"Pro bono? That's great. I wish I had time to take on a pro bono case." I meant it. I was supposed to be one of the good guys—that had been Gussie's mandate. So what was I doing? Helping rich people stay rich and get richer. I could get pretty depressed if I thought about it for more than a minute.

"It was—I loved that case. It was a custody dispute—a lesbian mother lost custody to her alcoholic husband."

"That's awful."

"It gets worse—he was sexually abusing the little girl."

"Unbelievable."

"Trial counsel really screwed up the case, but I took on the appeal and got it reversed."

"That's amazing. I mean, it's disgusting that she could have lost custody in the first place—but the fact that you got it reversed, that must have been incredible."

"It was the best thing I ever did. I mean that. If I died tomorrow, I'd go out knowing that I'd made a real difference in the world, at least for one family. There's nothing in the world like that feeling. You should have seen that little girl's face when she was finally reunited with her mother."

"It must have made your father so proud," I said, recalling our earlier conversation. "You really lived up to his standard—what did you call it? Noble."

Her face fell, and the light from her brilliant hazel eyes dimmed just a bit. "No, not really," she said in a subdued voice.

"What do you mean?"

"Well, he doesn't exactly approve of me."

"I see." But I didn't. Was she referring to politics only or something more personal? For some reason I had to know, but I couldn't think of any way to find out.

"If it's any consolation," I ventured—mostly to keep the conversation going—"my family doesn't approve of me either."

Her smile was soft and knowing—*shit*, I realized, *she must think I'm saying that I'm a lesbian.* Before I could explain what I meant, that I was referring to their disdain for lawyers, Janelle interrupted us with a new round of drinks.

"I think that girl wants your phone number," Janelle said as she handed me my scotch in a highball glass. "She had her eyes on you the whole time she was pouring. Now you be careful with that drink—she didn't leave a lot of room for soda. Renee, white wine for you."

"Thanks," said Renee.

"Don't go away—I'll be right back." I gave her a look imploring her to stay, but she shook her head. "Only two hands," she explained. "I left my drink with the bartender."

I wasn't going anywhere, and the look Renee gave me said she wasn't either. She clinked her glass against mine with a smile, and I smiled right back, and we both took generous sips. *What the hell am I doing?* I wondered in a brief moment of lucidity. *Here I am with this gorgeous woman—this gorgeous* lesbian, *if reports were correct—and she's flirting with me and I'm enjoying it. Worse, I'm flirting back.* I knew my blush was deepening, but there was absolutely nothing I could do about it but enjoy the moment.

It struck me that I hadn't experienced anything like this since—well, since longer ago than I wanted to remember. I hadn't flirted with Veronica; that much was certain. I'd barely even noticed her until that night after a long session of document review when we'd all gone out for a few drinks at the Tavern—that night when she'd cornered me outside the bathroom. She'd picked her moment carefully—in hindsight, I could see that clearly. We'd been alone in the dim hallway, and she'd pinned me against the wall to show me how Doug Collier had inappropriately made a pass at her an hour earlier. But when she'd demonstrated how he'd clumsily copped a feel, she'd flicked her finger across my breast, and I think she'd been as surprised as I was by the sudden and dramatic hardening of my nipple at her touch.

I'd been tipsy, and so had she, and I think that explained a lot of what followed—the widening of her eyes as she felt my excitement blossom, the little moan that escaped me as she started to massage my breast in earnest, the slow grind of her hips against me in response. I'd felt a wash of warm cream flood out of me—so unexpected that I'd wondered for a moment if I'd just gotten my period. All it took was a slight tip of her head toward me, and we were instantly locked in a deep, no-holds-barred kiss that had us both gasping for air. I'd heard the door unlock just in time to disentangle myself—but as soon as the bathroom was free, she'd dragged me inside and locked the door. When we'd finally made it back to our table much later, everyone was too drunk to notice our disheveled appearance or the distinct odor of sex steaming off of us.

No, there had been no flirting with Veronica—everything had been direct, and wholly devoid of any emotion except frank unbridled passion. Nor had I ever really flirted with David. Our sex life had always been more of an afterthought, at least for me—something tagged onto an otherwise comfortable and abiding friendship. Whatever this thing was with Renee, it was already far more complicated than I cared to admit. And much as it scared the shit out of me, I couldn't help myself—she was intoxicating.

"What are you thinking?" she asked quietly. I couldn't look at her.

"Nothing, why?"

"You're blushing."

Shit. "It's the heat."

"Mmm, I guess it is pretty warm in here," she said, and proceeded to remove her tailored suit jacket. I watched, transfixed, as she slipped off her jacket to reveal a slinky black halter underneath. I tried, but I was simply powerless to tear my eyes from the mesmerizing sight of her long dark hair cascading over those alabaster shoulders, with the deep V of the silk halter providing a tantalizing glimpse of perfectly rounded breasts. Was that a shadow playing tricks on my eyes, I wondered, or was I really seeing the outline of her nipples straining against the sheer fabric? Oh God, I became aware of a slow ache starting to hum in me somewhere below my waist—a lot below—and my mouth suddenly felt very dry.

"You look fantastic," I think I said. She smiled again and that got my heart pounding even more.

"Oooh, look at you," Janelle cooed at Renee as she rejoined us with her vodka martini. "Come on," she said, linking an arm through Renee's and one through mine, "you're sitting with us tonight. We'll have to beat the girls off with a stick."

Renee nodded. "You sure there's room at your table?"

"We'll make room, honey. Won't we, Ash?"

Fuck. "Yes."

Once we were seated and the rest of the Huxley Doyle crew joined us, Janelle kept up a running patter through most of the dinner, and generally spared me the need to say much of anything to anyone. Of course, she deftly engineered the seats to ensure that Renee was right next to me, but apart from that she pretty much behaved herself and didn't seriously embarrass me. On the whole, she could have been a lot worse.

Remarkably, the evening's swift decline into hell had nothing do with Janelle. If anyone was to blame, it was me—I should have left after the main course was finished. Instead, I stayed through dessert, and that's when it happened, when I'd excused myself to visit the ladies' room and get some air. I'd successfully nursed the same drink all through dinner, so I was feeling pretty clear headed, despite the insistent throbbing that hit me between the legs every time Renee smiled at me. Renee had invited herself along on my bathroom jaunt—a fact that did not go unnoticed by Janelle, who at least kept her thoughts to herself. As we headed for the ladies' room in the lobby, Renee made a little joke about my needing to earn the cappuccino I'd just ordered—something about having to indulge in chocolate cake—and that's when I suddenly stopped dead in my tracks. There was Veronica, smoking a cigarette, just beyond the lobby doors.

"What's wrong?" Renee asked.

"Nothing. Just someone I don't want to see right now." But it was too late—Veronica had spotted me, crushed out her cigarette, and was walking toward us. The smirk was once again plastered on her face.

"On your way to the bathroom?" Veronica asked me. She gave Renee a very obvious once-over, and I wanted to throttle her.

"Hi—um, yes."

"Aren't you going to introduce me to your friend?" she purred.

I did, and Renee gave me a questioning look as she nodded her hello to Veronica. "Look," I said, "I really have to go." *So just get the fuck out of the way.*

"I'll just bet you do," Veronica said.

"Look, Veronica—"

"Buckle your seat belt, Renee," she said. "She's famous for her trips to the ladies' room."

"That's enough. If you'll excuse us—"

"My, aren't we in a hurry?" Veronica said, shooting daggers at me.

"Maybe I should just leave you two alone," Renee said as she took a step backward.

"That's not necessary. Look, Veronica, you've had too much to drink. Just back off." She actually appeared quite sober, but she was angry—really angry—and I wasn't prepared for it.

"Is this the one you dumped me for?" she spit. "Does David know?"

"Renee is a client of mine, and you're making a spectacle of yourself. So why don't you just go back to your table?" I abruptly took Renee's arm and practically yanked her to my side. "Come on; I have to pee."

"Client, huh?" Veronica called after us. "Aren't there rules against that sort of thing?" I fumed without comment and prayed that she'd die a painful death. Right then.

There was someone in the ladies' room, so we waited by the door a good minute or so before I had my temper under control enough to say something. But what was there to say?

"I'm sorry about that."

"You don't have to apologize," she said. Her expression was one of concern, but with just enough reserve to let me know that she really didn't know what to make of the scene she'd just witnessed.

"I know, but you shouldn't have been subjected to that."

"It's not your fault. And I think you handled it very well."

"No, very well would have meant killing her. But then I'd get arrested and Doris Baker would have to come get me out of the pens."

She laughed, and it broke the ice a bit. It was going to be okay, or so I thought.

"I'm lucky it wasn't me," Renee said. "There are one or two of my exes here tonight."

Well, Veronica wasn't exactly my ex. But that would take more of an explanation than I felt up to at the moment, so I let it drop. I was much more interested in the fact that Renee had an ex or two in attendance here at a gay fund-raiser. What more confirmation did I need? The little shiver of excitement that passed through me was as delightful as it was disturbing. What the hell was I doing?

"Sounds like it ended pretty recently," she continued.

"Yeah." Last month, to be precise. "But it wasn't really . . . I mean, it was just this thing. Nothing, really. But I guess she's pissed off about it now."

"I think you've got that right," she said. "I'm sorry if I made things worse."

"No, it's not you. It's just—complicated." She nodded, and paused for a moment to bite a fingernail before she continued.

"Can I ask you a question?" Here we go. She was looking me square in the face—full, open, and demanding the same from me. My breath caught in my throat and I felt the world balanced precariously on a pin, ready to tilt in the next few seconds. I was drawn into her eyes, those deep pools of hazel cream, and knew I'd tell her whatever she wanted to know. I'd give her whatever she asked.

"Sure," I answered quietly.

She looked at me intently for a few seconds, and I was reeled in by the movement of her eyes as they peered into mine—first to the left one, then to the right, as if searching for something.

"Who's David?"

Although it wasn't the question I'd expected, wasn't the question I was prepared to answer, I could deny her nothing at this point. Lost in her searching look, I had no choice but to answer, whether or not I was ready to begin digging through all the layers of complexity that awaited us.

"Well." I took a breath and plunged in. "He's my husband."

   📖 📖 📖

I sat back in my seat on the Acela and perused the stack of briefs before me. As long as Renee wasn't accompanying me down to Baltimore, I'd figured I could cancel my flight reservation and just take the train—getting to and from the station was much easier than dealing with airport traffic, and I could use the travel time en route to spread out and get some work done. I was a little disappointed that the estate documents hadn't arrived from Texas by the time I'd left the office—I'd hoped to review them as well.

Yeah, right. I could barely focus on the revised motion to dismiss in front of me—the replay of last night was spooling on an endless reel in my mind, its abrasion rubbing me raw each time I got to the look on Renee's face when she'd learned that I was married.

I wasn't really surprised when Stella had tracked me down in a meeting around eleven this morning to say that Renee had called in with a change of plans. The phone had been suspiciously silent all morning, and I'd spent the time anticipating our trip to Baltimore with something akin to dread—anxious over the thought of facing her after last night, but at the same time afraid that she'd back out of the trip altogether. I still wasn't entirely sure which one had come to pass. All that she'd told Stella was that she wouldn't be on the flight, so I had no idea if she was planning to come later or not at all. And, chickenshit that I am, I didn't have the nerve to call her back to find out.

I'd never been in this predicament before—having my professional focus invaded by personal distractions. Whatever happened to "don't shit where you eat"? Veronica hadn't been a colleague, much less a client. She'd really been nothing more than an acquaintance, and once that document production was finished we never saw each other again professionally. This thing with Renee was precisely the kind of personal drama I would warn my friends to avoid—yet here I was, neglecting to call someone, a *client*, to get clarification about a business trip, solely because of some personal complications between us. All because I was afraid she'd want to discuss last night—or worse, that she wouldn't. It was the height of unprofessionalism, and I loathed being in this position.

The truth was, she hadn't given me a chance last night to explain anything—not that I would have known what to say if she had. *Gee, Renee, I'm not really a lesbian, I just play one at work. I'm not really gay, but I have slept with a woman before. But I'm also not really all that married—in fact, I'm separated, except that we're still living together right now. But I'd still really like to keep this thing going between us, except I'm not exactly sure what it is, but even if it's what I think it is, I don't really know what I want from it, or how far I can take it.*

I was giving myself a headache trying to sort through it all. Why was I having such a hard time getting my hands around what was going on with Renee? Part of it, I knew, was the fact that I'd known her only a few weeks. Yet there were those moments, especially last night, when it felt as if we were on very intimate terms. It was an intimacy that seemed both familiar and thoroughly enticing, comfortable yet laced with a palpable eroticism.

Sure, it was a crush. God, I felt like a teenager even admitting it to myself. But even an unexpected, powerful attraction to Renee didn't really explain it—I could just say fuck it and forget it, or I could just fuck her and then forget it. No, there was something far deeper than a simple crush working on me here—something that made me hyper-conscious of where she was standing in a room, something that made me feel homesick when her eyes crinkled at the corners. Something, I had to admit, that made me care very much about what she thought of me.

Which was the reason, of course, that I'd been twisted in knots since I'd told her about David. I'd known that I would have to tell her eventually, if we'd proceeded with . . . whatever it was we were doing. But I'd known that such news would necessarily—and understand-ably—set off a few clarion warning bells for her: it suggested that I was already in a relationship, and that I was straight. As to the first, I was sure I could make her understand that my marriage had been circling the drain for a long time. As for the second, well, what the hell did I expect? I was well aware that the specter of heterosexuality would ring more than an alarm bell—it would sound the death knell for us. A lesbian friend of mine at Farnsworth Crowley calls it the Lesbian Prime Directive: never, *ever* get involved with a straight woman. To Renee, I knew, my straight taint might as well be leprosy.

And the real killer, the appalling irony that I would probably never get to share with her, was that I understood her need to pull away all too well, because I'd once felt the very same thing. The look in her eyes when I'd told her about David was, I knew, the same look I'd given Claire fifteen years ago.

📖   📖   📖

Claire had a hard time getting around campus for a good month or so after her fall. Although her ankle wasn't broken, she had torn ligaments all along its side and couldn't put any weight on her foot. Wearing a large padded boot that resembled a ski boot, she was able to walk only by using crutches, and she tired very easily.

The logistics for getting around involved more than navigating a course that encountered as few stairs as possible. Her arms were required for the crutches, so she couldn't carry anything. Her books and things were either stuffed into her backpack or were left behind. Easier said than done—she had to pack each morning for the entire day, since she couldn't just run back to her room to pick up something. It wasn't easy, and after witnessing her first week or two of hobbling around campus, I volunteered to be somewhat of a gofer for her.

I was happy to do it. We'd started to become friends, in a way, since the time of her accident. We still didn't really hang out together on campus, but ever since that long night in the infirmary, we seemed to have arrived at a level of easy companionableness that most friends require years to develop. We never really went through the stage of exchanging meaningless pleasantries or polite small talk. Right from those first few weeks, ours was a friendship where we were perfectly comfortable with long silences, where the conversations we had seemed to start in the middle, as if resumed at the precise point where we'd last left off.

I'd never had a friend like Claire. She was in many ways a complete enigma to me—normally quiet and aloof but capable of total silliness too, especially if she went too long without sleep. I loved those moments of hilarity with her, usually very late at night after some long probing discussion about who-knew-what. She was a scientist by nature—although she hated her organic chemistry class that term—and hers was a mind such as I'd never before encountered. She saw the connections between the most diverse lines of thought, and she structured everything—her studies, her day, her life—around carefully considered and logically sequenced principles. Her belief in science bordered on the religious—she felt that it explained a grand order, organizing all things, and believed that with enough study and discipline, science could open all doors and answer all questions.

I have no idea what we said in those late-night talks when Janice was away and we had her room to ourselves. One night we'd be discussing the role of the hetaera in ancient Greece, and another would find us exchanging quotations by our favorite authors. I introduced her to the works of T. S. Eliot, and she especially loved one line in which he noted that "all time is unredeemable." We'd tease through that line from time to time, seeking to unravel the conundrum. Claire loved such games.

She, in turn, shared with me quotes from Colette, her favorite author. One passage she particularly loved to recite talked about a road having led to a sort of epiphany, to an inexpressible state of grace. Claire would quote that passage often, asking me what I thought of the mystery, what it was that Colette had found so incapable of expression.

One night, Claire told me about some graffiti she'd seen in one of the bathroom stalls in the library: "A woman without a man is like a fish without a bicycle." Her eyes lit up with glee as she told me about it, as if she'd discovered on that bathroom wall a philosophy in harmony with her essential self, both silly and profound. I knew she didn't have much patience for our housemates who seemed to live their lives through their boyfriends—who, like her roommate Janice, appeared to have no existence apart from their male counterparts. Although she never said so, it seemed to me that Claire took pride in her independence, and instinctively I knew deep down that she would not have tolerated my presence if I were attached at the hip to some Amherst guy. So when she relayed to me her discovery on the bathroom wall, she did it as if speaking to a kindred spirit, never doubting that I would love it as much as she.

What I loved, of course, was how she delighted in playing word games with it. We returned to the theme often over our next few late-night sessions, spinning it in new directions as we ran through all of the off-color permutations we could conjure: fish living alone in a fishbowl, fish riding on tandem bikes, fish swimming in schools. And one day, about two weeks after she first told me about it, Claire surprised me with a present—she'd had T-shirts made for us with the quote emblazoned across the fronts. As thrilled as I was to have this little token of our inside joke, and to have it proclaimed on T-shirts that only she and I had, her gesture also highlighted for me one of the big differences between us: she had money to burn.

We sometimes read aloud from an English translation of *Gigi*, one of the works by Colette that Claire especially loved. During one such reading, Claire stumbled over a phrase that had been kept in the original French. Despite her love of Colette, Claire spoke no French, and she turned to me for help.

"*Ce que je pense,*" she read. "What is that?"

"You know what."

"No, I don't—what's it mean?"

"That's what it means," I said. "'You know what.' Technically, I guess it's 'that of which I'm thinking.' But it's a euphemism—the old courtesan's talking about Gigi's private parts, and she wants to be delicate about it. It's from the turn of the century, after all."

Claire seemed delighted. "How do you say it?"

"*Ce que je pense,*" I repeated, showing off a little.

She tried it out. "Sicka-juh-puntz."

"Close," I laughed.

Well, that did it—Claire had a new word toy to play with. And since by this time she'd started referring to her despised organic chemistry course as "you know what," I knew just where she'd employ her new phrase from now on. I was right—for the rest of that semester, she never referred to organic chemistry as anything but *ce que je pense*. Of course, eventually, she applied the term to something else as well.

In the end, it didn't really matter what we discussed during those long hours in her room—the point was the exercise itself. We gave each other an intellectual workout on those nights, and we each grew stronger from it. At the time, full of the hubris that only a twenty-year-old can muster, I believed in the power of our minds, believed them to be truly limitless. I think I first fell in love with Claire's mind, awed by its elegance and challenged by its inspiration.

Our late-night sessions evolved slowly. At first, I was just a friendly neighbor offering to pick up odds and ends for her on my trips into town, but at some point those quick stops by her room turned into actual visits, and by mid-October or so I was deliberately blocking out certain evenings that we'd spend together studying and solving the problems of the world. Janice was hardly ever there, and I always got the feeling that her absence suited Claire just fine. Claire liked a lot of time to herself, and whenever I came by her room I always found her busy with something—engrossed in a book, tending to her plants, listening to music. Still, she never sent me away—seemed, in fact, to look forward to my visits, as if I were an ambassador bringing her news from the world in which the rest of us lived. Because Claire just wasn't a part of this world—at least, not my world.

Maybe it had something to do with the fact that I hardly ever saw her during the day—she never returned to Comstock until dinner time—but I think the otherworldliness of those evenings I spent with her had more to do with the fact that we spent them only with each other. None of the other Comstock residents had any interest in hanging out in Claire's room, and in the minds of our housemates we were soon associated with each other to the exclusion of everyone else. I felt proud of the association, exalted in my role as the ambassador to Claire, as if I alone had been granted this privileged access. I later came to realize that it wasn't so much a matter of me being special; it was just the way Claire was. She just gave so much of herself, focused so intently on whomever she was with, that she was overwhelmed by large groups, preferring the company of just a few at a time. I'd simply been the first at Comstock to crack through her glacial exterior, and only then because I'd been the first on the scene when she'd fallen from her desk. I often wondered how different things might have been if Shelly had been home that night.

The night that I knew, really knew, that there was something very different about this friendship, at least for me, was the night I came back to Comstock after work and found Shelly sitting quietly in our room listening to the music coming through the wall from next door. It was a Friday night, and most of the residents were either away for the weekend or already in bed, so the house was very quiet, and we could hear the music coming from Claire's room pretty clearly. It was a beautiful violin piece but, lovely as it was, I couldn't understand why Shelly would be listening to it so intently instead of putting on a tape of her own. I started to say so, but she held up her hand to quiet me, and waited until the piece was over before she spoke.

"Oh my God, wasn't that amazing?" she said breathlessly.

"Yeah," I said—and it was—"but what's the big deal?"

"Don't you know? That's Claire."

"Get out."

"No, really. Didn't she ever tell you she plays the viola?"

"No." I felt a little hurt that Shelly was privy to this detail of Claire's life, that Claire hadn't shared it with me. "Does she play in an orchestra or something?"

"I don't think so. I think she just plays for herself."

"How come we never heard her before?"

"She usually goes to a practice room in the music building. I guess she can't manage the steps these days."

I shook my head in wonder at this new insight into Claire. "That was beautiful."

"Yeah," Shelly said, "but don't get your hopes up—from what I know, she never plays for anyone. At least not intentionally." She grinned at me conspiratorially.

The fact that Claire kept her playing a secret, didn't share it with anyone, made me feel a little better. Not much. I couldn't really blame her, though—there were a lot of things she still didn't know about me, including the place where I worked. She would never ask, of course—Claire just didn't ask questions about people; it wasn't her way. And I hadn't found a convenient way to slip it into the conversation. Recently, I'd also been feeling a little uncomfortable about even broaching the subject—afraid that it might suggest something about me that I didn't want her to consider. Or reject.

She started in on another piece—soft, plaintive—and I realized that Shelly was right, it wasn't a violin. It had the dark, brooding tones of the viola. I turned off the light to sit quietly on my bed, listening with rapt attention, imagining her face with that earnest expression she gets when she's really involved in something. The tones were melancholy, breathtaking in their poignancy. And as I listened to the gentle crescendo, that mournful urgency of the strings rising to their painful pinnacle, I felt my chest constrict with an ache, a longing that I could not identify. It hurt, physically hurt, as if those notes of lacrymose beauty were reaching into my heart, each sweep of the bow scraping me raw and echoing some deep and directionless yearning of my own.

I didn't tell Claire what I'd heard. Weeks passed, and we kept up our rendezvous in her room every few days or so, occasionally returning to the theme of fish and bicycles, but I never let on that I knew how she spent some of her evenings alone. She tended to play only on weekend nights, when I guess she knew she had the floor pretty much to herself. I found myself on those nights anxious for my bartending shift to end, chomping at the bit for last call so I could dash back to Comstock, sneak into my room, and settle in for a concert—sometimes with Shelly, sometimes alone.

I suppose we would have gone on that way indefinitely, if not for the fact that Claire's ankle gradually improved. By early November she'd dispensed with the crutches and was managing stairs with far less difficulty. When an entire weekend went by with no music reaching through the wall to embrace me in the dark, I knew that Claire had returned to the practice rooms.

Disappointed as I was to see the concerts end, and much as I'd wanted to find some way of broaching the subject with her directly—

asking her right out if I could just listen to her practice sometimes—I'd decided to respect her privacy. I figured she'd mention it eventually. She'd drop an offhand remark about playing the viola—she'd say it matter of factly, as if we'd discussed it many times before and she was merely picking up in the middle of an earlier conversation. That was her way, I'd learned, with topics that made her uncomfortable—she'd dismiss their significance with a deadpan delivery.

It didn't exactly happen that way, however. Planning, it seemed, was often a pointless exercise when it came to Claire—her remarkable ability to surprise me, her capacity for the unexpected, was one of the things that delighted me most about her. But not in this case. She really pulled the rug out from under me with this one, and set in motion a chain of events that would change everything.

It was late on a Saturday night over Homecoming weekend, about two weeks after Claire's liberation from the crutches, and although I was making money hand over fist behind the bar at the Cave, I was looking forward to the end of my shift. The bar was packed with more than the usuals, filled with returning alums crowding several feet deep around my station and clamoring for booze. As a result, I'd been moving on automatic pilot since around nine, without a moment to pour myself a single glass of water during the relentless stream of orders.

Since September, I'd become fairly adept at dodging the attentions of the bar's regular flirts, who had early on decided that I was simply playing hard to get. Kat, by the this time, had learned the deep dark secret that I was straight, but she didn't talk about people—especially her employees—and probably figured that my ambiguous sexuality was good for business. She'd watch with amusement as I got a fair number of offers for after-hour trysts, but I tended to avoid eye contact when I was very busy, and was usually able to decline the invitations with a simple smile and "Not tonight, thanks."

That Saturday, with the bar so hectic, I made even less eye contact than usual—I'd often just lean my ear toward the customers so I could hear their orders over the din, and set about making the drinks before they even finished speaking. It was right at the start of a popular song, when the crowd dispersed to hit the dance floor that, without looking up, I tipped my ear in the direction of the next person in line, and heard the voice that froze me in my tracks.

"Why didn't you ever tell me you worked here?"

I looked up and there she was, her long blonde hair flowing across her shoulders, her blue eyes chipping into me like ice picks.

"Claire," was all I could manage. I was utterly speechless—unusual for me—and rooted to the floor. She just stared at me, the look on her face almost challenging, but also a little hurt. Or maybe that was just my imagination. I had to move, to say something, but all I could do was switch back to autopilot.

"Can I get you a drink?" I kick-started myself by reaching for a glass.

"Miller," she said, and promptly sat down on a barstool that was suddenly vacated. Shit.

I was nervous at the beer tap, self-conscious under her laser glare and careful not to give her too much foam. It shouldn't have mattered what she thought of my bartending, but for some reason it did. The smallest things, which had been so routine only a few moments ago, now took on an inexplicable prominence. *If only she would look away for a minute,* I thought, *I might be able to crawl back inside my skin.*

"Ash, baby," I heard from somewhere behind Claire as I passed her the beer. It was Lori, one of my more persistent suitors, and she was noticeably drunk. This night just seemed to get better and better. There was no rat hole for me to duck into, so I cupped my ear in her direction and asked her what she'd have.

"You, honey. When are you going to give in and let me show you a good time?"

I determinedly kept my eyes away from Claire and wiped down the bar as I shook my head. "Not tonight, thanks."

"Come on, Ash. What are you holding out for?" She was swaying on her feet, and I knew I should cut her off. I poured her a Coke, hoping that she was too buzzed to notice.

"Sorry, Lori. Here." I passed her the Coke. "On the house—just because you're such a good sport."

She seemed satisfied with that, and stumbled back into the crowd.

"Very smooth," Claire said. Unfortunately, there was a momentary lull in the drink orders, so I had no choice but to deal with her.

"She's harmless." I started drying glasses. Anything to avoid looking at her.

"If you say so."

I shrugged. It was surreal, having Claire sitting there glaring at me. I was hyperactive, brimming with nervous energy, while she was the same quiet, composed statue that I'd first met. I couldn't stand it anymore.

"So are you going to tell me what you're doing here?" I asked.

She simply looked away, over her shoulder, and there on the dance floor I saw the sophomore violinist I'd once seen with her outside the bookstore. She was dancing with someone I didn't recognize, maybe an alum.

"My friend Joan wanted to see someone. We just came from a recital."

"A viola recital?" I asked, looking at her directly. She didn't flinch.

"Yes, as a matter of fact."

"Why didn't you ever tell me you play the viola?"

She gave me a little half-smile. "I guess we're both pretty private about some things."

I knew what she was thinking, and was more than happy to set the record straight, but not here in the middle of the Cave on a busy Saturday night. I was about to tell her that we should talk about it later, but just then Joan walked up with her friend.

"Claire, we're going back to Connie's hotel. Do you mind?"

Claire shook her head. "I'll be fine," she said. "I think I'll sit here for a while." She took another sip of her beer and turned to lock her eyes on mine. "If that's all right with you."

Be cool; it's no big deal. "Sure," I said casually, and turned to Joan. "Claire lives next door to me. I'll see that she gets home okay."

Of course, I had no idea if Claire had been intending to stay until closing, still another two hours away. But she nodded, drained her glass, and handed it to me for a refill, so that appeared to be the plan now.

Remarkably, I was actually able to forget about her sitting there a few times—mostly during the busiest crunches, when I was handling three or four customers at once and had to dash through the orders with seamless choreography. The women generally ignored Claire. I suppose they sensed—as most people did—the invisible wall that surrounded her when she wanted to be left alone. Claire appeared perfectly content to sit quietly behind the little fortress she erected around herself, but whether or not she noticed it, she was receiving a fair amount of attention from the patrons. Small groups here and there were taking turns looking at her from across the room, and then exchanging some comments among themselves. And the conversations were probably about more than just her startling good looks. I was sure they were wondering why she appeared to be sitting with me. I smiled to myself at the thought—a little amusement at the irony, but also, for some reason, a little pride.

She nursed maybe three or four beers the whole time, and said very little—nothing more than asking for refills really. Kat was scheduled to close up, so I was free to leave soon after last call. Of course, my exit with Claire garnered another round of stares—and this time I felt certain that Claire noticed them too, but still she said nothing.

Once we were out in the chilly quiet of the night, my ears still ringing from the blaring music, I felt the perspiration quickly cooling on my skin. Despite her tender ankle, Claire took off toward Comstock at a brisk pace, and with my shorter legs I had to hustle to keep up. Her stride often gave the impression that she was angry—and maybe this time she was. I just couldn't tell.

She stopped at the corner to let a car pass on the deserted street, and I pulled up beside her to wait by her side. She stared at the car's retreating tail light for a moment, and that's when I knew she was going to say it. I'd become pretty good at reading the lexicon of Claire over the past few weeks.

"So, what, does this mean you're gay or something?" She didn't sound accusing—she seemed, in fact, to have a genuine inquisitiveness underlying her studied neutrality. But I was so antsy from the past two hours, so ready for a confrontation, that I breezed right past any possibility of just having a simple conversation, and went immediately on the offensive.

"Oh, so I must be gay if I work in a gay bar?"

She looked at me with the patience reserved for a recalcitrant child—which really annoyed me, so I pushed it even further.

"You know, some of us don't have a rich daddy paying for everything. Some of us have to work at whatever job we can find."

Even as I said it, I knew I was just trying to get her mad so she'd focus on something other than my sexuality. I desperately wanted to avoid that discussion—afraid that she'd pick up on some of the confusion I'd been feeling lately, afraid that she'd come out with some homophobic remark, and then I'd lose respect for her, and she'd lose respect for me, and we'd have no more talkfests until dawn.

But she didn't go for the bait. She just stood there on that lonely corner and looked at me, quietly waiting for me to get my emotions under control. She would have to wait a long time—my adrenaline was pumping on overdrive with her staring at me like that, and the knowing little half-smile that snuck onto her face just made matters worse.

"You didn't answer the question," she finally said.

Why did she want to know about this? What on earth could it possibly matter? I was tempted to shout it at her, but then held back, knowing that to do so would give away just how very much it did matter to me. For a moment, I considered making a crack about fish without bicycles. But in the end, I decided to just play dumb.

"What question?"

She wasn't going to give up. "Are you gay?"

Maybe it was my exhaustion at the hour, maybe it was my adrenaline bottoming out—all I know is that the fight suddenly seeped out of me like a dying wind. Defeated, depleted, I just gave up and answered her goddamn fucking question as best I could.

"Well, I never have been."

She nodded and seemed to digest that for a moment. What the fuck—in for a penny, in for a pound. I pressed on, to the place where I didn't want to go.

"Would it matter if I were?"

"Not to me," she said with absolutely no expression. She was behind her wall again, that much was clear, and the only way I was going to break through it was to shake her up, get her mad, or laughing, or distracted by a nonsequitur. But I just wasn't up to it—it would take far too much effort. What with this huge undiscussed issue hanging between us now, like a massive beast just waiting to devour us, I was spent. It had been a long night, and I just didn't have the energy, or courage, to maneuver her into an answer that, with each passing minute, scared the shit out of me.

Because at that moment I knew, as I had never known anything in my life, that what I felt for Claire was something totally unique—not just friendship, not even a deep and growing "best friends" kind of feeling. I was drawn to her in a way I'd never experienced with anyone before, in a way that had me thinking about her when I went to sleep at night, had me looking at her whenever I possibly could, had me avoiding eye contact but at the same time seeking it. It was so obvious, so simple really, that it clicked into place for me not as a thunderbolt from above, but with the dull quiet thud of a tumbler finally slipping into its notch. And it unlocked a door to another universe, a door that I hadn't even known was there.

It was as simple as it was devastating: I was falling in love with Claire. And as I regarded her on that dark street corner, awed by the sheer pleasure of seeing the breeze blow a few strands of that golden hair across her face, a cold sliver of excitement flashed through me. Because for one brief instant, I thought I glimpsed something in her eyes—a kind of recognition that suggested I wasn't alone in this new universe. Maybe it was just wishful thinking, or a trick of the eye, but I didn't think so. I was in some kind of hyperaware state, where something other than my brain was taking over and cluing me in, at last, to the things that my pitiful gray matter had been too blind or obstinate to accept. What I saw in Claire's face at that moment was nothing less than a miracle—it told me that maybe, just maybe, she was feeling it too.

❧ Chapter Eight

I checked into the hotel shortly before five. It was too early for dinner, so I clicked on CNN and set up my laptop. Sure enough, my e-mail Inbox was stuffed with useless crap, and for a moment I shuddered to think of the ramifications that all this technology would soon have on litigation. The simplest exchange of information, which formerly might have been the subject of a two-minute phone call, was now routinely memorialized in an electronic record for all the world to see. That's exactly the kind of thing that litigators hate, because it multiplies exponentially the number of documents that might be sought in discovery during a lawsuit someday. In every case, the parties typically request production of "all records relating to" this or that. With the advent of this technology, such requests would now call for the production of e-mails as well—with the result that some poor junior associate might be called upon someday to devote several hundred hours of his or her life to poring over the clients' network servers to locate and produce responsive e-mails, in addition to the multitude of other documents sought in discovery.

I didn't have any interest in weeding through my e-mails at the moment, so I called in to Stella for the highlights.

"Nothing much here," she said. "It's been pretty quiet. Oh, you got a FedEx from someone in Texas."

"Great, I was waiting for that."

"Well, I didn't recognize the case, so I asked Louise about it, but she didn't know either."

Shit, the last thing I needed was for Queen Bee to be nosing around in my business. *But wait,* I realized, *I'm not named in the will—there's no way they'd know it had anything to do with me personally. Unless—*

"But then Louise found the cover letter still inside, so we realized it wasn't a client."

Damn, I hoped Shawanna hadn't gotten too chatty in her letter.

"Does this mean what I think? Your grandmother was worth three hundred and fifty million dollars?"

Fuck, fuck, fuck.

"I don't know what it means yet," I said. "I have to go over it when I get back."

"Well, let me tell you, Louise's mouth was on the floor. I wish I'd had a video camera—I don't think I've ever seen her speechless."

"Listen, Stella, let's just keep this quiet for now, okay? I really don't want this stuff getting around the firm."

"Sure, sure. That's what I figured, once I realized what it was. I put it under the stack of papers on your desk."

"Thanks," I said, hoping that the damage could at least be contained. "Anything else?"

"Yeah, Parsons wants to speak to you. Should I transfer you over?"

Great, now what? "Okay. And thanks."

Louise was remarkably cordial when she picked up his line and I identified myself. You'd almost think she was a human being. She switched me in to Parsons, and when he answered with a cheery hello, I had to swallow past the lump in my throat. If he was in a good mood when I was on the line, it could only mean trouble for me. I wanted him to die in the worst way.

"Ashleigh, pleasant trip down to Baltimore?"

"Fine, thanks. What's up?"

"Just checking in, really. Huff wasn't too clear on what you're doing down there."

"Well, it was Renee's idea actually." *That's right, you shit, the client wanted me to go, so if you've got something to say about it, you can stuff it up your ass.*

"I see. So what's it all about?"

"Oh, probably nothing. She tracked down a former employee and she wants us to interview him—see if he knows anything about the FDA file."

He was quiet for a moment. "Sounds like a wild goose chase," he said. It did, but who am I to argue with the client? "She's not with you, is she?" he continued.

"Not right now, no. She might show up later tonight—she left it sort of up in the air."

"I see," he said again. I wished I did. "Well, make it quick and get back up here—we need to go over a few things," he said before hanging up with a friendly good-bye. I didn't like the sound of that, not one bit. But there wasn't a goddamn thing I could do.

After I hung up, I stared at my Inbox some more, without really seeing it. Try as I might, I couldn't shake the feeling of dread when I thought about what Parsons might have in store for me. And wondering what Renee was up to didn't exactly help. And David—well, let's just say that wherever I looked for a pleasant diversion to think about, I just hit more turbulence. All week, I'd had an itch in the back of my head that I really should call Mom. I needed to tell her about this Gardner thing, but maybe that was just the excuse—I think I really just missed my mother and wanted to hear her voice. So, with a few hours to kill and nothing but a fucked-up mess to occupy me otherwise, I picked up the phone and dialed DC.

She must have been out in the garden, since the phone rang a long time. She'd gotten rid of the answering machine after Dad had died—she couldn't figure out how to tape over the greeting he'd recorded years earlier, and she was sick of everyone starting each message with a comment on how difficult it was to keep hearing his voice on the machine. "What do I care if someone calls when I'm not here?" she'd said. "If they want me, they'll call back." She was Gussie's daughter, all right.

Of all the grown-ups who populated my childhood home, I think the one I knew the least was Mom. It's funny how so much of our energy was devoted to protecting this person who was, in some ways, not really there. For one thing, she worked long hours to help support the household, so she simply wasn't around when I was a toddler playing in the house while Robbie and Lizzie were off at school. It was Gussie who stayed home and kept house, Gussie who put me down for my naps, and when I was older it was Gussie who walked me to the corner to catch my school bus.

Sure, Mom put us to bed most nights, and taught us to say our prayers before we climbed under the covers. But looking back, I think

I related to her more as a kind of older sister who floated in and out of the house, kept to herself a lot of the time, and was always tired. I loved her dearly, of course, but in some sense it was from afar. Gussie was the grown-up I'd run to when I got into fights in the schoolyard and needed some babying.

It wasn't just Mom's physical absence that kept her apart from us all. It was her nature, too. She was just a very private person—strong and bullheaded like the rest of us, but her power was of the quiet, stoic variety. She just didn't take up as much space as the big personalities of my other relatives. And when she met Dad, I truly think she'd found her soul mate—they had their own world just between the two of them, and it didn't include us.

Not that we were neglected by any means—they monitored our homework and punished our misbehavior, and were probably as involved as any parents could be. But the quiet moments, when they'd collapse at the end of a weary day and exchange information about more than just the business of living—those times were reserved for just the two of them. I suppose that's as it should be, but what it meant was that I never really had the kind of relationship with Mom that I had with Gussie, or that I saw some of my friends share with their mothers. We never really learned to talk to each other.

"Mom?" I said when she finally answered.

"Hi, honey. I'm sorry—I was in the garage repotting some flowers."

"Is this a bad time? I can call back later." She was always busy with something whenever I called—she was handling this widowhood thing better than I would have expected, burying herself beneath a mound of tasks and appointments. Still, even before Dad died I always got the feeling that I was interrupting her when I called, that I should let her get back to whatever she was doing. She'd say, "No, no. That's all right," sounding as if she thought that's what she ought to say, and I wouldn't really believe it.

"No, no," she said. "That's all right. Is everything okay? I haven't heard from you in a while."

"Yeah, I'm busy at work, you know, but things are fine." She didn't want to hear about work—she never wanted to hear about my work—so I plowed right on. "Listen, Mom, I wanted to talk to you about something."

"What?" she asked cautiously, her radar alert for anything that might be remotely personal.

"Well, I got a letter from some lawyers out west. And it seems the Sperm Donor wants to talk to us. Me, Lizzie, and Rob."

"Oh," she said quietly. I could just picture her standing there in the kitchen, looking frantically for an excuse to get off the phone, racking her brain for a change in subject. I'd discharged my duty; I'd told her what I had to, what I felt she had a right to know, so why couldn't I just make it easy for her and let her go? Because I wanted something from her—information, a reaction, *something*—even though I knew I wouldn't get it. That just wasn't who she was. But still, I kept her on the line, and listened to the silence.

"Mom?" I finally said.

"Honey, Uncle Dink is stopping by on his way to Ellicott City. I really have to get dinner ready."

"Mom, what do you think? Do you think I should call him?"

I heard her sigh on the other end. "I don't know. I guess you should if you want to." She really didn't want to talk about it, but for once I was more interested in my own needs than hers, and I bullied my way forward.

"They said he wanted to talk about Grandma Edna. About her estate."

"So?"

"Did you know she was rich?" I tried to keep my tone casual, even inquisitive—tried not to let it suggest any of the hundreds of accusations that the subject stirred up in me.

"I suppose," she said. "Is that what this is about?"

"I don't really know. That's what the lawyers said, but I don't know what it means. I was hoping maybe you'd know something." What a laugh.

"I don't have any idea what it could be," she said. "She died a long time ago." I could tell I was running out of time—she was going to cut this conversation short any second—so I went for broke.

"I mean, do you think she could have left us something, and they're only now getting around to it?" I didn't for a moment think that could be the case, but I was hoping to spur her on, get her talking about Grandma Edna. No such luck.

"Honey, I don't know what to think about any of that," she said with a slight tremor in her voice, which made me hate myself for pushing it. "But if you want to talk to him, I think you should just do it." She was quiet for a few more beats, as if considering whether she should say her last piece. "I don't think you should get your hopes up, though."

I didn't know what she meant by that—my hopes about the money, which were nil, or my hopes about finally, after thirty-seven years, hearing the voice of the man whose existence had been a defining question mark in my life.

"Okay. Well, I'll let you know what happens."

"Was there anything else?" she asked in a tone that said she really hoped there wasn't.

"No, go fix dinner. I'll talk to you later."

I ordered room service and ate in front of the TV, with my laptop beside me on the bed. It occurred to me that I really should go over my notes for tomorrow, but I decided to fuck it—what did it really matter at this point anyway? Renee still might call to say she'd be coming after all, and if she did we could prep for tomorrow's interview then. Otherwise, I'd just wing it—it was probably a dead end anyway.

The news ended just as I finished the last bite of my Cobb salad, and I turned to my laptop to see if maybe Renee had sent me an e-mail. It took several minutes to scan through my Inbox, automatically deleting without reading all of the junk messages from names I didn't recognize. Just as I neared the bottom of the stack, I stopped before deleting one message from an address that seemed vaguely familiar. I stared at it for a moment before it hit me. The name was gibberish—CLM4026—but the domain jumped off the screen at me: meersboothe.com.

Claire and I didn't see much of each other during the week or so following that night at the Cave. For my part, I was happy to bury myself in schoolwork, using my pile of reading as a welcome excuse to avoid dealing with what I was feeling. I stopped studying in my room or Neilsen Library and started studying in the art library, where nobody knew me. I think Claire was avoiding Comstock too—I often heard her arrive back at the house very late at night, after I was in bed. I'd hear her key in the door and roll over, pulling the covers up to my ears and willing myself not to think about how easy it would be to just get up and go next door to talk.

Shelly didn't seem to notice that I wasn't spending as much time with Claire, and for that I was grateful. I didn't know what I could possibly say if she'd asked. We didn't see Claire at dinner, so Shelly didn't have an opportunity to witness how uncomfortable we were around each other, how resolutely we avoided even looking at each other. If I ran into her on my way to class, we'd say hello but not much more. She'd hold up her organic chemistry book as if to prove that she was too busy to linger, but then she'd smile when she said *"ce que je pense."* Just being near her was an exercise in conflict for me: She made me terribly nervous, but at the same time I was powerfully drawn to her. It was no better when I was away from her; I constantly had my eye out for her, yearning for the turmoil that her presence provoked in me. Eventually, I couldn't stand it—the situation was intolerable, whether or not I was with her. I had to get it out, had to get us past this awkward state of limbo, in order to reach some kind of resolution, for better or worse.

So I sought her out. I had a pretty good idea where I'd find her on a Thursday night, and I climbed the three flights of stairs up to the practice rooms in the music building with nothing in mind but an unformed plan to get her talking about anything, anything at all. Maybe if I could just get her talking, hard as that would probably be, I could figure out what she was thinking about me, or us, or all of the unspoken potential that was looming between us.

I listened outside each closed door along the hallway until I knew I'd found the one I wanted, the one with the somber viola concerto playing softly inside. I gently opened the door and peeked in. Her back was to me, and she seemed to be staring out the window. There was nothing on the music stand in front of her; she was playing from memory. I slipped inside, soundlessly closed the door and stood there, not daring to breathe, as I watched her play.

As often as I'd pictured it in my mind, the reality was so much more, and I took it all in, capturing and memorizing each nuance of the experience, as if afraid that this moment was all I'd get—my one and only chance to witness the unearthly splendor of Claire's playing. And, as before, the music gripped me in a vise, touching every nerve in my body, squeezing out of me every drop of well-hidden emotion and then coming back for more. I watched transfixed, transported, my eyes glued to her broad shoulders as she worked feverishly back and forth, her torso snapping to attention with the brief andante, then dipping low with a mournful adagio of angels weeping. The tremulous sound that she coaxed from this small, simple instrument pulled painfully at my heart. And as she neared a heartbreaking crescendo, which tickled the back of my neck and brought a stinging sensation to my eyes, I finally got it—I understood her adamant refusal to play in public. Her playing was simply too intimate, filled with too great a passion, for someone as desperately private as Claire to expose. And although I knew in that moment that I'd betrayed her by coming here, there was no way I could leave. This passion, so unexpected, was precisely what I'd been searching for in her, what I'd somehow sensed was there, but never really thought I'd find—and I was, quite simply, intoxicated by it.

She ended the piece all too soon, the final poignant strands coming to rest in a place of utter desolation and leaving a wide, gaping hole in my heart. She lowered the viola and bow, letting them dangle at her side as she continued to stare out the window, her back proudly erect.

"What do you think?" she said softly.

I was too swept up in the spell to worry about having been caught or to wonder how she knew I was there. Slowly, she turned around to look at me, and I closed my eyes, leaning back gently against the door for support. My legs were quivering, and I knew that I was flushed, knew that she could see the tears, but none of that mattered. I heard her lay down her instrument and walk over to me, and still I couldn't open my eyes. I searched my mind for something, anything, to say— but there was only one thing pressing to be said. I felt her standing there, maybe a foot or two away, and I finally opened my eyes to face her.

"I think I'm in love with you," I whispered.

She nodded, but didn't say a word. Instead, she gave me a little half-smile, almost a grimace, and reached out to wipe the tears from my cheek. I think the only other time we'd touched—other than her first day at Comstock, when I'd decked her in the hallway—had been the night she'd fallen from her desk, and the bolt that suddenly shot through me now was electrifying. Nothing, absolutely nothing I'd ever experienced could have prepared me for the riptide of raw desire that flooded me at that moment. And I didn't think twice: I lifted my arms around her neck and inclined my face to hers. She leaned in to me so slowly that for a moment I thought she might just leave me there in limbo. But no, she met me halfway, and when her lips finally touched mine, it was all over. The world simply dissolved—there was nothing but the fragrance of her shampoo, the feel of her hands slipping around my waist, and the unspeakable softness of her lips moving slowly under mine in a gentle rhythm that belied the enormity of what we were doing, so powerful in its simplicity. All of those late night talks, all of my unspoken, unnamed fears, all of the conflicting desires when I looked at her—it all came down to this simple, wondrous moment. And I was drowning in it, lost in the warm tide of her lips, like nothing on earth I'd ever imagined—and I didn't care.

I was the first to pull away—not because I wanted to lose contact with her, but because I'd forgotten to breathe and was having a hard time staying on my feet. One look at Claire, and the coals of my passion were ignited into a blazing flame. She tipped her head back just enough for me to take in the palpable arousal radiating from her, from her heavy-lidded eyes to the rapid rise and fall of her chest. The sight of her like that did me in—the scorching heat burning through my veins intensified a hundredfold. I had to dive in, had to taste those lips again. I pulled her face back to me, and felt her tighten her hold, encircling me in those strong arms and moving her hands up and down my spine. I felt her tongue dart against my lips, and I opened them willingly, without hesitation. Her tongue slipped inside and began a teasing exploratory dance around mine, fluid and smooth and unbearably erotic. I moaned my desire, my mouth filled with her, my tongue tasting, probing every inch of hers, and some primal animal instinct took over as I found myself unconsciously moving against her, gently moving my hips into her to seek I didn't know what.

But she seemed to know: All at once I felt her leg deftly maneuvered between mine, and discovered the subtle pressure for which I'd been unknowingly yearning. She broke away from my mouth, but only so she could cover my eyelids with her lips. She kissed a slow trail down my cheek to the hollow of my neck, where she suckled and nipped at the tender flesh, and I tried my best not to blank out. I didn't want to let go of her, but I couldn't breathe. I couldn't keep standing, and the liquid throbbing in my groin was becoming unbearable.

"I can't," I gasped, and she stopped right there, pulling back slightly to look at me with a mixture of hurt and confusion.

She took a step away and moved her hair out of her face—I'd really made a mess of it, and it looked fantastic. "I'm sorry," she mumbled.

"No," I said quickly, leaving my hands on her shoulders to keep her there. "I mean, I can't stand up anymore. I . . . I was afraid I was going to fall down."

She searched my eyes for confirmation, and when I smiled at her and gently stroked the little hairs on the back of her neck, she smiled back.

"Well, I'd offer you a seat, but—" she said, looking around the room. There was only a single folding chair in the corner.

I was still on pins and needles, the molten cream of my arousal still bleeding through my jeans, but in the past ten minutes I felt I'd already been through more than I could probably handle in a lifetime, and I knew that this was neither the time nor the place for taking it any farther. I think she knew it too, because she suggested we take a walk. "I guess we have a few things to talk about," she said with an embarrassed smile. I guessed she was right.

I watched as she put away her viola in her hall locker, marveling at the power of those hands to coax such unspeakable pleasure from the instrument, and from me. We left the building and headed toward town, away from the Quad, neither of us speaking. There was so much to say, but I really didn't know what, or how to start, and I guess I needed to talk it over with myself first anyway, because the whole thing still seemed totally unreal. She left me to my own thoughts on the walk into town, and I left her to hers.

She finally broke the silence when we hit Main Street. "I'm not sure it's a good idea for anyone to know about this."

Whatever I'd been expecting to hear out of her, that wasn't it. And my emotions had been through too much of a blender that night for me to react with any kind of forethought. I just came out with the first thing that popped into my head—and, naturally, it put her on the defensive.

"I'm not ashamed of how I feel about you," I said. And I wasn't. In fact, I was proud to be walking with her, proud to be seen with her.

"It's nobody's business," she said simply.

"So what do you expect us to do? Sneak around?"

A hint of exasperation crept into her tone. "Well, what do you expect us to do? Go out on dates? Make out in the Cave?"

Hmm, that might be nice. "I don't know. I've never done this before. Have you?" I had to ask, even though she wasn't likely to give me an answer, and I really didn't want to hear it if she did.

Amazingly, she did. "Not exactly," she said, staring straight ahead.

"What does that mean?"

She shook her head as if to brush away the question, but then decided to push on as long as she'd started down this path. "I've never actually had a thing with a woman before," she said, still striding along at a brisk pace.

"What's that supposed to mean?"

She didn't like personal questions, but I felt entitled to press for an answer. Hadn't we just been engaged in something deeply personal, something more intimate, frankly, than anything I could ask?

"You know, the physical stuff," she elaborated, clearly uncomfortable.
"But?"

"But I had feelings for someone once." She shot me a look. "And I
didn't go broadcasting it all over campus."

But wait, isn't that a little different? I mean, a one-sided crush isn't
exactly the same thing as a relationship.

"Is that what this is? A *thing*?"

"You know what I mean."

"No, I don't; I really don't. One minute you're practically making
love to me, and the next you're telling me that it's just some *thing* that
you can't even describe, and you want to keep it a secret."

She stopped in front of the Italian restaurant and turned to face me.

"Look," she whispered emphatically, "I don't know what you want
me to say."

"I want you to tell me what you want, what you feel. Because this
whole thing is kind of scary to me, and I'm not sure I can do it." There,
I'd said it, and I didn't regret it. Sure, I was still conscious of the sopping
puddle in my panties, still feeling a wash of desire when I looked at her
stoic, chiseled features, but I was perfectly prepared to turn tail and run
if she couldn't give me the answer I needed. Or so I told myself.

The candid look of hurt in her eyes cut me deeply. I loved this
woman. She was infuriating and exhilarating, and I couldn't bear to
cause her pain.

"I want to be with you," she said with conviction. "I don't know
what that means, but that's what I want."

Her words were a salve on my raw nerves, quieting the uncertainty
and bathing me in a glowing warmth. I was tempted to put my arms
around her right there, cradle her head to my breast, and tell her all
the things I never thought I'd say to anyone. But a couple walked out
of the restaurant just then, so we stood there, unmoving, and stared at
each other in silence.

📖   📖   📖

I plucked the twizzle stick from my double scotch, and looked
around the hotel bar without really seeing anything—nothing but

the look I knew had to have been on Claire's face when she'd sent that e-mail. I saw her, of course, not as the mature woman she must have become—no, to me she was, always and forever, the quiet twenty-something whose high-cheekboned face was sculpted from porcelain, whose perfect mouth would never be marred by the hint of little lines etched along its sides. Her smiles were just too infrequent to leave a mark.

I'd needed a change of scenery after rereading her message for the hundredth time—I simply had to get away from my room, away from the laptop, and the bar's picture window overlooking the lovely Baltimore harbor offered the ideal sanctuary. Fortunately, it was relatively empty in there, and the few men in business suits scattered here and there seemed to pick up on something emanating from me that told them to keep their distance.

David used to be pretty adept at picking up on cues like that—until his own needs began to override his common sense. During a visit from Shelly once, about a year or so after we'd been married, she'd casually asked if I ever heard from Claire, and he'd given me a quizzical look when he saw me cut her off with an abrupt "no." He'd never known about Claire, not specifically. He'd only known that I'd had a relationship in college, that it had ended very badly, and I didn't like to talk about it. Ever. He'd assumed, I'm sure, that my romance had been with a man, and I'd never said otherwise. But when I shut down Shelly's questions about Claire that night, I know I'd reacted just as I had when he would occasionally ask about my college romance. And he must have known it too. After his early, aborted attempts at digging into my past, he'd eventually come to respect my privacy, but over the years I knew he'd wondered about it, and about Claire—trying to wheedle something out of me at times by bringing up the topic of gay rights, or asking innocuous questions about the grossly exaggerated reputation for lesbianism that Smith enjoyed. I got pretty good at the shrug-and-grunt, and after awhile he stopped probing. We finally fell into a kind of truce whereby he didn't ask questions that neither of us wanted answered.

If I'd been asked to predict an e-mail that Claire would send me after all this time—frankly, if I had been asked to compose it myself—

I couldn't have come any closer to what she'd actually said. "Ash," it began. No "Dear Ash," of course, no superfluous endearment of any kind. Just Ash.

> Ash: I assume if you're reading this e-mail, you haven't deleted it and are curious to see what I have to say. See, I still know you. When I saw your address in Carla's mass mailing, I had to write to say hi. I heard from Carla that you became a lawyer. I shouldn't be surprised, but I am. I also heard you got married. I guess some fish ride bicycles after all. Anyway, I'm here if you feel like writing back.

So typical of Claire, divulging absolutely nothing about herself— no information about her life, no feelings. Just some observations about me, as if to deflect attention away from herself without coming right out and asking me about myself. She had never been the kind of person to ask personal questions, indulge in fluffy chitchat, or disclose any personal details about herself unless absolutely necessary. And she certainly wasn't going to delve into our past, at least not directly. With so vast a terrain roped off from discussion, I guess it left very little for her to actually say.

Hard as I looked, I could find no hidden message in it, nothing between the lines to suggest that she was saying anything beyond those few words. But I searched all the same, because Claire had always been a blank page on which I scribbled my most fanciful imaginings. I could just see her sitting at her computer, face expressionless as she typed out the lines in rapid fire, knowing that they would stop my heart, that I'd peruse them over and over to unearth their buried meaning.

From a remove of fifteen years and a thousand miles, Claire had blipped into my universe as unexpectedly as she'd once blipped out of it. She'd lobbed the ball into my court, and I could respond or ignore it—it was up to me. I suppose I knew that it took some guts for her to contact me at all, that the simple act of sending that e-mail, however innocuous, had been an uncharacteristically bold move on her part. But that's as far as she'd go; I knew with absolute certainty that if I didn't respond, I would never hear from her again. The only real questions were, what would happen if I did respond, and was I up to it?

And that thought, of course, sent me right back into the landmine named Renee Silver.

I drained my Johnny Walker Black and ordered another double on the rocks. Out of the corner of my eye, I saw one of the suits get up from a nearby table and start to amble his way over. Shit, I was in no mood for this. He stood beside my table with a big expectant smile on his face, too drunk or stupid to have a clue.

"Let me buy you a drink," he said as he pulled out a chair and plopped his considerable girth into it, none too gracefully.

"No thanks, I'm waiting for someone," I said politely. I've found that this lie is far more effective than saying I prefer to be alone, which for some reason men seem to take as a challenge that they can, and should, overcome.

"Aw, c'mon darlin', don't be like that."

"No really, please—"

"I think she asked you to leave," I heard over my shoulder. I looked up and there was Renee, dressed to the nines and ready to rip his lungs out through his nose.

"Well, pull up a chair and join the party," he said, practically salivating at his good fortune. She moved so quickly that at first I didn't know what was happening—Renee was suddenly behind him, leaning over and whispering something in his ear. The look of giddy excitement on his face was quickly replaced by uncertainty and then outright fear. He did a quick scan of the room before nodding and mumbling "okay." She seemed to accept that; she watched with cold detachment as he quickly got to his feet.

"Well, I guess you girls wanna talk, so I'll just leave you to it," he said as he took his drink and lit out of there.

I just stared at Renee, thrilled to see her and acutely aware of how fantastic she looked when she was ticked off.

"Did I look like a damsel in distress?" I asked, impressed as all hell with her chivalry.

"What's that supposed to mean?" she snapped as she looked around for the waiter.

"Nothing. What'd you say to him?"

"I told him we were part of a sting operation targeting the johns of high-class call girls, and he was about ten seconds away from getting arrested." I couldn't tell if she was joking, and before I could figure it out, the waiter came with my drink.

"What are you having?" she asked.

"Scotch."

"Glenlivet," she told him. "Double, on the rocks."

"Are we celebrating something?" She shot me another icy look— I wasn't going to be able to joke her out of this mood. Might as well face it head-on, or begin to, as long as she'd come all this way.

"Look, Renee, I'm really glad you could make it. I was hoping I could talk to you about last night."

"Not now. Something's come up."

I didn't like the feeling that started to creep under my skin. She was clearly upset, but it wasn't about me, I realized. She was all business.

"What?"

She took a deep breath and seemed to consider for a moment how to begin.

"Renee, what is it?"

"Okay, look, I had the MIS guys pull the network server tapes for the past three months."

"Three months? Wait a minute—how often do you back up the server?"

"Every day."

"And you keep the tapes for three months?" I'd never heard of such a thing. Most companies stored that kind of digital information for thirty days at most.

"We do now. I changed the retention policy just after I joined the company. It was too haphazard before. Sometimes they'd let a week go by without backing it up, and then they wouldn't get around to destroying the outdated stuff until it occurred to somebody."

I nodded. We'd both seen the bloody aftermath when a company didn't devise and adhere to a strict backup and retention policy. Still, ninety days seemed overly cautious, and I said so.

"I know, but I figured the longer the better with a company like CRS, since so much of what we do is developmental." She was right. The R&D department was involved with developing stuff that was so complicated that if you took a wrong turn and had to rework a whole section of the design, it might require you to revert to some point in the process farther back than thirty days.

"The point is, it's all one server—R&D, word processing, e-mails, the works—and I had the guys pull the last ninety days of tapes to search the e-mails."

"Why?"

"To see if maybe anyone on the inside was feeding information to Amtec. I figured if they got their hands on our FDA application, they didn't necessarily get it from the FDA."

She was not only ballsy, she was smart. But another thought occurred to me.

"Wait, e-mails can be deleted. Even if anyone was stupid enough to put something in an e-mail, I can't believe they'd just leave it on the system."

"That's why I did the search in deleted files. It isn't really deleted, you know, just because it disappears from your Inbox or your Sent box. It's still on the system until the system purges all of the deleted files around midnight. Even then, it's probably recoverable, but that doesn't matter, because I found something in the deleted files."

"So someone's working with Amtec?"

"Not exactly." She took another sip of her scotch, and then another for good measure. "Someone's a large shareholder in Amtec. Two people, actually."

"No shit! Who?"

She looked me in the eye, and I saw something that looked a lot like fear.

"Huff Chasen and Dick Parsons."

📖   📖   📖

Lawyers get a bad rap. The jokes about us may be funny—okay, very funny—but they're unfair too, because on the whole the profession is populated by honest, hardworking people. A few bad apples have put us, in the public mind, somewhere between the paramecium and the amoeba on the evolutionary ladder—and some would say that the amoebas deserve more credit.

I understand society's loathing, I really do, and not just because I was indoctrinated with it since conception. We lawyers wield tremendous power; we're privy to some dark secrets. And to those outside looking in, it seems that we're all part of some nefarious fraternity: we know the secret language and exchange the secret handshake.

What few of those folks looking in may realize, however, is that we have strict rules of conduct that we're required to observe, and we're carefully monitored in all of our activities to make sure we do. No other profession is so thoroughly policed or goes to such extraordinary lengths to weed out the bad guys. There are copious rules of ethical conduct for lawyers—yep, there's another example of a book with a list of rules—and they make it clear what we can and cannot do. The sanctions for a violation are as wide-ranging as the rules themselves, and include anything from a slap on the wrist to being called before the committee on character and fitness for disbarment. You can get fined; you can lose your license to practice; you can even go to jail.

And one of the rules, at least here in New York, is a whistle-blower rule—requiring that any lawyer who becomes aware of a fellow lawyer's illegal activity must report it to the bar. It's a tough rule, but absolutely necessary. Lawyering is a team sport, after all. We rarely work in isolation, so there are almost always other lawyers involved in everything we do. The whistle-blower rule works as a built-in system of checks and balances: any lawyer who learns of a colleague's misconduct had better report it or run the risk of being disbarred. It's a powerful incentive to keep your nose clean, and keep it down.

As I sat there and listened to Renee run through the details, I tried to piece it together in my mind. We didn't know anything for certain except that Huff and Parsons appeared to be involved in some sort of joint venture. That in itself was pretty close to the line—lawyers aren't supposed to have their finances mixed up with their clients'. The part we didn't know, but which smelled pretty bad, had to do with the possibility that they were somehow manipulating the mar-

ket in Amtec stock. And it didn't take a rocket scientist to fill in the
gaps: The thing that had impacted Amtec's stock most dramatically
in recent weeks was the rumor about a rush FDA application.

"So what do you want to do?" I asked after Renee ordered us another round.

"Get drunk."

"No, seriously."

"I don't know," she sighed. "And I'm sorry to dump it all on you,
but I didn't know where else to turn. And I knew you were clean—"

"Oh, how's that? My innocent face?"

"That face isn't so innocent," she said, smiling. "No, it's pretty clear
that you and Parsons aren't exactly chummy."

"You got that right." I laughed. "And I'm glad you came to me;
I'm still the company's lawyer, until Parsons drums me out. I guess I
don't have to remind you that you're the company's lawyer too: your
client is CRS, not Huff. You have to protect the company, even if it
means that Huff Chasen goes down in the process."

"But if he goes down, so does the company."

"Not necessarily. But if he's engaging in misconduct that could
hurt the company, you know as well as I do that you've got to bring it
to the board of directors. They're your client, and he answers to
them."

"I know. But we don't really know if he's doing anything illegal.
He just owns some Amtec stock; there's nothing wrong with that."

"I agree. But with the size of their holdings, and the sudden rise in
price, they stand to make a killing by manipulating the market; and
that's exactly what will happen as soon as they pull the trigger to have
us file that lawsuit. You can't just ignore a coincidence like that."

"You're right; they'll make a double killing, in fact. They'll cash in
at the high, then short it right before they send it in a tailspin to double their money on the way down."

I nodded. "Stands to reason."

"You're saying I should investigate Huff, aren't you?" I just looked
at her. "Do you know what that means? He would fire me the minute
he suspected something was up, so it wouldn't do the company any
good anyway. Or me." She looked scared, and I didn't blame her.

Losing her job might be the least of her worries if the rumors were true about Huff's more belligerent forms of persuasion. It was probably just talk, but I'd hate to put it to the test.

"Look, all I'm saying is that you can't go out of your way to avoid looking into it. If you come across something concrete, you can't deliberately look the other way."

"And we can't file that lawsuit."

"No, we can't."

✎ Chapter Nine

The funny thing about Robbie, the thing that very few people knew about him, was that he was capable of such astonishing kindness. He had a deep sense of family—we all did—and in Robbie it often came out as a hard-hitting defense of every one of us.

Like the time he beat the shit out of Louie Plough when I came home with a black eye after a particularly nasty scuffle in the back alley. Louie hadn't realized that Robbie was nearby, and neither had I: I didn't want Robbie fighting my battles for me. I was reluctant to give Robbie something to hang over my head, and I feared that it might just make Louie even more determined to seek me out at a later date. But Robbie had seen me playing that day with my friends Mary and John in the alley near Louie's yard, and when I snuck back to Gussie's a while later, with my eye already starting to bruise, Robbie lit out after Louie without asking any questions. I tagged along a few paces behind him and watched as he stood outside Louie's gate to call him out. Louie turned the garden hose on him, and I swelled with an unexpected sense of pride when I watched Robbie open that gate and march straight toward Louie, heedless of the water hitting him full blast in the chest. I swear, the spray bounced off him like bullets bouncing off Superman's chest.

But it wasn't just me who Robbie sometimes took upon himself to defend. Robbie saw himself as the champion of everyone in the family, and he'd pummel anyone who said boo about our mother being divorced or Cousin Ginny being cross-eyed. In high school, when one of his buddies went out with Lizzie but then unceremoniously dropped her a week later, Robbie stopped being friends with the guy right then and there.

He could also be gentle, although not usually with me. Like that time we found a dead sparrow at the foot of a tree by the south field at Aunt Tavia's farm. Robbie said it might have left a nest of chicks in the tree, and he risked his neck to climb up and crawl out onto a small limb that could just barely hold his weight. But he found the nest and, sure enough, there were three chicks in it—two dead, but one still alive. Robbie picked it up and slowly made his way back out of the tree one-handed, gingerly cradling the baby chick to his chest. He carried it in his hand the whole drive back to DC, feeding it now and then with an eye dropper, and he even let me pet it a few times. That night, Gramps arranged for us to give it to a guy from his office who raised birds, and Robbie seemed to tear up a bit when he had to hand it over. I didn't let him know I'd seen him almost cry.

Robbie was also the best baseball player in the neighborhood. He could throw a ball hard as a cannon, with pinpoint accuracy, and he could hit it a mile. Every kid on the block wanted him to play with us, but he rarely did—we were just too little. But he was the one who took the time to teach me and Lizzie how to throw and catch, patiently working with us, spending long hours in the backyard—making us stronger, improving our form, challenging us to throw it farther and straighter. Part of it, I'm sure, was simple expedience—to make sure he had someone to play catch with if ever there was absolutely no one else around. But there was also some pride involved. "You throw like a girl" was the most vile insult among the neighborhood kids, and Robbie made damn sure that no such epithet was ever directed at one of his sisters.

When I was first learning how to catch with a glove, around age five or six, I guess, Robbie invented the game Slide. It didn't require any throwing, at least not on my part. He'd toss the ball to me from a distance of about ten yards or so, and dash toward me to see if he could slide in before I could catch the ball and tag him out. He'd make sure he threw the ball on a slow sweeping arc, to give himself as much time as possible to beat the throw, and he'd toss it high enough that I'd have a hard time snagging the ball and getting my glove down before he slid into the base.

Of course, it wasn't a base he'd slide into: it was my feet. He'd slam into me spikes first, good and hard, time and again, but I never really complained about the pounding I'd get during those sessions: it was such a thrill to be playing ball with my big brother. Gussie would see my bruised and bleeding legs when I'd come in for supper, and she'd give Robbie a hard look, but he'd just shrug and say I was free to quit anytime I wanted. But I never did.

Despite those rare glimpses of humanity that he could display, the SOP around Robbie was avoidance: his temper could flare in a flash, and I never quite knew what might set him off. He could give me a soft little punch on the arm as a gesture of camaraderie or affection, but I could just as easily get a hard jab that would leave a bruise. When he hit high school, things got a little better in some ways—he was out of the house more often, or preoccupied with his friends talking about girls—but he also became even more moody, spending lots of time alone in his room. Our bedroom doors had no locks, but he had a rule that we were never, *ever* supposed to come into his room without knocking, and he was dead serious about it. I never wanted to go in there anyway: as far as I was concerned, it was a dead zone, full of a bunch of mysterious boy stuff and secrets that I sensed I was better off not knowing. But one day I did, and I lived to regret it.

I was about ten at the time, and we were off from school on our spring break. Some of the neighborhood kids had decided to break out the baseball gloves to have ourselves a little spring training—Louie Plough had moved away by then—so I'd gone in search of the brand new fielder's glove I'd gotten for my birthday. After scouring the basement, I remembered that I'd seen Robbie with my glove a few days earlier, so I ran up the stairs and called through his bedroom door.

"Robbie? You got my glove in there? I need it."

No answer. I knew he was in there; I'd seen him head upstairs as soon as Mom and Dad had left to take Lizzie to the dentist.

"Come on, Robbie, just give me my glove."

"Get out of here!" he yelled through the door.

I'd be damned if I was going to let him swipe my new glove. He had his own—two, in fact—and I really loved that glove.

"Look, if you don't hand it over, I'm coming in to get it," I called out.

"No! I'm warning you—"

But I was out of patience, and out of time—the kids might be leaving for the dirt field already. So I stormed through the door.

I didn't really notice what he was up to, not at first—I was too focused on finding my glove and making a quick exit, and deliberately avoided looking at him.

"Get *out!*" he screamed. I don't know if it was the bloodcurdling sound, or the sudden commotion I caught out of the corner of my eye, but something made me look at him. He was on his knees trying to scramble off the bed, with a bunch of magazines strewn in front of him. Even though his back was to me, I could see that he was fiddling with his jeans, desperately, and I stood there watching him for a moment—one moment too long. When he turned around to throw a book at me—the handiest thing he could reach, I guess—I didn't even flinch. I was too busy being shocked, staring at his erect dick in his hand.

"I'm gonna fucking *kill* you," he seethed, and that got me moving, because I knew he meant it. His eyes were bulging the way they did when he was really furious, and his face was beet red from embarrassment and rage.

I lit out of there quick and tore down the stairs, hoping to make it outside before he could catch me. But the front door was closest to the landing, and Mom had locked it before she'd left. I spent a few precious seconds struggling with the lock before realizing that the back door was my best bet. It was open, and led to the backyard where my friends could protect me. Robbie was storming down the stairs, screaming a blue streak at me, and jumped the last three steps to close the gap just as I took off for the kitchen. He snagged my arm as I made it to the middle of the living room, whipped me around to face him, and then backhanded me across the face so hard that I fell back against the fake fireplace.

I was too stunned to move for a moment. But when the stars in front of my eyes cleared, and I realized that my mouth was filling with a warm coppery taste that I figured must be blood, I looked up through a blur of tears to see Robbie standing over me, his cock still poking out from his fly—standing up even straighter, it seemed.

"Now you've done it," he said quietly, in the dark voice that always gave me the creeps.

"Robbie, I—"

He kicked me hard, right in the meaty part of my thigh, and although I tried to stifle the yelp of pain, I didn't quite make it.

The bulge of his eyes relaxed just a bit as he moved a hand toward his fly; I thought he'd finally realized he was hanging out like that and was going to put himself back together. But what he did instead turned my blood to ice. He started rubbing his hand back and forth on it, massaging it, and a sick little grin slowly appeared on his face.

"Get a good eyeful, missy? Is this what you were looking for in my room?" he said darkly.

"Leave me alone," I yelled, determined not to beg but scared nevertheless. I didn't quite understand what he was doing, what it meant, but something told me that it could get a whole lot worse very quickly. I tried to scoot myself backward and away from him, but he immediately dropped to his knees on top of me, straddling me, using his legs to hold me in place and pinning my arms to my side.

"Oh no, missy, you're not going anywhere," he said, still massaging that thing, which was now just a few inches from my face.

I tried to buck him off me, and he lost his balance just enough for me to wedge one arm out from under his leg. I didn't even think about it—I grabbed the fireplace poker that had been knocked to the floor beside me, and swung it at his head for all I was worth.

I didn't hit his head, but I got him good across the back. He couldn't really block the blow because it came from his right-hand side, and his right hand was busy pulling on his dick. The full force of the blow was enough to knock him off balance, and that shift in his weight gave me just enough room to bring a knee up into his crotch with every ounce of my strength.

The howl that erupted from him was not human. He doubled over, and although he weighed a ton, he was in too much agony to try keeping me pinned under him, so I pushed him off me and scrambled away, the poker still in hand.

He looked up at me, and I guess he saw the fury in my face and the white of my knuckles clutching that poker like a spear—and he was afraid. I never thought I'd see that look on his face, but there it was. And he was right to be scared, because I was absolutely resolute: I was going to kill him.

I gripped the poker with both hands and steeled myself to run him through, wondering if I had the strength to pull it off but determined to try. But then an amazing thing happened. There, within the space of a heartbeat, I saw how my life would change forever if I did this thing. I didn't think it through—I didn't have to. I only knew that everything would change for the worse—much worse. I wanted him dead, but I didn't want to be a murderer.

"Don't you ever lay a hand on me again," I said quietly, trying my best to mimic his dark voice.

Years later, when I would think of that day, I'd remember it as something of a defining moment—laying out a critical difference between me and my brother. Because we'd both been ready to cross the line that day, but at the last minute, I'd stepped back. And all the family loyalty in the world couldn't make me believe in my heart that Robbie would have eventually stepped back too.

📖 📖 📖

When I rolled over, I saw that the lights in the living room were still on. David must still be up, or he fell asleep in front of the Saturday *Late Show*. I wanted to go to the kitchen for a glass of water, to shake the lingering effects of my dream, but I didn't want to run the risk of another confrontation with David. I got up quietly to check the door. Assured that it was locked, I returned to the bed, pulled the covers up to my chin, and tried to go back to sleep.

📖 📖 📖

Around noon on Monday, I entered the firm through the oak paneled reception area, and took what I assumed might be one of my last looks at the elegant Huxley Doyle sign in gold letters. When I'd called this morning to make an appointment with Dennis, he'd said he could see me around one, so I'd used the morning to lounge around the hotel room I'd moved into on Sunday—the Mayflower, not the Excelsior—and tried to sort through in my mind all the detritus I'd assiduously ignored while caught up in the whirlwind of the last forty-eight hours. It didn't take much sorting: the categories were basically Shit, Fuck, and I Don't Know.

David was the star of the Shit column. He'd been waiting to pounce as soon as I'd gotten back from Baltimore and walked in the door on Saturday night, evidently impatient with how long it was taking me to give up and admit that he was right, that we could salvage this dead marriage. He had let me have it with both barrels, zipping right past the cajoling stage to get to the pleading. But all that was just the warm-up act; he'd been stewing for two days, and had lined up all the weapons he could marshall—a catalog of every hurt and slight and indignation that he'd stored away for future reference over God knows how many years.

I don't think it had ever before occurred to me that the seeming harmony we'd enjoyed over the years was due to the fact that, when it came to a lot of the big stuff, I often shared his views. I hadn't acceded to his positions, I'd simply agreed with them, so we'd never really gone head to head on any major issues. I think that's part of what he found so infuriating about my resistance now—he simply wasn't used to not getting his way. And so he came out fighting, hard and ugly, and I took it for as long as I could. It seemed to go on all night, but it was really just a few hours. All I know is that I'd let him hit me with everything in his arsenal: he'd take the apartment, he'd take half of Grandma Edna's (nonexistent) bequest, and he was entitled to an equitable share of my law license. Then he threw me the zinger: I'd be sorry if I took him to court, he said, because he'd be only too happy to tell the world about my lesbianism, and wouldn't Dick Parsons just love to hear about that? "Thought I didn't know about your little friend Claire, huh?" he'd sneered. That was the one that finally got me moving: I'd walked in the bedroom, shut and locked the door behind me, and the next morning I'd taken a single bag with me to check in at the Mayflower.

Which brings us to the Fuck heading, with Claire's name in bold letters under it. I'd had less success in keeping that whole mess on the cerebral back burner since I'd spent so much of my time in Baltimore—basically every waking minute—with Renee, who was properly situated in the I Don't Know category but took a few scenic detours into the realm of Claire, passport courtesy of Dr. Mbaye, fuck you very much. It might have dawned on me eventually, in a decade or so, but the good doctor had brought it front and center for me with that simple devastating question about who it was who had me thinking so much about Claire.

There really wasn't any question about whether I'd respond to Claire's e-mail: I was no more capable of turning my back on her than I was of forgetting the way her eyes would dance with mischief when she wanted to make love. God knows I didn't want to write back, but she'd brought me to the ledge of a tall building and I was acutely aware of the dizzy temptation pulling at me, the irrational urge to jump. Not now, though. I had to step back from the ledge, knowing that there were just too many other things to resolve before I could think clearly enough to figure out what I would say.

Which is why there were so many entries under the I Don't Know heading. The details of the will—well, that question would be answered fairly quickly, as soon as I retrieved it from under the pile of papers where Stella had hidden it. The thornier issue was what I was going to do with the answer: Tell Rob and Liz? Call Gardner? I didn't feel up to any of it, but it had to be done. I resented that he'd come out of the woodwork after all this time to drop this pile of shit in my lap, and I guess part of my determination to call him was to find out why. And maybe while I was at it, I could get some answers to the thousands of other questions that I'd spent a lifetime not asking.

Then there was the issue of that departmental meeting last Friday. There too, I'd find out what had happened soon enough. Although it seemed almost irrelevant after what we'd learned in Baltimore, it still mattered to me. Ego maybe, or just morbid curiosity, but I still wanted to know if, at the end of the day, I'd had the support of my department, the only people whose opinions of me I really gave a shit about.

When it came to the remaining items in the I Don't Know column, they came in different flavors but could all be summed up in a simple word: Renee. It was amazing how well I'd kept my mind off the profound confusion she sowed in me, given how closely and constantly we'd worked together in Baltimore. But we'd been thrown into hyperdrive by the swiftly changing events, forced to focus every ounce of energy on dealing with the suddenly shifting terrain. Side by side, we'd worked feverishly through Friday night, strategizing our options about Chasen and Parsons, and preparing for the interview of Irwin Knowles on Saturday.

Up to that point, I'd already compiled an impressive list of things I admired about her—her brains and integrity right near the top, not to mention her smoldering beauty, which turned my legs to water if I thought about it for too long. But in those long hours, my list grew immeasurably as I was granted a cherished opportunity to see the Renee she rarely let people see: the one whose incomparable strength was susceptible to self-doubt, and whose commitment to do the right thing overcame her innate need to go it alone, allowing her to ask for help. As my list grew, so did my attraction to her, although I deliberately avoided acknowledging it at the time.

Okay, I have to admit, a few twinges crept into my consciousness now and then. When she'd suggested we leave the hotel bar on Friday and continue working in her room, for example, I'd felt a little sizzle grab my groin, but it quickly dissolved as soon as we drew up chairs by the desk and started going through the e-mail printouts. Then there was that moment, sometime after three, when she'd decided to get more comfortable. The sight of her emerging from the bathroom clad only in shorts and a long T-shirt delivered a swift blow to my chest, and my throat closed up for an instant. But she didn't appear to notice, she just gave me a friendly smile as she pushed her long dark hair behind her shoulder, and didn't react at all to the deep blush I felt burning on my face as my eyes caressed her unbearably gorgeous legs and the lovely curve of her breasts outlined against her shirt.

There were also a few times when I sensed it wasn't just me—that she was feeling something too. That moment on Friday night—well, technically, Saturday morning—when we'd run out of steam and decided to call it a night. As we'd stood there by the door, we abruptly found ourselves enveloped in an exhausted stillness. She'd leaned against the door, legs casually crossed and her lovely swan neck tipped invitingly to the side, and she'd held me there for a second, held me with her eyes, as if she'd been about to say something but then decided against it. And then on the train back to New York, when I'd been running through all the ways that the information we'd uncovered was probably going to fuel the political fires that were already consuming my career—she'd reached out and taken my hand. A simple gesture of friendship perhaps, but she hadn't let go—had, in fact, rubbed her thumb against my fingers for a few moments, until I'd rubbed back. She'd withdrawn her hand then, and I'd felt embarrassed, so I got up to visit the rest room. "Don't rush," she'd said with a smile. "You might run somebody down."

We'd have to talk about it, that much was clear. And it was up to me to bring it up, make her understand that whatever this thing was that we were dancing around, she needn't be afraid: it wasn't nearly as complicated as it appeared. In fact, it was no longer as complicated as it had been the night of the Lambda dinner, because since then I'd been able to put at least one item in the I Know column. There wasn't any use in pretending I wasn't drawn to her in a way that scared the shit out of me. And whether or not she felt it too, I could no longer deny the enormity of what it meant for me, because I knew this nightmare. I'd been there before. I was falling in love with Renee.

As I approached my office, debating whether I would read the will after all, something in the back of my consciousness registered the oddly spirited greetings being directed at me from the open doorways I passed. Stella wasn't at her desk—probably at lunch—so I scooped up my phone messages and retreated into the sanctuary of my office, closing the door firmly behind me. I was tempted to call Renee but resisted the urge. She had a lot on her plate today, and as we'd said good-bye at Penn Station on Saturday, she'd promised to call as soon as it was over.

The will was right where Stella had put it, safely hidden under a stack of deposition transcripts on my desk. I turned on my computer, felt queasy at the sight of my Inbox, and turned it off again. Unable to come up with a single excuse for putting it off any longer, I opened the envelope from Texas and started to read.

I can't help but be a lawyer when I read a legal document. I knew this was my flesh and blood I was reading about, the will of someone as closely related to me as Gussie was, but it might as well have been a client's for all the attachment to it I felt. It didn't really begin to feel personal until I got past the massive assets of the estate and arrived at the beneficiaries. There was faceless Uncle John, described to me by dear Aunt Nell on a few occasions as "a troubled soul"—he was to receive one-half of the estate. But the bequest was to John Gardner "and his issue"—meaning that Uncle John's half went to him as well as any children he had at the time of Grandma Edna's death. But then, as I read the bequest to my father, a small coal of anger was stoked in the pit of my stomach: "Kenneth Gardner, and his issue Daniel and Elaine."

The words sliced into me as surely as they'd sliced me, Liz, and Rob from this estate. By identifying the children of his second marriage—and them alone—Kenneth Gardner, the self-interested drafter of this will, had ensured that none of his other "issue" would share in the bequest.

Although I'd been prepared for it, the stark reality of the words on that page still sent my mind into an irrational tailspin. I felt betrayed, as deeply as Mom must have felt it thirty-seven years ago. I wanted to call him up just to tell him to go to hell, to tell him that he's fucked with me and my family enough. I was awash in feelings as old as I was, feelings so deep I could not name them, that centered on the sense of orphanhood and unworthiness and utter desolation of a small child who sees a gaping, nameless hole in the family net and cannot understand what she did to cause it—but cause it she must have, since he was there for the others, and only left when she came along. Much as my grown-up mind knew better, understood rationally that embryonic little me had nothing to do with his desertion, I couldn't talk myself out of the tidal rush of emotion that swept me—feelings that pre-dated any conscious thought and had lurked beneath the surface, hibernating, for all these years.

Damn, I thought as I brushed away the unbidden tears. *I'm in no state to face Dennis. Not like this.* I tried to tap into my safety, the reservoir of anger that usually served me so well, but it was running a bit dry. I heard a knock at the door, and before I could tell whoever it was to go away, Janelle burst in.

"Ash," she said breathlessly, "it wasn't me, I swear to God." One look at my face and she closed the door behind her. "What's wrong?"

"Nothing. What are you talking about?"

"You haven't heard? It's all over the firm. They know about your inheritance. Parsons made a little speech about it at the partner meeting on Friday, and told them he was planning to support you."

"What?!"

"I swear I didn't tell a soul; I haven't even talked to Shawanna about it. Honest."

I tried to get my mind around what she was saying, but it wasn't making any sense. There was no inheritance, but that was irrelevant if everyone thought there was. The bigger question was why Parsons would latch onto it to throw his support behind me. Parsons wouldn't do such a thing unless there was something in it for him. As the pieces began to settle into place, I felt his oily grip snaking around my neck. He knew about what we'd found in Baltimore—or he suspected. And he was setting it up as a trade-off: partnership for my silence.

There it was—my good buddy anger finally reared its ugly head and helped me to think a little more clearly. My teeth itched to rip his goddamn head off: but for now, I'd settle for playing it cautiously and keeping the cards close to my vest. I knew what I had to do.

"Ash, is it true?"

"I don't know what to think, Janelle." I glanced at my watch. "Look, I've got a meeting. Can I talk to you later?"

"Sure."

"In the meantime," I said as I got up and headed to the door, "you know nothing, okay?"

"That's easy. I know nothing anyway."

As I strode down the hall to Dennis's office, I politely smiled and nodded to secretaries and associates who offered congratulations, not sure if they were acknowledging my fortune or imminent partnership. It hardly mattered; one was as illusory as the other at this point. Dennis waved me into his office as soon as he saw me, and I shut the door before taking a seat opposite his long mahogany desk.

"Well, it seems you're certainly the talk of Huxley Doyle these days," he said with genuine pleasure. "I don't know if you've heard, but it looks like you're going to sail right through when the vote goes to the full partnership later this week."

"Yeah, I heard you had a meeting on Friday."

"I was ready to go to the mat for you, Ash, but Parsons saved me the bother. I guess he likes the idea of having such a deep pocket among his partners. Which reminds me, congratulations on your inheritance; I certainly hope you're planning to stay with us."

Well, that remained to be seen. "Well, yes, but listen, Dennis—there's something I need to talk to you about."

He picked up on my ominous tone right away, and sat back to give me his undivided attention. I'd toyed with the idea of going to Alan first—he's one of my closest friends at the firm, after all—but I'd decided to bring it directly to Dennis for a number of reasons. First, he was the head of the department, so it would eventually land on his desk anyway. Most important, he seemed to have an axe to grind with Parsons, so if anyone was likely to confront him and make sure it wasn't swept under the rug—or turned around against me somehow—it was Dennis. Still, it was a gamble on my part—I trusted Dennis, but didn't know if he could outweigh Parsons if it came down to an all-out war. And with Parsons' career on the line, that was definitely where it was heading.

I took a deep breath, more to stall than anything else. It wasn't so easy to plunge in, now that the moment had come.

"I just got back from interviewing a guy in Baltimore named Irwin Knowles. He used to run the R&D department at Amtec."

"The competitor that CRS thinks got its hands on the FDA application?"

Dennis was amazing that way—he had an unbelievable ability to remember details—even the facts of a case he wasn't working on.

"Right. Although they didn't steal it from the FDA. We found out they got it directly from CRS. From Huff Chasen himself."

"We?"

"Renee Silver went with me."

He nodded. "Go on."

"Well, this guy got it from Chasen so that Amtec could develop the same process and rush it through the FDA too; they were about six months behind CRS at the time."

"Knowles had options, I assume?"

"Right, and he was about five years from retirement."

"So the stock would spike and he would cash in. But what was in it for Chasen?"

"Turns out he's a major shareholder of Amtec too—through a series of dummy corporations and joint ventures."

"More than five percent?" A holding at that level or more would have to be reported to the SEC.

"Not in any one entity, no. But as best we can make out, the holdings altogether amount to something around fifteen percent."

"So in addition to the securities violations for not reporting the aggregate holdings, we've got a client who positioned himself to manipulate the market."

"Right. And he did—the stock's way up on rumors of a rush application."

"Did Knowles cash in?"

"No. Seems he got cold feet. He knew it was illegal, and he didn't want to risk it. Also, he's a real company guy—been there for thirty years, knows everybody. He knew everyone else in the company would get burned if it ever came out and the stock tanked. So he pulled the plug—or thought he did."

"He reported it?"

"Not really. He took the file to the company's General Counsel, told them he'd gotten it from Chasen but that he hadn't used it."

"You believe him?"

"Yeah, I do. They said thank you very much; you did the right thing. But a week later he got canned."

"So why didn't he report it then?"

"At first, he thought they'd fired him because they didn't believe that he hadn't used the file. That's what they told him—they promised they'd keep silent about his misconduct if he would just take early retirement and go away quietly. They froze half of his options, though—basically forever—and made him exercise the other half and sell right away, while the stock was still in the toilet. So they held him hostage through the second half of his options, and through his pension."

"But once the stock started to go up, he must have known they were using the file he'd given them."

"I know. This guy's a twerp—scared of his own shadow. He said Chasen had threatened him when he'd handed over the file, said that once he took possession of it, he'd be implicated just as much as Chasen, and as long as he still had any Amtec stock in his name— which he did, of course—the SEC would be all over him."

"So why talk now?"

"At first he wouldn't. In fact, he was pretty shaken up when we told him we were lawyers for CRS, and he said we didn't have to worry about him talking. We had no idea what he meant, so we played along to get him talking."

"How do you mean?"

"We acted as if we already knew the whole story and were just getting him to confirm it. About halfway through, Renee pulled out a tape recorder, and he let us tape the rest. By then, he was on a roll, filling in all the details. He was pretty pissed off about how he'd been treated. I think it made him feel vindicated in some way to finally tell his side of the story."

Dennis nodded slowly, and I saw his mind racing through the implications for the firm, which were many. But he still had some questions.

"You can't file that lawsuit, you realize. And Renee has to report all of this to the board."

"She's there right now."

"Isn't Chasen on the board?"

"Yes—she's going to one of the outside board members first. But there's something else, and that's really what I need to talk to you about."

"What?"

"Chasen's got a partner in the joint venture. Dick Parsons."

Dennis didn't move. He just stared at me as I continued. "Parsons was with him when he gave the FDA file to Knowles, and it was Parsons who told Knowles that the SEC would be on his tail if he ever talked."

"You're sure of this?" he asked softly.

I pulled out a copy of the tape and put it on his desk. "Absolutely. Knowles identified him by name. To top it off, Renee found the paper trail of a joint venture he's in with Chasen. There's no mistake."

He shook his head in wonder. I looked in his eyes and saw in them the look of a man who has just dodged a bullet. I knew as well as he did that if Parsons had gotten away with it, the whole law firm would have been at risk. Lawyers are supposed to stop their clients from engaging in illegal activity—not facilitate it, and certainly not benefit personally from it. If that lawsuit had been filed, every one of Parsons' partners at the firm would be implicated. That's the way a partnership works: the acts and knowledge of one partner can be imputed to all the others, whether or not the others actually know anything about it. Of course, if the case had been filed, the first bodies in the hot seat would be the litigators—with Dennis as our head, and me as the one who had drafted and filed the damn thing.

"It's not the first time," he said finally, more to himself than to me.

"Parsons?"

"Chasen. It's his MO—setting up a company for a takeover."

"So he'd use the windfall from his stock manipulations to turn around and acquire the company after its stock has tanked?"

"I guess. Or maybe just to get richer. Either way, it's insider trading." He looked at me and gave me a confident wink. "Only this time, he got his lawyer involved, so now they're both going down."

I smiled, knowing that, if Dennis handled this just right, I'd just given him a ticket onto the Management Committee—and, just maybe, I'd handed myself a Get Out of Jail Free card in the process.

He punched the speakerphone. "Jen, get me Doug Wendall." He was going right to the head of the firm's Ethics Committee. If there was any group to which every lawyer at Huxley Doyle answered—even the gods on the Management Committee—it was the five-member Ethics Committee, which was charged with blanket authority to do whatever it took to keep us all honest.

"Okay," she said. "And Stella's transferring a call for Ash from Renee Silver. Do you want to take it in there?"

He looked to me and I nodded. "Yes, plug her in."

After a few seconds, Renee's voice came over the box. "Ash?"

"I'm here with Dennis. Go ahead."

"Good, I'm glad you're both there."

"Did you meet with the board?" I asked.

"The meeting's set for four. But I don't think I'll be there."

"Why?" asked Dennis.

"I just got escorted out of the building. I've been fired."

📖   📖   📖

Claire and I danced around the subject for a few weeks following our escapade in the practice room. I guess we were so careful about not alluding to it whenever we were around other people that the self-consciousness seeped into our private moments, which were few and far between anyway. Claire didn't show up at the Cave while I was working, and I was too uncertain about what it all meant to continue my routine of wandering into her room when Janice was away. I even retired the T-shirt she'd given me—too uncomfortable with the loaded message it seemed to convey. So we ate dinner together sometimes, and studied together in the library a few evenings, but otherwise saw very little of each other.

I have to admit, I was thankful for the slow pace, at least at first. My sexual experience up to that point had been limited to a few clumsy gropings by my high school boyfriend in the backseat of a Mustang, and exactly three uninspired copulations with a U-Mass boy during my sophomore year at Smith, notable only for how quickly they'd been consummated and how uninvolved I'd felt. Frankly, I'd been more turned on, more deeply touched, by Claire's simple engulfing kiss than by anything I'd experienced or dreamed before, and that fact alone gave me pause. I didn't know if I was ready to call myself a lesbian, or what that would even mean. And while I knew that what I felt for Claire was like nothing I'd ever felt in my life, I wasn't at all sure that I was ready to proclaim it from the rooftops. I really needed to think about it, and somewhere inside me I knew that I'd never be able to consider it clearly from inside her intoxicating embrace. So I kept my distance, and so did she, as we tiptoed around the subject.

All that ended one Saturday night just before exams, when I got off work and donned my parka at the door of the Cave, preparing to brace myself against the western Massachusetts cold. I felt her eyes before I actually saw them, two blue beacons shining through the smoky haze of the bar, and when I looked up I saw her standing there just to the right of the door. She smiled, walked up to me, and reached out to clasp the hand that was working the zipper.

"Janice is away," she said, just loud enough for me to hear over the music, and slowly proceeded to zip my coat up to the neck, her eyes boring into mine the whole time. She said it matter of factly—it might as well have been a weather report—but the overall effect on me was powerful and immediate. A mixture of fear and longing did battle in my chest as I gazed into her inviting look, but then she leaned over and kissed me so tenderly that I barely felt it, and desire won out. She had that kind of effect on me, always—she could make my knees tremble with the tilt of her head.

"How long have you been here?" was all I could think to say.

She gave me a little smile, and I melted all over again.

"Long enough to be dying for you right now."

Another aching surge gripped me as she said it, and the twinkle of devilment in her eyes did me in. The stickiness in my panties gave way to an all-out flood, the juices pouring out as my cunt throbbed in yearning anticipation. I could barely stand there, much less walk back to Comstock, but I was sure going to try.

"Let's get out of here," I said as I grabbed her hand and pulled her out into the cold. We practically ran back to the Quad.

The house was still as we climbed the stairs, but we were careful to keep our tread light anyway. I didn't even bother dropping my stuff in my room; I didn't want to run the risk of seeing Shelly, although I was pretty sure she'd gone to Amherst with Janice. I followed Claire into her room, closed the door softly behind me, and leaned back against the door to await whatever was going to happen.

I didn't have to wait long. We'd arrived at some unspoken under-standing that Claire was in charge, that she was going to lead us into wherever we were going. In some ways, it had been that way since we'd first laid eyes on each other—I took my cues from Claire, react-ing to her moods, waiting to intuit what she wanted before doing any-thing. Why should it be any different now? It wasn't. She turned and walked toward me and, just as she had in the practice room, she merely reached out and pulled my face to hers.

I blanked out; I know I did. I really can't remember much beyond the heartrending urgency I felt as I allowed myself to drown in that kiss, as I felt her arms strengthen their hold to crush the air out of me and pour me into her body. I know I was the first to touch skin; I reached under her shirt, awestruck at the splendid length of her soft torso rippled by tiny goose bumps. And when I brought my hands around to the front to cup her breasts, she let out a moan that em-boldened me and dispelled any lingering doubts about where this was going and whether I wanted it to. In one swift move, so deft that it seemed rehearsed, I pulled her turtleneck over her head and stood looking at her long, beautiful, bra-clad chest, fascinated by the little buds I saw in each cup and the deep crimson that was blossoming from her cheeks down her neck.

She stepped back and held me with a look that dared me to glance away, her blazing blue eyes digging deep in a teasing half-lidded look that took immediate control of my howling center. She reached be-hind her back to unclasp her bra, but didn't remove it; she left it there, unhooked but in place, and gave me a smile that said it all.

"Now yours," she whispered in a throaty rasp that betrayed the depth of her desire.

That was it. I walked over to the bed, high from the sensation of cream lubricating my swollen clit with each step, and turned to face her as I pulled off my T-shirt, unhooked my bra, and unzipped my jeans. I could see it in her face—surprise at my unexpected bold-ness—and I reveled in the power I felt from it. I stretched out on her bed, draped my arms on the pillow above my head, and smiled at her.

"Get over here and fuck me," I said softly.

She smiled at me, teasingly. "Or what?"

Never tearing my eyes from her, I reached my hand between my legs and sampled the sopping wetness she'd inspired. "Or I may just come without you."

She did. My God, did she ever. She played me like a virtuoso, taking me places I'd never imagined. She started slowly, her tentative fingers strumming the curly hair between my legs and occasionally, maddeningly, dipped into the pool of cream to answer the siren call of my yearning cunt. But I couldn't take the teasing, not for long, and soon I was pulling her to me, inside me, begging her with my beseeching mouth and frantic pelvis to take me there—take us both there—to the place where we'd been headed since that first life-altering kiss. She coaxed me to the pinnacle as deftly as she massaged that unearthly music from her viola, and when she finally entered me, slipping her fingers inside my gaping wet maw, I felt myself clutch at her hand as surely as my arms were clutching those powerful broad shoulders, and I came long and hard—crying out her name, weeping it, as the waves crashed over me and spun me headlong into a steaming vortex of torrential, quaking orgasm.

Numb, but at the same time tingling right down to the last nerve in my body, I lay there cushioned in her arms, unable to move, to think, to do anything but savor every exquisite sensation. But then I opened my eyes and saw the merriment dancing in Claire's face, the confidence and sense of achievement she seemed to exude from having rendered me nearly comatose. And I couldn't resist—I had to meet her challenge, bring her to the same place. So I rolled her onto her back, kissed my way slowly down her neck to those adorable buds that immediately puckered under my tongue, and swatted away her hands as they tried to direct my fingers to the place where her spread legs were inviting me. No, I wasn't going to give her my hands—not yet. It wasn't until I had her moaning audibly that I continued my trail of kisses, lowering my mouth slowly, unmistakably, to the center of her need. So when I finally touched her, it was not with my fingers—it was with my tongue, pushing past the sweet folds of her honey-drenched lips and onto the twitching hard button, where I suckled with abandon. She didn't give me long, however, not that first time; she came within seconds, an animal cry erupting from her as her legs thrashed wildly beside my head and she collapsed in a weeping heap beneath me.

So this is it, I thought. *This is what it is to be a lesbian.* Somehow I'd known what to do, as if it were the most natural thing in the world. And it struck me then and there that, for me, that's just what it was.

We spent the rest of the night in much the same way, exploring every nuance of each other and coming back for more. And when finally the dawn started peeking in her window, we slept—she, deeply and sated, and I, with a peace and centeredness such as I'd never known. I'd been transported, taken to a whole new realm of existence—blipped into a new dimension, through the portal of her arms. And as I lay there in her embrace, I knew that whatever universe it was, it was a place where I belonged, it was where I was connected and fully alive. For a crazy minute I was tempted to wake up Claire, to tell her I'd finally seen a glimpse of that road described by Colette, the one that had led me, for just a moment, to an inexpressible state of grace.

📖   📖   📖

I entered my hotel room and shut the door hard, just shy of the slam I'd been tempted to give it. With the CRS case on hold, basically indefinitely, and Dennis locked away behind closed doors with the Ethics Committee, I'd had no reason to stay at the office, and every reason to get the hell out of there. I looked longingly at the bed—sleep would have to wait. There was just too much to do, and I reluctantly admitted that the long-delayed call to Gardner was at the top of the list. I threw the will across the room, just because it made me feel better to act like a five-year-old, and kicked my pumps under the bed. I hoped I would remember that was where they'd landed.

I ordered up a scotch from room service, and considered checking in with David to make sure he was all right. Okay, stupid idea, but I was stalling for time—anything to delay making that phone call. Renee was going to be coming by later after meeting with Dennis, and I wanted this Gardner mess out of the way by the time she arrived. So I decided to make the call. Then I reconsidered, and decided to wait for my drink before calling. I phoned room service again and changed my order to a double.

The thing that really killed me about this prick was that he was still pulling the strings. He'd just reached out across all those years, from the other side of the country, to disrupt all our lives—especially mine—for no apparent reason. It burned me that I allowed him such power over me, and I began to gain an inkling of why Mom never spoke about him. Maybe she didn't want to insert him into our lives, situate him in our imaginations, only for him to betray us as he'd betrayed her. Or maybe she just didn't want any connection to him at all, because he *was* a string puller. Maybe he had a history of pulling her strings.

"You're not missing much," was her pat answer if ever anyone— okay, I—had the insensitivity to ask about him. As if she were doing her bit to erase him, adding an exclamation point beside the question mark.

What did I want from all this? I honestly didn't know. Not the money, certainly—that was a dead issue. Ha ha. Information, maybe— about why he'd stayed out of our lives all this time, and what he wanted now. But I didn't hold out much hope for getting any of that either. I guess I mostly just wanted to see where it went, to let him have the connection he seemed now to be asking for, so I could see for myself what that connection might be.

My drink arrived just as I was about to chicken out. I drank half the damn thing in two gulps, and walked around the bed to retrieve the scattered pages of the will. My grandmother's will. The woman worth millions who had sent fifty bucks every Christmas—at a time when we were so poor that we were eating off a dining room table that Dad had built by removing the basement door and putting legs on it. She had probably never even seen a picture of me. I took another sip—this time a reasonably sized one—and picked up the phone.

"Yeah?" a deep voice grumbled after about the fifth ring.

"Kenneth Gardner?"

"Who wants to know?" he said cautiously, and with the barest trace of a slur. Although it was only about two in the afternoon out in Arizona, I had the feeling he was drunk.

"This is Ashleigh Moore."

"Who?"

Well, this was off to a great start. *Your daughter, you dumb fuck.* He had to know my name—how else could his lawyer have contacted me?

"Ashleigh Moore," I repeated, tempted to just hang up.

"Ashleigh, oh my God," he said quietly. I didn't know what to make of that, so I just pushed on.

"Is this Kenneth Gardner?"

"You're damn right it is," he said brightly, his twang gentle but noticeable. "I'm your father."

As soon as he said it, I felt the biting around the rims of my eyes, and I swear to God I wanted to smash that phone against the wall. *How dare he call himself my father,* I thought. My father was twice the man this sorry sack of shit could ever be, and now that he was dead and gone I wanted to rip the lungs out of anyone who'd pretend to take his place, who'd sully his name that way. There's Us and Them, and this worthless asshole was most definitely Them.

I got my temper under control with another sip of scotch, and decided to let it pass for now. I swallowed past the lump in my throat. *Just keep going.* "I understand you wanted to talk to me."

"Damn, girl, you sound all grown up." Well, what the fuck, did he think they'd kept me in a deep freeze for thirty-seven years? "I guess you must be; that's right. You and Elizabeth and Robert." He seemed to be almost thinking out loud, but I found it curious how he referred to us—as if he only knew us as names on a birth certificate. Which, I guess, he did.

"Well, tell me, girl, how the hell are they? Your brother and sister?"

Gee, thanks for asking about me. "Liz and Rob are fine. They asked me to call to see what it is you wanted."

He gave a little "hrrmph," but it was less the sound of indignation than just a vocal tick, sort of acknowledging what I'd said.

"And Linnie?"

Who, Lizzie? He lost me. "Who?"

"Linnie, your mother."

That one really turned my stomach, and threatened to dislodge the boulder in my throat. My mother's name was Caroline, but it was pronounced Carolyn—and no one, to my knowledge, ever called her anything else. I hated that this stranger had a nickname for my mother, a pet name that bespoke an intimacy I knew nothing about.

"My mother's just fine." *Certainly better than the last time she saw you.*

"Augustina and Francis?" Jesus, was he going to run through the whole family tree? I got the feeling he was trying to impress me with his memory of us, to prove that he had indeed occupied a place among us once upon a time. My patience for such posturing was wearing thin.

"Gramps is doing very well, but Gussie died about ten years ago." *Damn, I wish she was here now.*

"That's right, Robbie started calling her Gussie. She got such a kick out of that," he said with a kind of fondness. "That boy had brains." *Could have fooled me.* "I suppose he made a fine man of himself." *Not exactly.* "Probably a lawyer now, huh, just like his old man?"

My slow burn was stoked up a few degrees by his galling insinuation—the suggestion that he had the right to take even an ounce of credit for our achievements. Especially mine, since I was the one who'd gone into the law. God knows, it hadn't been in his footsteps, which had been erased into oblivion before I could even walk. I decided right then and there that, no matter what, I'd never give him the satisfaction of knowing that any of his issue—that's right, the issue he'd gone out of his way to cut from the will—had become a lawyer.

"No, Rob works in computers. He hates lawyers."

Gardner came right out and chuckled at that, a deep bubbling sound that could only come from a lifetime of cigarettes and booze.

"So what was it that you wanted to talk about?" I tried again.

"Where are Rob and Liz? Are they there with you?"

"No."

"Well, why the hell not?" he said with impatience. He must have been loads of fun as a father to my faceless half-siblings, the famous Daniel and Elaine, whom Aunt Nell had once described as "nice," followed by the observation that they took after their mother.

"You had your lawyer contact me," I said reasonably, "so they just left it to me to call."

"So let's get 'em on the horn! You're in New York City; can't you do one of those conference call things?"

I really didn't get the connection, but it hardly mattered.

"Look," I said, "the truth is, they don't want to talk to you."

He did that little "hrrmph" again, this time more emphatically. "Now that's just plain silly. Hell, girl, can't you talk some sense into them?"

"It's up to them. They have their own minds, and I guess they've made them up."

"Damn, you sound just like your mother." Okay, that one really made my skin crawl. He must have had some genetic intuition about how to press my buttons. "At least you had the good sense to pick up the damn phone." Well, I wouldn't call it sense—more like a death wish.

I was getting pretty sick of his dodging, and I knew my temper was beginning to show, but I couldn't help it. "It makes no difference to me," I said. "I have nothing to lose." Except my self-respect.

He chuckled again—I really hated that sound by now. "Yep, you're Linnie all over. Tell me, you got a boyfriend?"

Ugh. "I'm married."

"Well, that's real nice. Kids?"

"No." They'd be his grandchildren. I thanked God I could say no—there was already too much of his DNA polluting the species.

"Well, there's plenty of time for that. You just take your time."

Please, spare me the pearls of fatherly wisdom. "Look, I've got to get going in a minute, so—"

"Right, right," he said absently, as if his mind had started wandering. He was probably getting drunker as we spoke. I took another sip of scotch, enjoying its fire on the way down.

"See, what I wanted to talk to you about was my mama's estate. Your grandma."

Finally. "That much I got. What about it?"

"Well, she had some trust papers put together before she died. I just came across them. And you three are named in them."

No fucking way. That estate was closed—probated and distributed twelve years ago. And half of that estate went right into this shitbag's pocket. I'd known it would come to this, that he'd lie outright to me, and that I'd have to play dumb to see where he'd take it. So I dug in.

"So what does that mean?"

"I can't rightly tell. See, the one I found isn't signed. So unless we can find a signed copy, I guess it doesn't mean anything."

Well, that last bit was probably the first honest thing he'd said during this whole call. Play him some more. "When did she die?"

"Oh, I don't know. Ten years or more."

"And you're saying the money in her estate has just been sitting around all this time? It was supposed to go in a trust, but it didn't?"

"Well, I guess that's about the long and short of it."

I was frankly astonished at the transparency of his bullshit. His story was ludicrous even to a layperson—and there was no way he'd offer up such crap if he'd known he was speaking to a lawyer. But the question persisted: what the hell did he want, and why employ such a pathetic ruse to get it?

"Listen," he continued, "if you'd like to come on out here, I thought maybe I could show you the papers—you know, go over it all for you. And maybe we could talk a bit."

So that's what he wanted? To meet me?

"You and your brother and sister."

To meet us? Boy, that sounded like fun.

"Well," I said, "I'd have to talk to Rob and Liz—"

"Now you just do that," he said with satisfaction, assured that I'd do his bidding, that he'd get his way.

"—and I'm pretty busy myself these days," I continued, bludgeoning my way through his condescending tone. Weirdly, it was almost as if I were talking to Rob.

He retreated just a hair. "Of course you are. I understand how busy you little city girls can be. But I sure wish you'd think about it."

My eyes no longer stung; they were dry and clearly focused on the string he'd just handed me. I had to admit, I derived a good deal of pleasure from the thought of him sitting by his phone, waiting for a call back from me. A call he'd never get. It was a petty payback, sure, but it was all that I had, and I took it.

"Yes. Well, we'll see," I said. Growing up in my house, I too had become pretty adept at the art of dodging.

"You do that. Bye now, honey."

I hung up without a good-bye, because the one I would have delivered would have been anything but cordial. "I taught you better than that!" I heard Gussie silently reprimand me. But I just couldn't help it—how dare he address me with anything like that last little endearment? Who the fuck did he think he was? I threw the will across the room again, because it had felt so satisfying the first time. My drink was nothing but a pool of scotch-flavored ice water, so I decided to go downstairs to the bar for a refill and to give myself a change of scenery. While I was at it, maybe I could think over how I'd report back to Liz and Rob.

I was flat out on my stomach under the bed, trying to reach my damn pumps, when I heard a knock at the door. One shoe retrieved, I clambered to my feet and strode to the door, ready to rip the head off whoever had interrupted my tantrum.

"Shit," I said as I opened the door and saw Renee standing there. I'd totally forgotten she was coming by to fill me in on her meeting with Dennis and the Ethics Committee.

"Nice to see you too," she said cautiously.

"I'm sorry. Come on in," I said, standing aside to let her pass.

"What's all this?" she asked as she tiptoed around the pages scattered all over the room.

"Yeah, excuse the mess. I was just—" What? I shook my head. "You caught me in the middle of something."

"So I see," she said with amusement. "So do you want me to come back later?"

"No, no, that's all right. I was actually about to head down to the bar, if you'd like to join me."

"On two conditions. One, you have to wear both shoes," she said, looking at the solitary pump in my hand. "And two, you have to tell me what the hell is going on."

Chapter Ten

The pilot announced our descent just as I completed the finishing touches on my CYA memo. Renee had been right—I needed to get it down in writing while it was all still fresh in my mind, and to preserve everything we'd done in case Parsons and Chasen later tried to point fingers our way. It was exactly the kind of advice I would give to a client in my situation, so it was ironic that my client was the one who had suggested it to me. "CYA, Ash; cover your ass," she'd said, holding up her own memo. It wasn't the first time, or the last, that we would switch roles in this way.

She'd more or less assumed the role as soon as we'd been seated at the bar in my hotel the night before. Frankly, I'd been relieved that what she'd ended up asking me about had been the will; I'd been afraid that she was planning to ask me about the on-again off-again weirdness that had permeated our time together since the night of the Lambda dinner. But no—after she'd given me the rundown on her uneventful meeting at Huxley Doyle, we'd conceded that both of our futures were in limbo, at least for the time being, and there was nothing we could do about it. So she'd switched gears to inquire about the papers scattered all over my hotel room and my obviously agitated state.

I supposed I could blame it on the scotch, but the truth was that I really needed to talk about it to someone—someone other than a family member. If anyone was to blame, it was Dr. Mbaye, who'd opened the hatch by getting me a little less panic-stricken at the idea of airing the things that every nerve in my body screamed at me to keep under wraps. And I had my safety, my anger, right there with me as I started in with the whole sordid story. It took a while—dinner and two more drinks, in fact—but she listened through it all. Sometimes she was just a friend—a good one—sitting there across from me, commiserating with my angst and fury. But as the tale progressed, she began to don her lawyer cap as well, and served as the kind of intelligent, quick-thinking sounding board that I'd come to expect of Alan or Janelle.

I'd been reluctant to call Liz and Rob to fill them in, because their likely reactions—from curt dismissal to annoyance at my attempts to keep them involved in this nonsense—were going to be aggravating at best. But Renee had wisely pointed out the need to make those calls anyway, distasteful as I might find them, because like it or not I'd assumed the responsibility for acting on their behalf. And, of course, once she'd pointed it out, the lawyer in me had to agree.

I guess the moment that really brought it home for me that she could be—she was—a trusted ally in this mess was when she'd come out with a suggestion that seemed preposterous at first, but which I quickly recognized as trademark bull-by-the-horns Renee.

"Why don't you just go there and confront him?" she said with a noticeable crinkle at the corner of her eye. She had the same tone of inspiration that I'd heard when she'd suggested we go to Baltimore to confront Irwin Knowles.

"Wait a minute," I'd stuttered. "What, you mean now?"

"Sure, why not?" she said, her enthusiasm growing. "Now, when he's not expecting it—just show up."

"What for?" But I knew the answer, and knew she was right.

"Look, you want answers, right? Real answers—not some rehearsed script that he's prepared in advance."

Did I? Part of me did. But another part—the part that still recoiled at the memory of Robbie's dark voice and the torture it always preceded—just wanted to take my lumps and crawl away to hide.

"And this Ethics Committee mess is going to be going on for a few days; you might want to make yourself scarce around the firm while it's blowing up. It's not like you'd be able to get any work done, you know."

She was right, I thought. I'd been planning to stay away from the office anyway—out of town might be even better.

"But suppose he gets pissed off?" I said. "What if he slams the door in my face?"

"What if he does? At least you'll know that you're not going to get anything real out of him. That's an answer in itself."

Damn her, she was making some sense.

"But I think it's much more likely he's going to invite you in. He asked you out there for a reason, and I think the only way you're going to find out why is if you go. But do it on your terms, not his."

I sat there a moment and let the idea sink in. Once again, she'd impressed me with her in-your-face approach to fact-finding, and I only regretted that I hadn't thought of it myself.

I nodded slowly. "Maybe you're right."

"And one more thing," she'd said, "I think you need to be sure that, no matter what he says, you've got a lawyer's eyes looking at the whole picture. This is a big thing for you."

"I know." I'd just been wondering the same thing: how could I possibly keep it together and think clearly when everything about this situation was yanking at my deepest childhood emotions?

"As it turns out," she'd continued, a devilish grin on her face, "I happen to be without a job right now."

"What are you saying?"

Her steady gaze was reassuring, giving me something that I hadn't felt in a very long time—the sense that I was not alone, that someone was there to help.

"I'm going with you."

As the plane's wheels touched down, I knew I was landing in a place I'd never been, to see a man I'd never met, with the impossible hope that maybe, at long last, I'd capture a piece of who I was, see a few pages of the opening chapter of my life which had been ripped from the binding before I was born. I turned to Renee in the seat beside me and took her hand.

📖　📖　📖

I left open the door to our adjoining rooms as I unpacked my small bag. Next door, Renee turned on CNN, and I reflected on how nice it was to have her here, to hear her puttering around a few feet away. This thing between us had to get talked about—it was getting more intense by the hour, at least for me—but we both had to keep our eye on the ball for now, and a discussion about it at this point would only muddy the waters. Still, the hour was coming when I'd have to get it out or explode.

I still had a few minutes before we'd have to leave if we were going to hit Gardner's house around four-thirty—the hour that we predicted he'd be sloshed but still coherent—so I decided to check my voice mail at the office. I'd left word with Stella that I had to leave town unexpectedly, and fortunately she didn't ask for details. Stella was a real pro.

I only had one message, and it was from Janelle, sometime the night before.

"Ash? I don't know where you are; I tried your house but David said you moved out. Thanks a fuck of a lot for telling me. Anyway, girlfriend, wherever you are, you'd better be calling in for messages like always, because you need to hear this. Parsons is on the warpath, and he's gunning for you. I'm telling you, I've never seen him like this. What the hell did you do? I thought you two were all buddy-buddy, now that he's supporting your partnership. Well, whatever you pulled, it's got the whole firm turned upside down. And Parsons says he's going to have you disbarred and I don't know what-all. And Dennis is nowhere to be found. Alan said he thought he was in a meeting, but no one knows what's going on and, let me tell you, the rumors are flying. So call me, Ash. I mean it, this is serious. Call me."

"You look like you were in a train wreck," Renee said from the doorway against which she was lounging.

"Close," I said as I deleted the message and hung up. "That was a message from Janelle; seems we made quite a stir at the firm. Parsons says he's going to have me disbarred." I suddenly wished just then that Janelle were here with us—someone from the normal world, someone from my recognizable life. I should at least have brought along her crystal; its good energy would be very welcome right about now.

Renee smiled confidently as she picked up my jacket from the bed and tossed it to me. "Come on, let's go. Your lawyer will handle it."

📖 📖 📖

I think I saw a picture of Gardner once. I'm not positive, but I'm pretty sure. It was shortly before David and I got married, when we were down visiting the family and trying to convince Gussie not to go whole hog on a big wedding. I was starting law school in the fall, then a month or two away, and I was already worried about pinching pennies—my own, of course, since there was no way that anyone in Washington (other than the government) was going to help me out on that treacherous little adventure. I just couldn't bring myself to let them spend a lot of money on my wedding; I'd have to share the cost with them. And it rubbed me raw to think that I'd have to piss away all that dough on a wedding—which, let's face it, was really a party for them, since I was fairly lukewarm about the whole thing. I guess I'd held my wedding hostage: they weren't going to contribute to law school, which I cared about so much, so I deprived them of the big wedding they wanted.

Mom and Dad seemed content to keep it simple. Not happy about it, but resigned. This was the first wedding for one of Gussie's grandkids, however—and I suspected she'd have a good long wait before Rob or Liz gave her another—so Gussie was practically bursting with excitement to stage a grand affair. And in my typical fashion, adding to the growing list of transgressions I'd regret in a few years when she was gone and I had no way of making it up, I stole this little sliver of joy from her.

We didn't talk about it a lot—she knew that tone I could get when I'd made up my mind. But she tried to wheedle us into it by subtly appealing to the deep sense of family that she'd instilled in me. I knew her so well, I had no doubt what she was up to when she had Gramps pull out the slide projector during our visit, but I dutifully sat beside David through that long Saturday afternoon as Gramps showed off his photography skills and Gussie narrated the history of each picture. It was fun, in a way—reminiscent of so many afternoons we'd all spent huddled in Gussie's living room to witness the photo passage of time. I especially used to love seeing the old pictures of Mom as a little girl—running on the beach at Ocean City with a ten-year-old Uncle Dink, sitting proud and confident atop an enormous horse at Aunt Tavia's farm in Virginia. Those shots had afforded a cherished opportunity to glimpse an unrecognizable Mom, a Mom I couldn't begin to imagine—one who was carefree and full of life. I always wished I'd known that little girl.

Coming back from getting a Pepsi in the kitchen that afternoon, I'd heard Gussie snap at Gramps about the slide that was up on the screen just then.

"What in tarnation is that thing doing in there, Fran? I thought you got rid of them all." It was unusual to hear that tone—Gussie hardly ever spoke sharply to Gramps—and I guess that more than anything perked up my ears. I looked hard at the slide, but there was nothing remarkable about it—just a fuzzy old black and white of a man leaning against a Chevy from the early 1960s. The scene might have been outside Aunt Aurelia's old house, but I couldn't be sure. All I knew was that I didn't know the guy, but there was nothing unusual in that, since Gramps was famous for using that old camera of his to chronicle nearly every trip we took and every person we met.

It was gone before I knew it. Gramps softly mumbled, "What do you know, I thought I got 'em all," as he clicked the tray to the next slide. David looked up at me in the doorway, an inquisitive arch in his brow telling me that he was just as clueless as I about what had just happened. But part of me knew, and if Mom hadn't been right in the next room, I might have said something. As it was, I was left with that shadowy image burned into my memory. Because, stranger though he was, there was one thing about him that did ring a bell—the hair-line on that young man followed a distinct contour that was all too familiar, receding dramatically above the temples before jutting out again over his forehead in the middle. It was the line to which I'd seen Robbie's hair retreat over the past few years.

📖 📖 📖

"I don't get it," Renee said from the passenger seat of our rented Honda. "How do you know where you're going? I thought you said you've never been here before."

"I looked at a map in the hotel."

She shook her head and looked out the window. I knew what she was thinking, had heard it all before—that a quick glance at a map

couldn't fully explain how I knew which way to turn as we left the hotel garage, or how I knew that the interstate would be just a few
blocks to our left as we headed north. But the truth was, Tucson was
remarkably simple to navigate, laid out in an elementary grid on a
north-south axis. Compared to DC, it was a piece of cake. The plan-
ners of most modern cities made it so damn easy; they took all the fun
out of it. Now London or Rome, *there* were some challenges.

It was a straight shot up Interstate 10, and I imagined briefly how
easy it would be to just keep going all the way to Los Angeles. But
Gussie didn't raise me to be a quitter or shy away from the hard tasks,
so I kept my eyes peeled for the exit to Gardner's place, and tried not
to think about how fantastic Renee looked in profile.

I honestly had a moment of doubt about my magical navigational
skills when we pulled up in front of the address I'd memorized. The
house was nice, but nothing spectacular, and certainly not what I'd
expect of someone who had inherited 175 million dollars. Three stories, I'd guess maybe four or five bedrooms, the place would probably
run around half a million in a New York suburb, so it had to be worth
considerably less out here. I could see by the look on Renee's face that
she was thinking the same thing. Unless he had a Xanadu tucked
away for himself on his own private island, this guy didn't pour his
loot into housing. Or he didn't really have any loot.

"Ready?" she asked.

"Guess so. Remember, you're just a friend of mine. If he gets a whiff
of lawyer, he'll clam up."

"Yeah," she said with a smile. "I'm glad you reminded me, because
you've only mentioned it seven or eight times, and I'm really not too
bright."

I loved that look on her face, and wanted to just sit there and stare
at her for a few days. Instead, I opened the car door and got out.

The driveway was empty, but their car might have been in the garage. Still, as we approached the door, I sensed a sort of stillness about
the place—no television or stereo, no shadows crossing in front of the
window. Renee looked at me when we reached the porch, waiting for
me to ring the bell. I did.

Nothing. Not even a dog barking inside. Just . . . nothing. I gave it a few beats, and tried again.

"Well," I said, "I guess we could wait around and see if they show up."

Renee looked around and shook her head. It would look pretty strange for us to hang out in the car waiting for Gardner and his wife to come home. The street was deserted, with cars parked in garages or driveways. And it was a quiet street—not a single car had driven past since we'd arrived. Besides, who knew how long we'd have to wait? They could be out for the rest of the evening.

"I've got a better idea," she said. "Let's bag it for today. We can go back to the hotel, have a totally decadent dinner—with dessert, of course—and try again tomorrow. They aren't going anywhere, and I'm hungry."

I was too. Although it wasn't even five yet, we were still on New York time, and lunch on the plane had been pretty pitiful.

"Deal," I said with a smile, feeling as if I'd been granted a twenty-four-hour reprieve.

"Besides," Renee said as she walked me back to the car, hooking her hair behind her ear and shifting a sidewise glance my way, "I think now might be a good time for us to talk about a few things."

📖　📖　📖

It's a wonder I didn't flunk out my last year at Smith. Claire and I roomed together that year; it only made sense, since Janice and Shelly were hardly ever there, and everyone knew that Claire and I had become great friends. Only Kat knew the real story about Claire, and that was as it should be.

Junior year, while we'd still had separate rooms, our lovemaking had been sporadic—stolen hours here and there dependent on Janice's absences, which became frustratingly infrequent after she broke up with her Amherst boyfriend in February. Entire weeks would go by with little more than some hurried kisses and a few achingly brief embraces behind closed doors, where we'd tease each other senseless—but we had very few chances to actually make love. By the time April rolled around and we had to put in room requests for our senior year, I couldn't stand it anymore; I was a bundle of raw nerves, walking around in a constant state of arousal and desperate for any change that would assure us of some real privacy. When I mentioned to Shelly that Claire and I were thinking of rooming together for our last year, I'd had a whole speech planned—how Claire really wanted to stay in Comstock but didn't want to room with Janice anymore—but I needn't have bothered; Shelly just looked at me with a smile that was understanding but kind of sad, and said quietly, "I guess you know what you're doing."

I have Claire to thank for any studying I managed to squeeze in during our senior year. She was a ruthless taskmaster when it came to schoolwork, and would not let us fall into bed if either of us had reading to do. Even so, I daydreamed away many of my classes in a hormone-induced drunk, and skated by by doing the barest minimum of studying, so I could spend every possible minute with Claire. The only time I really tried to study was when we worked together in the library; Claire was adamant that we not study together in the room, knowing too well that we'd just wind up in bed. Still, even at the library, I often found it difficult to buckle down, and couldn't wait for the moment when she'd look across the table at me and say, "Okay, I give up. All I can think about is your *ce que je pense*." She got very good at saying it.

Now and then, Claire would mention the fact that we didn't have boyfriends, and would wonder out loud if we ought to accompany Janice and Shelly on one of their Amherst junkets, just to keep up appearances. I'd assure her that no one was paying any attention to our social lives, and that lots of our classmates devoted themselves to studying instead of boyfriends. Besides, the thought of Claire out on a date with some guy—even a platonic double date with me—galled me no end. There was just no way I could put myself through that.

It never occurred to me that her concern could have something to do with keeping up appearances in the eyes of anyone other than our housemates or friends around campus. But as the winter term progressed and we started talking about our plans for the future, she became somewhat distant, and started mentioning with increasing regularity that her parents were planning for her to come home for a year before starting graduate school. She knew I hadn't yet decided on a grad school, and was considering the possibility of just getting a job instead, but she was maddeningly noncommittal when I suggested that I might follow her to Chicago to find work.

"Ash, I just don't know where I'll end up," she'd say. "Can't we just play it by ear? You settle wherever you decide, and we'll make plans around that."

She made it sound so simple, as if she intended to work out her grad school plans around me—but at the same time she wouldn't let me go to Chicago, which made the most sense to me. And I couldn't understand her reluctance to just take charge of her own life anyway. I'd never met her parents, and had only spoken to them a few times on the phone, but they seemed reasonable enough. I couldn't imagine they'd react with anything but approval if Claire announced she was going to grad school right away.

And so we spent that winter of our senior year in a carefully choreographed waltz—from the books, to the bed, to the discussion of our plans, which would border on a fight. For some reason, we always made love in Claire's bed, never mine, and as graduation approached I began to regard her bed as a DMZ—the place of truce where we'd put aside our divergent desires for a few hours to focus on our immediate needs, but which in the end always brought us back to our differences. Because for me, the communion of our bodies in those hours only seemed to reinforce my need for permanence, but for Claire, it seemed to have the opposite effect—once she was sated, she could withdraw, think clearly, and insist with even greater force that she had to do her parents' bidding; she had to return to Chicago. And I couldn't follow.

So that spring, when I got accepted to the history program at NYU, there was really no more discussion to be had. She acted as though my grad school acceptance were a grand achievement—which, considering my grades at that point, I guess it was—and that everything might still work out for us, because there were so many schools in New York from which she could choose when her year of filial indenture in Chicago was over. She still had me believing at that point that she might actually join me in New York, now that I'd finally decided where I'd be.

The possibility that she'd come to New York—I don't think she consciously held it over my head, deliberately used it to keep peace in our room, but that's how it worked out. We'd reached a kind of tacit agreement: I didn't bug her about coming to New York right away, and she still fucked my brains out. But my orgasms in those last few weeks were bittersweet, laced with uncertainty and a kind of dread. A distance had found its way between us, a vast terrain of dust and uncertainty, and I didn't know how to bridge it. I knew she was worried about her parents coming to graduation and meeting me, and I assured her that I was perfectly capable of keeping our secret. Hadn't I kept it all this time? Still, as graduation weekend approached, she told me she would be making plans for entertaining them alone—adamant that we should see our families separately. I understood her paranoia to some extent: I could never hide anything from Gussie, and she would need only one look at me sitting beside Claire to know exactly what was up. So I agreed, and on that Saturday night before the Sunday commencement exercises, we went off to our separate family dinners. "Don't wait up for me," Claire had said as I was about to go meet Mom and Dad and Gussie and Gramps. "My parents said something about having me stay with them at the hotel tonight."

She didn't come home that night—didn't show up, in fact, until just before we had to leave for the ceremony the next day. She seemed a little disappointed to find me still in the room when she came in, and avoided looking at me as she hurried to change and grab her cap and gown.

"Why don't you just go on ahead—I'll catch up," she said.

"No, that's okay. I thought we could go down together—sort of our last stroll through the Quad."

"No, really, you go without me."

I didn't like this feeling I was getting from watching her buzz around the room. "Claire, stop. Look at me and tell me what's going on."

She must have heard the determination in my voice, because she stopped what she was doing and shook her head. "I really didn't want to do this now," she said softly.

"Do what?"

She sighed and went to her backpack to pull out an envelope. Avoiding my eyes, she walked over to me, handed me the envelope, and went over to sit on her bed. The bed we always made love in.

"What's this?"

But I didn't need her to tell me—it was written all over her face.

"You're not coming to New York," I said dully. I'd known, of course, even while harboring an irrational hope. But I saw from the look on her face that it was more than just not coming to New York now; she was never going to come.

"I can't do this, Ash," she said in a near whisper. "I'm sorry."

"What do you mean? Do what?"

"I'm not gay. I'm—I can't be with you like that anymore."

What? "I don't understand."

"Look, I can't just say 'fuck you' to my parents, to everything they've done for me and planned for me. I'm sorry, but I just can't."

I was hearing the words, I know I was, but they weren't registering. She couldn't be saying that—she couldn't be turning her back on everything we'd had for two years.

"Don't stare at me like that," she said. "I really can't stand that."

Well, her feelings were certainly the most important thing just then. I choked back the *fuck you* that sprang to my lips. "I can't believe this—that you'd pretend to be someone you're not."

"I'm not pretending to be anything. I know who I am, and I'm not gay."

"You can't be serious. What do you think we've been doing all this time?"

"That's not the point. The point is who I am, and the life I'm prepared to live. And it doesn't include making a life with a woman." She looked me right in the eye. "With you."

I may have bitten off the *fuck you*, but I couldn't restrain the rest of what needed saying just then. "Your father's money is really that important to you? There's a word for women who sell themselves like that, you know."

"I knew you'd be like this," she said softly. Her jaw was clenched in that resolute clutch I knew so well, hard and immobile. Yes, the wall of ice was firmly in place, and I'd never chip through it.

"I don't believe you're doing this," I whispered, the reality beginning to sink in. "After everything we've planned, everything—"

"You, Ash—everything that you planned. I didn't agree to anything. And you just didn't want to listen when I said I needed to keep things loose for now."

"So that's it? You're saying we're through?"

"Ash, don't." She was calm—eerily so, and that just gave me more of an outlet for my fury.

"I was good enough as a fuck buddy, but now that college is over it's time to grow up and join the real world? Is that it?"

"I never left the real world, Ash. And I don't think I ever could. I'm just not like you—I can't give the finger to the world. Not now, not ever. I'm sorry."

I don't think I heard one word of that commencement ceremony. Gussie was the leader of my family's cheering section about midway back on the left, but I didn't hear any of it. Carla Oakes was seated next to me—that much I remember, because she had to poke me in the ribs when they called my name. All I know is that I sat there staring at that unopened envelope in my hands, staring through dry eyes because I was too numb to feel anything at all. It wasn't until I returned to the room after a graduation dinner with my family that I finally read the damned thing, alone on my bed, facing Claire's stripped bed and empty closet. She'd packed up and left with her parents right after the ceremony. The last I'd seen of her, right after the ceremony, she'd been standing in a corner of the Quad, sandwiched between her parents and staring at the ground. As hard as I'd glared at her from across the lawn, she'd never looked up.

📖　📖　📖

"And you never saw her again?" Renee asked as she finished the last bite of her chocolate cake. It had been a long dinner, and an even longer dessert—and I had done most of the talking. I shook my head. To Renee, I'm sure it must have sounded inconceivable that I'd just graciously accepted Claire's severing of herself from my life—although the truth was I'd been anything but gracious.

"What did the letter say?"

I shrugged. "Oh, you know, more of the same. All about how she wasn't gay, how she couldn't just chuck everything to be with me."

Oh yes, that and so much more—her words may have been sparse, but they'd cut right to the bone. She knew how to phrase it in unanswerable terms, laying it out for me that we were such different people, wanting such different things out of a relationship: me needing to give my all, prepared to mold my life to someone else's; her needing to keep it simple, like everything else in her life, carefully compartmentalized. But beyond that, she knew I'd ignore the words and look for the message underneath, which was the point she'd delivered with devastating clarity—what we had shared simply hadn't meant as much to her. She could walk away from it because she didn't, and couldn't, fully invest herself in it. I wasn't enough.

"And you never talked about it after that?"

"No."

She looked at me incredulously.

"I tried—I tracked her down at her parents' house after graduation. But her mother said she was traveling in Europe for the summer." Her letter had popped that little surprise on me, but I hadn't believed it.

"So?"

"So nothing. I figured if she was so desperate to get away from me that she'd leave the country, what was I going to do? I went to New York and started grad school in the fall."

"And that's where you met David."

"A year or so later, yeah. He was finishing up an MBA at Columbia."

She nodded thoughtfully, as if the last few hours had finally started to cast some faint light on several questions that had been puzzling her. I wished the same were true for me.

"And all this time, you've never heard from her? You have no idea where she is?"

"Well," I said with a sad smile, "it's funny you should ask."

        📖   📖   📖

We took our drinks up to the adjoining rooms after dessert, more for a change of scenery than anything else. Renee was clearly intrigued at my reluctance to answer Claire's e-mail, but she didn't push it, and I was grateful. The truth was, I didn't feel any great urgency to respond just yet—partly because my plate was plenty full with other more pressing matters, and partly because the face I saw when I closed my eyes at night was no longer Claire's. And that was something that I just didn't know if Renee was ready to hear. Or if I was ready to say.

The fact that she was so easygoing with me these days didn't help matters. If I was drawn to the "business Renee"—and clearly I was—it was nothing compared to the indescribable pull I felt in the presence of this one, the "casual Renee," whose cherry lips beckoned me with every coy half-smile, whose hazel eyes had shone with understanding as I'd explained my separation from David. I knew I should say something. Just lay it on the table, tell her I was attracted to her and hoped it wouldn't interfere with our friendship—a friendship that meant more to me with each passing day. But I didn't know how to do it without potentially spoiling everything, making us uncomfortable again around each other. And I didn't dare let myself hope that she might feel the same way, despite the hints I'd been picking up. They could so easily have been the product of wishful thinking and an overactive libido—especially the latter, which was rearing its ugly head in direct proportion to the amount of time I was spending with her.

"Be right back," Renee said as she strolled next door, leaving the door open between our rooms. Maybe having adjoining rooms had been a bad idea—I wanted to change into sweatpants and a T-shirt, but I didn't want her walking in on me. I took my clothes into the bathroom to change, and when I emerged I found her in the doorway we shared, clad in shorts and a tank top, lounging against the door in a posture I'd come to recognize—one long tanned leg crossed in front of the other, her hair brushed to a sheen and hanging loosely in front of her shoulders, her eyes glued to a fingernail she was picking. Casual, centered, gorgeous—thoroughly Renee. It took my breath away.

"Nice toes," I remarked, noticing her bright red toenail polish.

"Thanks," she said as she kicked off from the threshold and strolled toward the table where we'd placed our drinks. "I guess I could try it on my hands, too, but . . ." She gave a little half-smile and shrugged as she lifted up her fingernail to bite it.

We reached the table at the same time, but instead of reaching for her drink, she caught my hand.

"Do you mind if I tell you something?" she asked.

There was something about her tone, a note of caution, that put me on alert. Something had changed—or was about to—and my stomach clenched involuntarily. She looked at me, no doubt seeing the apprehension all over my face, and gave me a soft smile of reassurance. I nodded her on.

"You can tell me I'm way out of line here, but I have to say it."

The gentle pressure of her hand started my clit yammering again, and all the moisture in my body seemed to pool between my legs—my throat was bone dry, so I could only nod again.

"Okay, here goes," she said and looked up at me. "I've been dying to kiss you all day."

The look in her eyes as she said it was so tentative, so unsure, that it emboldened me to raise my hand to her cheek and brush her hair behind her ear. I don't know if I was smiling as I did it, but something in my face must have told her that she wasn't out of line at all—that she'd said exactly what I wanted to hear.

With my hand in her hair like that—and God, it was so soft— I slipped onto autopilot without thinking, and it took nothing for me to reach around her neck and draw her face to me. Her free hand came up out of nowhere to slide up my shoulder, but by that time I lost track of it because I felt her breath just an inch from my mouth, and then the soft, heavenly press of her lips became the center of the universe.

Her lips moved gently under mine—a delightful massage so subtle, so different from the bricklike kisses of David or the hard flaming passion of Veronica, that I was awash in a symphony of sensations from another time, familiar yet nearly forgotten. *How could I have lived so long without this,* I thought, *this feeling like nothing else on earth?* I melted into her, my limbs liquid from her touch, and I opened my mouth to receive the warm tongue I felt cautiously tasting my lips. Her tongue felt its way inside with luxurious strokes as she thoroughly explored me and claimed me as her own.

We pulled away slowly, our lips lingering to the last in an effort to milk every delectable tingle from the kiss that had left us trembling. I opened my eyes first—her face was a deep crimson, and a little vein in her neck was pulsing rapidly, adorably. I was tempted to lean in and kiss it, but before I could, she opened her eyes and gave me a look so filled with lust, drilling so deeply into my core, that my breath stuck in my throat and I gave a little cough.

She got a kick out of that—gave me one of her patented half-smiles, and then bit her lip to suppress it.

"It's been a while," I said, sheepishly.

She circled my waist with her arms and started nuzzling my neck with little kisses. "I guess it's like riding a bike," she said between nips. "You never forget." I lost myself again in the texture of her hair, in the delicious taste of her tiny perfect ear, and eventually, once more, in the unspeakable magnificence of her tender, beseeching mouth. Only this time when our lips met, there was nothing tentative about it. Soon she was swallowing my mouth with an urgency that was immediate, insistent, telling me with the crush of her arms and every thrust of her tongue that she was aching just as desperately as I, that we were sweeping each other far past the point of teasing and would soon be in over our heads.

She broke the kiss with a deep sigh, and stepped back before I could reach for her again.

"I should have known I couldn't do this," she said, pushing her hair out of her face.

Her words slammed into me, dousing the white-hot embers that had engulfed my cunt, and allowing some neural activity to begin registering through the steam.

"What are you talking about?"

She fought to get her breath under control, and reached for her drink.

"I thought I could just kiss you and say goodnight." She swirled the drink a little and shook her head. "I had no idea it would be like this."

I picked up my own drink, just for something to do. "Like what?" I said, taking a sip.

She looked up at me. "That it would be so hard to stop."

"So why stop?"

She leaned against the table and swirled her drink some more as she stared at the melting ice cubes. I couldn't think much past the long graceful fingers holding the glass, imagining how they'd feel on my breasts.

"Because you've got an awful lot going on right now, and I don't think you need any more complications."

"But—"

"And," she cut me off, looking at me with determination, "when I finally get you in bed, I want your undivided attention."

I nodded—I knew she was right, although the molten lava between my legs said otherwise.

"Just for the record," I said, taking her hand, "I'm capable of chewing gum and walking at the same time."

She smiled. "Oh darling, when the time comes, I want you to chew a lot more than gum."

Chapter Eleven

The last voice I expected to hear on my office voice mail the next morning was Mom's. But sure enough, when I called in after a restless night of dreams—largely populated by Renee fighting off polar bears, for some reason—it was my mother's cautious monotone that greeted me.

"Honey, David said you moved out." As if she needed to explain why she'd placed a call to the den of iniquity. "What happened? Well, anyway, the reason I'm calling is that I've been thinking about what you told me. And I don't think it's a good idea for you to get in touch with that man." That man—in my whole life, I don't think I'd ever heard her refer to him by name. "Whatever he's up to, it's no good, and nothing good can come from it." She paused there, as if waiting for an argument from me, or maybe just deciding whether she should say any more. "Well, that's it. I just wanted you to know. And please call me and tell me where you are."

Well, Mom, I'm in Arizona on my way to see the fuck, if you must know. It irked me that she would go to the trouble of leaving me a message like that. She knew very well that I couldn't just leave it alone—especially after she'd already given it her halfhearted approval.

Renee knocked at the door just then, and poked her head inside. "Damn, you're up," she said as I deleted the message and hung up. "I was hoping I could wake you up with a kiss, Sleeping Beauty."

I shook my head and smiled. "I haven't recovered from the kiss last night. Don't start in again."

She came over and sat beside me on the bed. "You forgive me?" She kissed me gingerly, but with just enough pressure to make it interesting.

"No," I said when she pulled back. "I was up all night masturbating."

She smiled. "That makes two of us."

"Well, in that case, go wash your hands so we can get going. I want to be at Gardner's place by ten or so."

On the ride over, I filled her in on Mom's disturbing phone call, and spent the rest of the drive trying not to think about the magnetic pull of her presence. Much as I'd hated saying goodnight to her last night, and watching the door close behind her, it was the right thing to do. I could barely concentrate as it was, and if we'd taken things as far as I'd wanted, I'd be operating on even less sleep and my mind would be filled with much more distracting images.

We pulled up in front of the nondescript house, and this time saw a Camry parked in the driveway. I felt my resolve start to falter—now that the time had come and I knew he was there, I really didn't want to do this. The sun was shining brightly, the grass was green—why spoil such a beautiful Wednesday morning? Renee looked over to me, and reached out to give my hand a squeeze.

"Ready when you are," she said.

"How about never?"

She smiled, and waited until I opened my door before getting out.

The quiet of the neighborhood struck me again—no one watering their lawn, no one washing a car in the driveway, no dogs barking in any of the backyards. Such a momentous occasion, it struck me, but no one was here to see it. No welcoming committee.

We reached the door and stood there a moment. Maybe it was too early; they were still sleeping, and we should just come back later. Then again, maybe I should just get it over with.

I rang the bell. Nothing. I looked at Renee, ready to chicken out, but she gave a little nod that said to try again, so I did. This time, we heard a muffled "hold your horses" coming from somewhere inside the house, and stood frozen on the porch. It took a little while longer before we heard the sound of the latch clicking, and then the door swung open.

"Who the fuck are you?"

📖 📖 📖

From the time I was three or so, my best friend was Mary Boyle. She and her little brother John lived on the next street over from

Gussie's, so our backyards butted up against each other, separated by the back alley that ran the length of our block. Mary was witness to every major event in my young life, as I was to hers: we learned to ride two-wheelers on the same day, we shared our first days at nursery school, then kindergarten, then first grade, and together we fought untold battles with Louie Plough when he moved in down the block. Her mother, although a good deal younger than Gussie, liked to spend summer afternoons with Gussie, either in their backyard or ours—gabbing away about grown-up stuff as Mary, John, and I dug in Mary's sandbox or splashed in Robbie's wading pool. And my first sleepovers, starting at the ripe old age of five, took place at Mary's house, where we'd stay up long past my usual bedtime to draw pictures and tell secrets.

It was during my very first sleepover at Mary's house that I came face to face, in a very real sense, with my fatherless state. Up till then, I hadn't thought much about it—it was just the way it was, and I knew no different. My bedtime routine in Gussie's house was set in stone. Gramps, usually watching TV with us or seated at the dining room table working on papers from the office, would give a kiss goodnight to me and Lizzie (Robbie, of course, got to stay up later), and Gussie and Mom would herd us upstairs, where Mom would sit on my bed or Lizzie's to hear our bedtime prayers and tuck us in. The word "Daddy" had been included in the litany of "God bless's" before I came along and, although it was never excised, I never thought about attaching a face to it—any more than I thought about the meaning of "to the republic for which it stands" when I'd recite the Pledge of Allegiance. They were just words, which I learned to recite by rote.

But it was that first night at Mary's house that made it real for me; I didn't have a face to pin that word "Daddy" on. Mary and I had exhausted ourselves that day, running around the neighborhood selling the trinkets we'd collected from gumball machines, frantically trying to raise ten cents so we could buy a popsicle from the ice cream man when he came by in the early evening. We hadn't made it—business was slow, and by day's end we had only seven cents. So when we heard the familiar tinkle of bells after dinner, Mary's daddy, Mr. Fred, chipped in the rest so we could hurry outside and flag down the white truck before it turned the corner.

That night, Mr. Fred had come into Mary's room to tuck us in and kiss her goodnight. And as I lay there in the dark, I heard Mary say the words that suddenly, unexpectedly, had me choking up: "Goodnight, Daddy." There was just no way I was going to let her know I was starting to cry—she was my best friend, but she might think I was a baby. Or worse, her parents might think I was homesick and send me home. So I lay there, holding the tears inside, as she kissed him goodnight.

In a way, it really was a kind of homesickness I was feeling—but not for Gussie's house, not for the room I shared with Lizzie and Mom. I was homesick for something I'd never had. I too wanted someone to call Daddy, I wanted someone who would dig into his pocket and pull out an extra three cents for a popsicle. I wanted someone to whom I could say "Goodnight, Daddy," in just the same way Mary did, and hear him say "Goodnight, honey," with that big deep voice that said he'd take care of everything.

So I tried it out on Mr. Fred. I knew it wasn't the real thing, I knew I was just pretending, but I thought it would make me feel better saying it. Well, it didn't. He chuckled a little bit, and said, "Goodnight, Ashleigh," before plopping a quick kiss on my forehead and walking out, but I was left feeling pretty empty.

The face over which I'd superimposed Mr. Fred's gentle features that long ago night remained a mystery until that door opened on a blazing Arizona morning, and I looked at long last at the man whom every adult in my life had tried to wipe from the slate. But he was very much alive, very much there, in all his wizened, grizzly glory.

He was short—*so that's where I got my shortness,* I thought, *one more thing to hate him for*—and he was ancient. Sparse white hair, sallow complexion buried under a road map of wrinkles and liver spots. His eyes were partially obscured by thick horn-rimmed glasses, but I could just make out a blazing blue in the irises, and the wild white eyebrows overhanging them were furrowed in a deeply creased frown that might have been permanent.

"I'm Ashleigh Moore," I said, surprising myself with the smooth calm of my delivery. "Just think of it as a cross-examination," Renee had coached me. She'd been right—if I could keep myself in trial mode, I might be able to pull this off.

"Ashleigh," he whispered. I didn't exactly hear it; he might have just mouthed the word.

He looked at Renee. "Lizzie?" he asked hopefully.

"No," she said, stepping forward to extend her hand. "I'm Renee Silver, a friend of Ashleigh's."

He shook her hand limply, still somewhat dazed, and turned back to me. "Ashleigh. Well, damn," he muttered, and stared at me with a puzzled expression on his face.

"May we come in?" I said.

"Well, hell, yeah, come on, come on," he said, shaking the cobwebs from his brain. "Don't know where I left my manners." He stepped aside and ushered us into the dark hallway. As I passed him, I picked up the distinct odor of gin on his breath. Renee's polite smile was firmly in place, but she shot me a look that said she'd picked up on it too.

"Girls, why don't you take a seat right in there," he said, pointing to a living room off to the right, "and I'll just get us something to drink. What'll you have?"

"Iced tea, if you've got it," I said. I was tempted to join him in whatever he was having, but thought better of it, at least for now.

"I think I've got some of that crystal stuff, if that'll do."

"Sounds perfect," said Renee. "Same for me."

He shuffled off toward the kitchen, and Renee and I entered the living room to take seats on the sofa. The room wasn't particularly cluttered, but it smelled musty, as if it hadn't seen much Pledge or Windex recently. The overstuffed chair to the side had definitely seen better days, and the worn look of its seat cushion told me that it must be his special chair. The devil in me almost got up to go sit in it, but I told that devil to stay quiet a while longer.

The thing that struck me most about the room was what wasn't there—no flowers, no framed photos on the walls or end tables— nothing to indicate that anyone actually lived here, except for an overflowing ashtray and a stack of old *Sports Illustrated* magazines on the end table beside his chair. The walls, in fact, were totally bare but for a large mirror opposite the window, which reflected some of the sunlight pouring in through the drapes and gave the room more of an open appearance than it would have otherwise. I caught Renee's eye and she gave me a little wink.

"Here we go," Gardner said as he entered the room carrying a little metal tray with three drinks on it. He put his down on the table beside his chair before bringing the tray to us.

"My God, Ashleigh, I just can't believe it," he said when he returned to his chair and practically fell into it. I knew he couldn't be much more than sixty-five, and some of his movements were quick—like the dart of his eyes when he'd first opened the door—but at rest, he came across as a broken old man who'd never see eighty again.

"You're the picture of your mother," he said with another slow shake of the head. "I'd know you anywhere."

Not the first time I'd been told this, but still, I didn't really like hearing it from him. *Move on, counselor.*

"Well," I started in, "you asked if I might come by, so here I am. Now what was it you wanted to go over with me?"

"Robbie and Lizzie coming?" he asked expectantly.

I got some perverse pleasure out of his reference to "Robbie," but even more out of being able to burst his little bubble.

"No, they're very busy these days. I had some time on my hands, so they asked me to handle it."

"Well, hell, here you are—tell me about yourself, girl. What's keeping you busy these days?" he said, lifting the glass to his cracked lips.

Renee and I had rehearsed the story—close enough to the truth that I wouldn't have to actually lie to him, but keeping my profession out of it.

"Oh, this and that. My husband David works for a big dot-com company"—as if my soon-to-be ex-husband's job would explain what kept me busy, but he seemed to buy it. "And I run down to DC as often as I can to see my family." *That's right, you shit—my family, not yours.*

"And Robbie?"

Didn't we cover this in our phone call just two days ago? I guess I got my good memory from Mom.

"He's in Washington—the state. He works in computers."

Gardner nodded to himself and appeared to speak to a cigarette burn on the carpet. "I guess he got right in on the ground floor of all that. Should've known—he always was smarter than all get-out. That boy was taking apart my transistor radio as soon as he could walk."

"And Lizzie's in New York with me," I offered, just to close the loop so we could get on with business. "She works in publishing."

He was still nodding at the cigarette burn, and I wasn't sure he'd heard me.

"Too smart for his own damn good, that boy," he muttered.

"So about this trust," I said politely.

"What did they say?" he asked, looking up at me. His eyes were clear and looking directly into mine, and his tone had a little bite to it.

"Nothing. Just that they were busy," I said evenly. I was tempted to relay how adamant they'd been, how impatiently they'd dismissed my suggestion that they come with me, or even call. But there was no sense in sidetracking the discussion into something that might just piss him off. Not yet.

"How about Augustina? Bet she had something to say about you coming out here," he said with a knowing little chuckle that grated on me. I wanted to wipe that smirk right off his soupy old face—how dare he speak of her that way? Even if he was right—she certainly would have had a boatload to say about it, if she weren't long gone.

"Gussie died about ten years ago," I reminded him.

He looked confused for a second, until something clicked into place, and he quickly rearranged his features into a manufactured look of sympathy.

"That's right; that's right," he nodded. "I'm sorry to hear about that."

"So what was it that—"

"Now tell me about your mama. You see her much?"

I saw out of the corner of my eye that Renee was fidgeting slightly, mirroring my own annoyance at his determination to keep this conversation off track.

"Mom's doing just fine." *And she does not send her regards.* "I was hoping that we could talk a bit about this trust you mentioned."

He looked at me sharply, and I got the feeling he didn't like my ballsy change of subject. Good.

"There's plenty of time for that, girl," he said with a touch of rebuke. "Hell, I haven't seen you in thirty-some years. Let an old man ask some questions."

That did it. I wasn't going to sit there and take shit from this worthless bag of flesh. "That's right, you haven't. And whose fault is that?" I said calmly, but a little louder than I'd intended.

He chuckled at me and picked up his drink, the smirk reappearing on his face.

"Oh, you're your mama, all right. You're Linnie all over." He took a sip and I waited him out, composing myself, I hoped, into an attitude of poise and patience. "I suppose she gave you an earful of nonsense about me."

I shook my head, grateful to be able to deliver the next blow in all honesty. "Actually, she never talks about you."

It worked—but the look of bafflement on his face quickly changed to incredulity, and then outright disbelief. He finished his drink and shifted in the chair, preparing to get up. Renee beat him to the punch.

"Here," she said, rising quickly and crossing to his chair. "Let me get you a refill."

He slumped back only enough to get a better grip on the arms of the chair, and then hoisted himself to his feet.

"No," he said between huffs, "that's awfully kind of you, but I'll just see to it myself." He looked over at my half-empty glass, then at hers. "Can I top you ladies off?"

"Thanks, I'm fine for now," I said evenly. Renee shook her head as well, and we watched him shuffle his way back toward the kitchen. End of round one.

Renee arched an eyebrow my way as she strolled over to look out the window. I would have loved to know what she was thinking, but it was probably not much different from what was going through my own head—there wasn't anything for me here. I'd gone to the hardware store to buy oranges.

"You girls interested in a little tomato soup?" he called out from the kitchen. "It's getting to be lunchtime."

I looked at my watch and saw that it was barely eleven. He must get up pretty early.

"I get up pretty early," he said from the doorway. "Had my breakfast hours ago."

I looked at Renee, and she caught my eye as she turned to face him. "That would be very nice," she said. "Thank you."

"Three bowls of Campbell's, coming up," he said, disappearing again into the kitchen. Renee was already crossing the room to follow him, so I got up too.

"We'll just come keep you company," she called out to him, "if that's okay."

He didn't answer, but he didn't shoo us away either when we walked into the kitchen just in time to see him opening a cabinet over the sink to pull down a can of soup. I couldn't help but notice the sparse contents—a box of Triscuits, a few cans of soup, some vinegar, a package of paper plates, a carton of salt. It was lonely, that cupboard, bereft of the things that make a home. Bereft, I realized, of a woman's touch—a thought that prompted me to ask a question that had been occurring to me on and off since we'd first walked in.

"Is your wife at home?" I asked from the kitchen doorway as Renee took a seat at the small square table against the wall.

"What's that?" he mumbled, looking for a can opener.

"Your wife. Where is she?"

He gave a little snort—I realized it was the "hrrmph" that had annoyed me on the phone. "Gone," he said, examining the can opener and picking something off its blade.

I didn't know if that meant she'd died or had left him, but I figured some gesture of condolence was in order either way. "Oh, I'm sorry," I offered, taking a seat beside Renee.

"No need," he said as he struggled with opening the soup can. "Good riddance, I say." *Well,* I thought, *I hope that means she left him— I hate to think he'd talk that way about her death. But you never know.*

"Took my kids too," he continued. "Poisoned them against me." He turned and fixed those sharp blue eyes on me. "Guess I just don't have much luck picking out the ladies."

If he intended it as an insult to Mom, it worked—but I was damned if I'd give him the satisfaction of knowing it. I smiled benignly, and he turned back to work on the soup can. Once he got the lid off, or at least mostly off, he poured the contents into the single saucepan sitting on the stovetop.

"I suppose Linnie did the same thing," he said, almost to himself.

I wasn't going to get into it with him again, so I let it pass, and tried one more time to steer things in a more productive direction.

"Now about that trust, there's a few things I don't understand," I said. "If she died such a long time ago, how is it that her estate could have just been sitting around all this time? Didn't she have a will? Wouldn't the courts or somebody have just divided everything up a long time ago?"

With his back to us, Renee gave me a little smile, letting me know I'd said it just right—not informed enough to be the words of a lawyer, but displaying just enough commonsense knowledge of how such things worked to expose how ridiculous his story had been.

"Hell, girl," he snapped, "can't you think about anything but that damned money? Let me tell you something, missy, that money's a curse." He stirred the soup vigorously, and since his outburst had left me wondering just what the hell he was talking about, I chose to sit quietly and watch his stooped shoulders, waiting to see where this little detour might take us.

"Your mama knew better. I'll give her credit for that. She never wanted a damn thing to do with it. Wouldn't take a dime, that one. Stubborn as her mama."

Wait a minute, he lost me. "You mean you offered her money?" I said, trying not to sound shocked.

"Hell, yeah," he said, then turned around to shoot me a wary glance. "Why, did she say I didn't?"

"She never said anything at all about it," I said with a matter-of-fact tone that belied the churning in my belly. "When was this? When Grandma Edna died?"

He snorted again, only this time it turned into a hacking cough. He didn't even have the decency to turn his head away from the saucepan. I decided to skip lunch.

"Fuck no," he finally wheezed, "long before then. But she wouldn't let me see my boy." He coughed some more, and then took a healthy gulp of his drink. That seemed to settle him. "Damn women," he said quietly, resuming his stirring, "keeping me from my own kids."

"Wait, let me get this straight. After you left, you offered her money so you could still see us, but she wouldn't take it?"

"I didn't leave," he said, turning off the flame under the saucepan. "She threw me out."

His words blipped into my plane of existence as if from another dimension, flying in with no warning, from out of nowhere, and rooted me to that chair. Never, not once in my entire thirty-seven years, had anyone ever suggested such a thing. It simply couldn't be true. *Focus,* I told myself. *Hang on for dear life, and pay attention.*

"I wasn't going to pay for any kids after she cut me off from them. I got my daddy to get me a divorce right quick, nice and simple, and that was fine by her." He poured the soup into three bowls on the counter, and picked up two of them to bring to the table. "But I wanted to see you kids, and don't let her tell you otherwise." He placed the bowls on the table and stood looking at me, stooped and frail, but with a menacing gleam in his eye. "She can be mean as a hornet's nest when she gets an idea in her head, but don't you go listening to her stories."

He turned back to the counter to retrieve his bowl, and I looked at Renee, who gave me a reassuring nod and picked up her spoon.

"The soup's delicious," she said to his back—although she hadn't touched it.

"Well, thank you," he said as he ambled back to the table and eased himself into the chair to my left. "So you girls ever been out this way before? Arizona's right pretty this time of year." End of round two, no decision.

Lunch was polite; the strong pull of manners that Gussie had drummed into me forced me to take two or three spoonfuls of the watery red mess, and I smiled amiably as Renee engaged Gardner in a little chitchat about the Arizona wildflowers in bloom at this time of year. It was astonishing to hear him talk with such fondness and authority about flowers—a subject on which my mother, of all people, was a true expert. Could they have shared a love of flowers? Could they have actually cared about each other at one time? It was next to impossible to imagine my mother sharing anything with this crumpled old shell of a man, especially her bed. But I couldn't help trying to picture it, searching for something, anything, that Mom could have once seen in him.

Gardner got up to refresh his drink when the horticulture lesson ended—and given that we were there in the kitchen with him, he couldn't exactly sneak a little spike into it, so he came right out and announced that he was going to switch to something a little stronger, and did we want to join him? Renee answered before I could say no.

"That might be nice," she said, looking at me with big eyes. Maybe she was right, I thought. He might be more relaxed about drinking if we joined him, and he'd definitely open up more if he kept drinking. So I nodded too, and he poured us three tall gin and ice teas. It was truly disgusting, but I took a polite sip and swallowed it anyway.

"I left my cigarettes in the other room," Gardner said as he lifted his drink. "Care if we retire in there?" He didn't bother to wait for a reply before heading out the door in his slow gait. "And I might just be able to lay my hands on that damn trust agreement."

Renee and I exchanged a look behind his back, and she reached out to squeeze my hand before falling in line behind him.

Gardner set his drink on the end table beside his chair, pulled out a cigarette, and lit up with a snap from a heavy metal lighter—the kind Gramps used to use for his pipe, the boxy type that needs refilling with a good soaking of lighter fluid every so often. I hadn't heard the sound of that snap in many years, and there was something surreal about hearing it here and now, of all places. After a few puffs to make sure it was properly lit, Gardner took the cigarette with him and scuffed his way out to the hallway.

"I know I left it out here somewhere," he said, more to himself than us. We took our seats on the sofa and watched him through the archway as he shuffled through a pile of mail and newspapers on the entry hall table, cigarette dangling from his puckered mouth. He finally picked up a sheaf of papers that looked yellowed with age, and nodded his head.

"Here it is," he said as he came back into the living room. I got up and met him by his chair, and he looked at me with eyes that were brilliant blue and keen—the look of a lawyer about to deliver his summation.

"Like I said," he said, handing me the papers without breaking eye contact, "nothing there. It's not signed." He reached for his drink, removed the cigarette from his mouth just long enough to take a sip, and lowered himself into the chair.

I slowly walked back toward Renee on the sofa, scanning the document quickly. All I was really interested in seeing was the last page, and when I got there, I paused, looked at Renee, and then handed it to her.

"You don't mind if I have my friend Renee look at this, do you?" I said innocently. "She's much better at understanding these things than I am." Which, under these circumstances, might even have been true.

"No, no, go right ahead. Look as long as you like," he said confidently, sitting back and taking another slug. "Best as I can figure, she'd planned to set up this trust just before she died, and all of her grandkids were included in it. But then she up and died before she ever got around to signing it."

Well, it was a little more complicated than that, and Renee and I now knew it. The trust instrument he'd handed us had been dated two months before the will we'd seen, and had been drafted by another lawyer; presumably Grandma Edna's own personal attorney. Which meant that either she'd had a change of heart, or someone had changed her mind for her. Most likely the same someone who put together the will she eventually signed—the lying sack of shit who was now sitting in front of us.

"Yes," I said evenly, determined to nail him in his bullshit once and for all, "but that still doesn't explain what happened to her estate. I mean, lots of people die without setting up a trust."

"You want to know who got the money," he said with a cool smile that sent a little shiver down my spine. I really hated him.

"That's right." I simply stared back at him, waiting for the lie.

He gave another of those snorts that I'd come to detest; it said my questions were a nuisance and not worth the trouble of a response. But still I stared, waiting.

"Let me ask you something, girl. Supposing I was to tell you that it's all tied up in a big court mess, and no one's ever gonna see a penny, not in this lifetime. What would you say to that?"

"I'd say it sounds a lot like a Dickens novel I read once, and not very believable."

"Don't be naive," he said patronizingly. "Things like that happen all the time. Take it from this old country lawyer, I've seen it more times than you can shake a stick at."

"What's your point?"

"Does it look to you like I'm living here in the lap of luxury? Does it look like I'm living on a hundred and seventy-five million?"

I smiled sweetly. "I don't recall seeing the size of the trust mentioned in these papers," I said, taking the document from Renee again.

He gave me a look of pure menace, but recovered quickly. "Don't talk smart with me, missy. You know what I mean."

"No, I don't, not really. Are you saying that her estate never went through probate? That there's just a pile of money sitting someplace and no one can touch it?"

He was quiet for a minute as he stared at me. "I'm asking you to suppose something like that. Would you still have come all this way out here to see me?" He lowered his eyes and, suddenly, seemed terribly fragile sitting there with his gin in one hand and cigarette in the other. "Would you ever consider coming back?" he asked, almost in a whisper, eyes fixed on the cigarette burn by his feet.

I shook my head, not at all sure what to say. "I really don't know," I finally answered, and that was the God's honest truth.

He crushed out his cigarette with another "hrrmph," and lit up another immediately. I wanted to open a window, but figured I could breathe his toxic air a little while longer—this interview was just about over.

"And how about your brother and sister?" he said through a puff.

"What about them?"

"Well, the prospect of all that money wasn't enough to get them out here to see their old man. Do you think they'd give me the time of day if they thought there wasn't any money in it?"

I just couldn't get a read on him, where he was heading with all of these hypotheticals, but I was running out of patience. Time to end it right here.

"No, I don't. The truth is, they don't want anything to do with you, and the money has nothing to do with it."

He smiled, a feral grin that made my skin crawl. He seemed to think he'd scored some points, but I couldn't see how. He took another sip, a big one, which started another hacking fit.

"Well," he said cheerily once he had his voice back, "now we're getting somewhere."

"What do you mean?"

He looked at Renee, and then back at me, leaning forward to rest his arms on his knees. He looked like a metal folding chair about to collapse on itself. "That's the first honest thing you've said all day."

"I don't know what you're talking about," I said, meaning it. Sure, I'd been polite up till then, but not dishonest. Not really.

"Oh yes, you do, missy. You know very well why they won't come out here. You came for the money, that's plain, but you also wanted to see if you could find out if it was true. Well, you can just pack yourself right up and get the hell back to New York, because I'm telling you right now it's nothing but a pile of lies."

I swear to God I had no idea what this crazy old bastard was talking about, and I started to wonder if perhaps he'd lost his mind, or was suffering from Alzheimer's. Maybe a kind of alcohol-induced dementia. But something told me to wait before dismissing his nonsense— to see if maybe there was something here, buried in all the cigarette ash and booze. Maybe he wasn't crazy—maybe, under all his horseshit, I might find a little piece of what I came for after all. I decided to play him, to see where it took me.

"Oh, I don't know," I said carefully. "It seemed pretty believable to me."

"Who says so?" he asked, eyeing me warily as if I were a witness on the stand.

"Gussie," I said, figuring she'd be the most likely to blab about whatever had him in a tizzy.

"Well, there you go," he said, raising his arms as if he'd just kicked a field goal, and nearly spilling his drink in the process. "That dizzy old bird was so full of stories, you can't never tell the truth from what she made up. And when she got a bee in her bonnet over something, there was no talking sense to her. Now am I right, or am I right?"

As a matter of fact, he was right—but that was beside the point, since Gussie never said a word. "Gussie wasn't the only one. Mom said so too."

He nailed me with a mean glare. "I thought you said she never talked about me."

"I lied. I was being polite."

"No sense in being polite now, huh?"

"You asked for honesty."

"Well, let me tell you something, Little Miss New York, I don't care what anybody says, your mother's got a sick, perverted mind to fill your head full of all that filth."

A little river of ice water started seeping into my gut as I started to piece together what he was saying. The realization slowly dawned on me, but I didn't want to consider it, didn't want to think it. But what else could he be talking about? What else could make Mom shut him out of our lives so completely? I went for it.

"And then, of course," I said, looking him squarely in the eye, "there's Robbie."

His body seemed to fold in on itself, his face a mixture of pain and panic. With a little spittle lodged in the corner of his mouth, he drew back his lips to suck in some air, exposing yellow tar-stained teeth and giving his face the look of a rabid wolf. He leaned forward again to point a single bony finger at me.

"Now you listen to me, missy, and you listen good," he said, his tone eerily reminiscent of Robbie's dark voice, "because after this, the subject is closed."

I sat there and nodded, knowing with cold certainty what he was about to say.

"I *never* laid a finger on that boy. I never did any of those things they've been telling you. Now you get the fuck out of my house."

✎ Chapter Twelve

The letter from Liddle, Barrington and Sweet arrived almost exactly three months later, on a Friday. Coincidentally, it was also the day that I last laid eyes on Dick Parsons. He was in the hallway outside the appellate division, where I was called to give evidence before the committee that was considering his disbarment. I'd been kept blissfully removed from all the proceedings up to that point—his expulsion from Huxley Doyle and the subsequent SEC investigation. It had been the talk of the firm for weeks, but all of the activity had buzzed around in the upper echelons, requiring no input from me beyond two interviews with investigators from the SEC and the Justice Department, and the turnover of all my notes, including my CYA memo. One of the perks of being a lowly associate was that I could just plug along doing my work, and leave the reshaping of the world to the higher-ups. Ironically, I wouldn't be an associate for much longer; the firm had unanimously voted me in, and I'd be joining the partnership ranks at the start of the next quarter.

I had one small regret about the way things had been handled—I didn't get to witness the firing of Queen Bee. When the shit first hit the fan, Louise had erected an iron curtain around Parsons but, consummate political animal that she is, she had quickly detected the changing winds and had dropped her allegiance to him even before the partners had voted him out. Her face a mask of wide-eyed innocence and manufactured earnestness, she had immediately set out on a course to ingratiate herself with the new power structure, and Dennis in particular. Too little too late—Dennis was no fool, and Queen Bee's eleventh-hour attempt to make herself appear indispensable to those who had borne her bullshit for so many years was as insulting to Dennis's intelligence as it was transparent.

But Dennis was too decent a man to subject her to a public dressing-down. Much as I'd wished that I could be there, he'd insisted on firing her quietly, behind closed doors, with no fanfare. Even so, the entire litigation department—hell, the entire floor—rejoiced at the sight of her cleaning out her desk that day. And no one's smile was bigger than Stella's.

Having the Queen Bee deposed was nothing compared to the satisfaction I got out of being the one to testify against Parsons. When he had seen me sitting with Renee in the hallway outside the courtroom, he'd pointedly turned his back on us and whispered something to the lawyer he'd hired to represent him before the committee. While it would have been improper for me to speak to him, I nevertheless stared at him good and hard—and I got a happy little jolt of pleasure out of the furious look he'd given me in return. The greater his hatred, the more he'd lost, and the sweeter my victory. As petty as it sounds, I rejoiced in his downfall. Renee, a much better person than I am in so many ways, simply felt sorry for him—and for Chasen, who was most certainly going to jail. Not me; I'd hated them both, especially Parsons, with a passion that burned hot in me. Hated what he'd tried to do to the firm, to me, to her. I still thought of lawyers as a noble bunch, and this disbarment proceeding was, to me, a welcome weeding of the profession—just one more example of how we keep our house clean. *He may very well end up in prison with Chasen after the SEC gets through with him,* I thought as I passed him on the way into the courtroom. And that was just as it should be.

After such a great day, my heart sank when I got home that night to find a letter from Arizona waiting for me. Ignoring it for the moment, I kicked off my shoes and dumped the stack of mail on the sideboard to sort out David's stuff. After he'd been served with the divorce papers, we'd finally hammered out the terms—I got the apartment, and he took a sublet across town. It was amiable enough between us—as friendly as such things can be, I guess—and we were both trying to be reasonable in going our separate ways. Frankly, I assumed he'd found himself a girlfriend, although I couldn't be sure, and I wouldn't dare ask, especially because I didn't want him to ask me the same question. He already knew I spent a lot of nights at Renee's apartment, so I was sure he had his suspicions. Still, we kept our conversations on safe ground, and once he understood there was no pot of gold at the end of the Gardner rainbow, we'd been able to agree on the division of our assets pretty quickly. Except for the apartment, we split everything fifty-fifty, even though I'd been the sole contributor to our savings account.

As soon as I saw the return address, I wanted to rip up Barrington's letter without reading it. Whatever games that sick old man Gardner was playing now, he could just do it without me. I still shuddered at the memory of that animal gleam in his eyes as he'd lied to me, and the putrid odor of decay wafting off him when he'd had the outrageous gall to try hugging me good-bye at the door—as if he hadn't just ordered me from his stinking home. As if he actually had the right to pretend he was any kind of father. I'd given his bony old shoulders a halfhearted pat and backed away quickly, but not before I caught sight of his red-rimmed eyes leaking behind those thick glasses.

My family had been only too happy to hear the half-lie I'd given them when I'd reported back that I'd spoken to Gardner—I didn't mention the visit—and that he'd just spun some nonsense about a trust that had never been signed. I had no idea what Liz remembered of him, but I assumed that any memories she still retained could only be bad, and I didn't want to stir them up for her any more than I already had. The question of what to tell Rob and Mom had proven a bit more thorny, not so much because I wanted to enlighten them on what I'd discovered, but because some part of me—the part that for so long had sought some kind of connection to them other than pencil lines on a family tree—wanted to let them know, without saying so, that I understood and would keep their secret.

Dr. Mbaye, damn her, had patiently walked me through the process. I'd started seeing her regularly for individual sessions after I'd gotten back from Arizona. In fact, I'd refused to continue the marriage counseling at all, but instead of trying to convince me to keep up the joint sessions, as I'd expected, Dr. Mbaye had actually seemed to breathe a sigh of relief, as if satisfied that something important was finally starting to dawn on me. David didn't like the idea, of course, but he could do nothing about it.

I think Dr. Mbaye had been a little frustrated with me during those first few post-Arizona sessions, her big-eyed glare waiting me out through the long silences following my pronouncement, at least once per session, that I had it all figured out, that the taboos I'd danced around as a child were finally beginning to make some sense to me and I could now close that box up tight. At first, I'd assumed she was just annoyed at my ability to reach this place on my own—on the plane back from Arizona, in fact—so I could just present it to her neatly wrapped as I sat on her comfortable old sofa. Sometimes she'd tap her hook against her leg with a hint of impatience, but after a few weeks of listening through the same self-satisfied monologue, she started to turn things around by speaking up.

Her comments were few at first, and mostly concerned the box in which I'd put Mom. I'd decided that a lot of what Mom had covered up all those years hadn't been the pain of a broken heart, but a kind of guilt over not protecting Robbie. In talking it out in that West End Avenue living room, I started to see Mom in a new light. She'd kept that man away from us not for her own sake, but for ours. Far from the retiring little wallflower whom everyone had to circle and protect, she started to emerge in my eyes as our champion, standing up against poverty and the threat of a powerful family to keep us safe.

One thing that puzzled me was why he'd backed down if he really wanted to see us, and why he'd been willing to give her a divorce. But Renee had helped to shed some light on that one for me. A fight, she'd reasoned, was bound to result in a very public airing of the things that both Mom and Gardner would have wanted kept quiet. He had a law practice and his family name to maintain—especially the latter. In fact, his father the judge might well have insisted on the quick divorce in order to keep a lid on the whole story. Yes, I could see him caving in quietly under the circumstances, much as it must have galled him to let my mother win that round and get a clean break. He didn't strike me as the type who'd take kindly to resistance from an uppity woman, and Gussie sure knew how to breed uppity women.

Gussie was still a puzzle. I was certain that Gramps had no idea; Gussie was the captain of the house and hoarded everyone's secrets for herself. But I couldn't for the life of me imagine how she could have kept something this big to herself if she'd known; she'd certainly have let something slip, if for no other reason than to play up her own wisdom in having warned Mom not to marry the son of a bitch in the first place. But if she hadn't known, then why would she have circled the wagons around Mom as she had? Was it just the call of maternal duty? It was a question to which I'd probably never know the answer.

The biggest kick in the butt I got from the good doctor had to do with Rob. I guess she just got tired of sitting around and waiting for me to catch up to where she thought I ought to be, and it annoyed the hell out of me that she seemed to be trying to get me to look beyond what I'd compartmentalized for her so neatly. But eventually she got me to unwrap the box where I'd put all my age-old resentments, by making a simple request at the end of one of our sessions—a request that both surprised and perturbed me. She asked me to bring in a picture of him.

Although she hadn't said so, I knew the picture she would want would be a shot of Robbie as a small boy, and I knew just which one I'd bring, if I could find it—the shot of little four-year-old Robbie standing in the living room of a house I didn't know, holding a stuffed white bunny I didn't recognize. As soon as I got home that night, I went looking for a box of old pictures that Gussie had given me the year before she died, and I finally found it in the den closet, on a shelf way in the back. "Hold onto these pictures, Ash," I remembered Gussie telling me, as if she were handing me the family jewels, "and look at them now and then." Another of her requests I'd blown off.

There were maybe a hundred of them piled in the box in no particular order, all prints made from Gramps' slides—mostly black and whites, along with a few color shots from the 1970s, now turning orange. The picture of two-year-old Lizzie with our old cat, Pox, Mom standing beside a beaming Uncle Dink at his wedding—I went through each one, Gussie's familiar narrative running through my head, and tried to blink away the tears that were soon stinging my eyes. By the time I came across the one I was looking for, I could barely see—and that, I guess, had been good Dr. Mbaye's whole point.

I'd handed it over to her the following Thursday, and she got to see for herself what I'd been studying all that week—that sweet, angelic face looking up at the camera through blond bangs, a look of trust and unbridled delight beaming from his sparkling eyes. She saw then, as I had, what that filthy bastard had stolen from Robbie—had stolen from us all. The innocence and purity that he'd poisoned. She'd stared at the picture a good long time before lifting her eyes to me and nodding quietly. And although I knew what she was waiting for, I made her ask anyway. "What are you feeling?"

I struggled for the words, my throat tight and my tongue thick. I looked for a clean, edited version to give her, stripped of the tumult that was threatening to break loose from within my chest. But in the end, it came down to something that I couldn't homogenize, so I just said it, surprised as much by the realization itself as by my ability to articulate it in words that, in my entire life, I don't think I'd ever uttered about my brother. "I love him," I said, nearly choking as I whispered it. She gazed at me peacefully, and filled in the second half of the equation for me—the part I still couldn't get out: "And you forgive him."

That did it. I wept like a baby, wept for the little boy who had been lost, for the man he might have become were it not for the polluted touch of that monster whose poison had, in some way, infected us all. It was crushing, literally, to feel such things for someone I'd spent a lifetime hating, but there it was, and under the protective gaze of Dr. Mbaye, I bore it, let myself feel it, and tried to accept it. In her typical fashion, she'd ended that session with a simple observation that lingered with me long afterward. "I think," she'd said, "that you have found something of what you were looking for, even if you did not know you were looking." I'd looked up at her quizzically through a blur of tears. "Interesting, isn't it?" she'd continued, her expression neutral as always. "The answers that are there for us don't always come from the questions we ask. Sometimes they come from the questions we don't ask."

I thought about her words late that night. The fourth dimension was indeed round, I'd discovered, and it did span both space and time. I'd taken off to Arizona to find out what the hell that miserable shit wanted, and had ended up right back in my childhood bedroom in Gussie's house, curled on my side under the covers, with a missing piece of my life puzzle clutched tightly in my hand. What I would do with it now was up to me.

No, Rob didn't need to hear about any of it. He didn't need to ever find out what had prompted my change of heart toward him. It was enough for me to know that, the next time I saw him, I could give him a hug that had something genuine in it, that was not completely filled with fear or loathing. And maybe, if I didn't bristle so readily at his foul temper, he wouldn't lose it quite so often with me. It was a thought.

As I stared at that envelope, debating what to do with it, the phone rang and gave me a much-needed excuse to put off making up my mind. I could tell from the caller ID that it was CRS, and there was only one person there who'd be calling me at home. I snatched up the phone right away.

"Hey, what are you still doing at work?"

"I'm just leaving," Renee said. "Why, what's wrong?"

"You're never going to believe who I'm holding a letter from."

"Parsons. He wants you to represent him."

"Funny. No, Gardner's lawyer."

"Get out! What's it say?"

"I haven't read it. I was thinking of burning it instead."

"Don't you dare. I'm getting in a cab right now. Wait for me."

"I've been waiting for you all my life," I told her.

"I love you too. See you in a few."

I hung up, feeling the familiar warm glow that came from hearing those words. It was a miracle, really, how just the sound of her voice could put everything in perspective for me and bring order to the chaos. As hectic as things had gotten with the upheaval at Huxley Doyle and the management change at CRS, she'd been my ballast— as I'd been hers, I guess.

Not that it had been entirely smooth sailing, not by any means. Renee herself had been a major source of turmoil for me when we'd first returned from Arizona—for the simple reason that I'd been dying, literally dying, to make love with her. And she hadn't helped matters; she'd held my hand during the entire movie on the flight back to New York, and had pushed my throbbing center into near climax with her casual remark at one point that she couldn't concentrate on the film because all she could think about was crawling into bed with me.

But she wanted to wait, and I really thought it would kill me. She was absolutely adamant that we do nothing while David and I still technically lived together. In my clearer moments—which were few, believe me—I think I understood her reasons. She'd been seriously burned once by a straight woman, and had a hard time really trusting that I wasn't just a tourist on holiday from my marriage. Deep down, I think she kind of used my desire for her to hurry along my formal separation from David. She'd kiss me sometimes in a way that greased my gears big time, teasing me silly with her roaming fingers and tongue—only to break it off at a critical point to leave us both dizzy and frantic. I can't say I really minded being manipulated in this way—it certainly had its perks. And although it left me horny 24/7, with my swollen labia incessantly massaged in their own juices, it also worked, giving me the extra push I needed to be extremely accommodating with David: the sooner he got the hell out of the apartment, the sooner I could get her into bed.

With this game plan in mind, we'd early on realized we shouldn't spend much time alone together in my hotel room at the Mayflower. We'd come pretty close to breaking our chastity vow the very first night after we returned from Arizona. Amazingly, I'd been the one to pull the plug on that encounter. We'd landed in the middle of the night and, exhausted as we both were, we'd agreed she should just come back to my hotel, where we'd naively assumed that we might actually just fall asleep. So much for good intentions—we'd fallen on the bed together as soon as the door was closed, and she had my shirt over my head, with her face buried between my breasts, before I could even come up for air. Finally I did, though, and I forced myself to think beyond the magic she was working under my bra. There was no way I was going to be able to stop if I didn't do it right then, I'd realized, so I took her hands, stilled them, and looked into the lust in her eyes. God, she was breathtaking—but she nodded, rolled off me, and sat up. "This was a mistake," she said with a defeated smile. I nodded. And the very next day, I'd contacted the divorce lawyer Janelle had recommended, to start the apartment negotiations with David.

We'd had a few more close calls, but finally David had moved into his own place, and that night, Renee had come over to my reclaimed apartment to celebrate. We never got around to eating the dinner I'd prepared. When I greeted her at the door, she simply walked in, dropped her bag in the entry hall, and took my hand to lead me into the bedroom without a word. I had her skirt unzipped before we were halfway into the room, and by the time we hit the bed, she had her blouse off and my slacks around my ankles.

I don't remember the rest of the disrobing—I know her breasts were in my hands while she was unhooking my bra, and her mouth was devouring my nipples at around the same time that I was reaching under the waistband of her panties to take up handfuls of her smooth bare ass in my hands. The image that stands out most clearly in those first frenetic minutes was the moment when it all came to a standstill, when she was lying there looking up at me through strands of brown hair strewn across her face. She took my hand and slid it between her legs with a look of such quiet compelling need, her eyes brimming with tears, and she whimpered softly, "Please, I can't take it anymore." As I slipped my fingers between the creamy folds, her face simply crumpled, and I licked the tears that spilled down the side of her face. I wanted to go slow, to circle the twitching little nub under my fingers and savor the unearthly sweetness of her sopping center—but she started bucking her hips in an insistent, desperate rhythm of agony and want. "Please, Ash," she cried. "Oh God, please, just fuck me."

Yes, warmed with a glow of memory and anticipation, I dropped that damn letter on the sideboard to let Renee read it if she wanted, and I went to the bedroom to change into jeans and a polo shirt. Once Renee got there, I thought as I zipped up my jeans, I didn't plan to stay dressed for long.

I was making dinner when the doorman rang the bell, so I told him to let her up, and went back to finish cleaning the salad. She had me eating better: I actually enjoyed taking the time to prepare a real meal these days, something I virtually never did during thirteen years of marriage. The most remarkable change in my diet, however, was something that had nothing to do with Renee and everything to do with that poor drunken slob with whom I shared some genes: I stopped drinking. Not just a cutback—I stopped altogether, my resolve to do so firmly in place the minute I'd left his house. I didn't think about it beforehand, and hadn't given it much thought since. Go figure. I'd probably tell Dr. Mbaye about it eventually, just to give her a little treat on a slow day, and let her try to make some sense out of it. All I knew was that it felt right.

When I greeted Renee at the door, she looked so good that I almost suggested we just skip dinner and go straight to dessert. But she had that crinkle in her eye that told me she was eager for adventure—the kind that didn't involve the bedroom—and all I could get out of her was a distracted kiss before she asked about the letter.

"It's on the sideboard," I said as I turned toward the kitchen. "Be my guest."

I was slicing some tomatoes to put atop my salad—Renee hates them, so I keep them separate—when her "Oh my God!" rang out and she rushed into the kitchen.

"Ash, take a look at this," she said, holding out the letter toward me.

"What's he want now?"

"No, honey." Her tone was quiet, serious, and matched the intense look on her face. I took the letter and scanned it quickly, my heart accelerating with each word. Finished, I looked back at her, wondering what the hell this would mean.

Kenneth Gardner was dead.

📖   📖   📖

"Mr. Barrington? It's Ashleigh Moore."

"Ashleigh! I'm so glad you called. I was just on my way out the door."

I gave Renee a wink. She'd been right to suggest that I call right away; he was still there. And why wouldn't he be, since it was only a little after five out there?

"I got your letter."

"Yes, and I'm sure you have a few questions. But first, I want you to know how sorry I am about your father's death. He was so happy to have seen you a few months back. He mentioned it to me a number of times."

I'll just bet.

"Well, thank you for letting me know about his passing, but I don't understand what it is you wanted to talk to me about."

"You mean he didn't tell you?"

"Tell me what?" I asked, swatting Renee away as she twisted the receiver in my hand to try to listen with me.

"Why, honey, you're one of his beneficiaries. You and your brother and sister. Together with Daniel and Elaine, of course. Congratulations!"

Gee, one-fifth of a house in Arizona that's probably mortgaged to the hilt. Lucky me.

"Well, that's very nice," I said. "Thank you for letting me know. I guess I'll be getting some papers from you in the mail?"

"Ashleigh, I'm not sure you appreciate what I'm saying. This is a pretty sizable estate we're talking about."

"I don't understand. He told me he didn't have any money—that Grandma Edna's estate was all tied up in litigation and there wasn't anything there. Or wouldn't be, I guess, after probate." Not that I believed a word of that, God knows.

He laughed. "Well, he was right that there was a lengthy lawsuit, but it wasn't probate. It was matrimonial."

"What do you mean?" I asked, shushing Renee, who was practically bouncing on the couch beside me.

"Oh, he got his share of his mother's estate all right, back when she died. But Eleanor had initiated a divorce proceeding just before then, and he was concerned about her getting her hands on his inheritance. Let's just say that, on paper, he never had a cent of it."

"Are you telling me he hid his assets because of the divorce?" I was starting to get a numb kind of feeling in my body, and slouched back against the sofa cushions.

"Now, you wouldn't be asking me to disclose a client confidence, would you, counselor?" he asked jovially.

"Wait, you know I'm a lawyer?"

"Your father knew. He looked you up in the Martindale directory right after you left."

"But—"

"Ashleigh, nobody refers to probate unless they know something about it. And let me tell you, he was damn proud of you. Couldn't stop crowing about his daughter, the lawyer."

I didn't know if I was going to throw up or cry. It was all moving way too fast for me.

"I'll tell you something else," he continued, "and I don't think it's betraying a client secret to say it. He changed his will right after your visit. Came right in the next day."

"But wait a minute," I said, the lawyer in me slowly starting to kick in, "his second wife is going to contest this. I mean, I don't understand how he could have hidden his assets during the divorce proceeding, but she's certainly going to start sniffing around now that there's a sizable estate being probated. If he cheated her in the divorce, she might have a claim against the estate now."

"He didn't cheat her, so let's be clear about that first off," Barrington said carefully. "But Eleanor isn't going to be bringing any claims anyway. She died a few months ago, and her only family was her two kids. They're not going to make any fuss, believe me—not when they understand that a fight over the estate will tie it up for years on end. They'll be happy to take the money and run, I guarantee it. And there's plenty in it for them."

Which brought me to the question that I was suddenly afraid to ask. But I had to, so I did.

"And how much is that?"

He gave another of those little chuckles, and I could tell that he'd been dying to say it all this time.

"Well, it's divided up five ways, of course, in equal shares. Altogether, I'd say the estate is somewhere around two hundred and fifty million dollars."

📖　📖　📖

Renee was asleep when I finally climbed into bed beside her. It was late—sometime after three. Unable to keep her eyes open after my hours-long phone call with Liz, she'd retired around the time I'd called Rob to fill him in. My head was swimming by the time I hit the sack but, exhausted as I was, I knew I was too wired to sleep.

She rolled toward me and I stared at her lovely sleeping form, enjoying the peaceful respite it evoked in me. I wasn't ready to deal with the idea of being someone with fifty million dollars. I wasn't ready to deal with the fact that it was tainted money, poisoned at its source. All of that could wait—I'd be dealing with it soon enough, and would surely devote several years to hashing it through with Dr. Mbaye. For now, what mattered was that I had this miracle of a woman lying beside me—an anchor to hang on to, connecting me to the rest of the universe. The peace that blanketed me as I gazed upon her gentle sleep got me thinking of that Colette quote that Claire had so loved. I might have taken a few detours, but that road had finally had brought me full circle, and Colette was right—here was the road, now was the hour, and it was indeed a numinous state of such exquisite purity that it defied expression.

Renee stirred and opened her eyes. "Everything okay?" she murmured.

"Yes. Perfect."

She smiled and brushed the hair from my face. "What are you thinking about?"

"Claire, actually," I said. "I was just thinking that I still haven't answered her e-mail."

"Oh yeah," she said, kissing my cheek. "What do you think you'd want to say?"

"I don't know. Nothing, really. I'm just curious about why she decided to contact me after all this time."

"Well," she said, slowly sitting up, "I've got an idea."

"What?"

The little crinkle appeared at the corner of her eye. "How do you feel about a quick trip to Chicago?"

About the Author

Author of the best-selling *To the Edge,* **Cameron Abbott** is an attorney in New York City, where she litigates complex commercial disputes involving a variety of high-tech industries around the world. She also serves as an arbitrator in the securities industry, teaches as an Adjunct Professor of Law at a law school in New York, and has appeared as a television commentator on various legal issues.

SPECIAL 25%-OFF DISCOUNT!
Order a copy of this book with this form or online at:
http://www.haworthpress.com/store/product.asp?sku=4932

AN INEXPRESSIBLE STATE OF GRACE

_____ in softbound at $13.46 (regularly $17.95) (ISBN: 1-56023-469-5)

Or order online and use special offer code HEC25 in the shopping cart.

COST OF BOOKS_____

OUTSIDE US/CANADA/
MEXICO: ADD 20%_____

POSTAGE & HANDLING_____
*(US: $5.00 for first book & $2.00
for each additional book)
Outside US: $6.00 for first book)
& $2.00 for each additional book)*

SUBTOTAL_____

IN CANADA: ADD 7% GST_____

STATE TAX_____
*(NY, OH & MN residents, please
add appropriate local sales tax)*

FINAL TOTAL_____
*(If paying in Canadian funds,
convert using the current
exchange rate, UNESCO
coupons welcome)*

Prices in US dollars and subject to change without notice.

☐ **BILL ME LATER:** ($5 service charge will be added)
(Bill-me option is good on US/Canada/Mexico orders only;
not good to jobbers, wholesalers, or subscription agencies.)

☐ Check here if billing address is different from
shipping address and attach purchase order and
billing address information.

Signature_____

☐ **PAYMENT ENCLOSED: $**_____

☐ **PLEASE CHARGE TO MY CREDIT CARD.**

☐ Visa ☐ MasterCard ☐ AmEx ☐ Discover
☐ Diner's Club ☐ Eurocard ☐ JCB

Account # _____

Exp. Date_____

Signature_____

NAME_____

INSTITUTION_____

ADDRESS_____

CITY_____

STATE/ZIP_____

COUNTRY_____ COUNTY (NY residents only)_____

TEL_____ FAX_____

E-MAIL_____

May we use your e-mail address for confirmations and other types of information? ☐ Yes ☐ No
We appreciate receiving your e-mail address and fax number. Haworth would like to e-mail or fax special
discount offers to you, as a preferred customer. **We will never share, rent, or exchange your e-mail address
or fax number.** We regard such actions as an invasion of your privacy.

Order From Your Local Bookstore or Directly From
The Haworth Press, Inc.
10 Alice Street, Binghamton, New York 13904-1580 • USA
TELEPHONE: 1-800-HAWORTH (1-800-429-6784) / Outside US/Canada: (607) 722-5857
FAX: 1-800-895-0582 / Outside US/Canada: (607) 771-0012
E-mailto: orders@haworthpress.com
PLEASE PHOTOCOPY THIS FORM FOR YOUR PERSONAL USE.
http://www.HaworthPress.com   BOF03